WEDDING NIGHT REVENGE

Mary Brendan

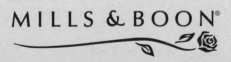

MILLS & BOON®

DID YOU PURCHASE THIS BOOK WITHOUT A COVER?

If you did, you should be aware it is **stolen property** as it was reported *unsold and destroyed* by a retailer. Neither the author nor the publisher has received any payment for this book.

All the characters in this book have no existence outside the imagination of the author, and have no relation whatsoever to anyone bearing the same name or names. They are not even distantly inspired by any individual known or unknown to the author, and all the incidents are pure invention.

All Rights Reserved including the right of reproduction in whole or in part in any form. This edition is published by arrangement with Harlequin Enterprises II B.V. The text of this publication or any part thereof may not be reproduced or transmitted in any form or by any means, electronic or mechanical, including photocopying, recording, storage in an information retrieval system, or otherwise, without the written permission of the publisher.

This book is sold subject to the condition that it shall not, by way of trade or otherwise, be lent, resold, hired out or otherwise circulated without the prior consent of the publisher in any form of binding or cover other than that in which it is published and without a similar condition including this condition being imposed on the subsequent purchaser.

MILLS & BOON and MILLS & BOON with the Rose Device are registered trademarks of the publisher.

First published in Great Britain 2001
Harlequin Mills & Boon Limited,
Eton House, 18-24 Paradise Road, Richmond, Surrey TW9 1SR

© Mary Brendan 2001

ISBN 0 263 82757 7

Set in Times Roman 10½ on 12 pt.
04-1201-80292

Printed and bound in Spain
by Litografía Rosés S.A., Barcelona

Prologue

'You changed your mind.'

The pure pleasure in the young man's voice dug pain deep beneath Edgar Meredith's ribs. But he managed a smile.

No...Rachel has, was immediately in his mind, and an irrepressible mordant humour wrenched his smile into a grimace. His chest constricted with a piercing regret that left him breathless, unable to respond to the greeting.

After nineteen and a half years of tears and tantrums, he was quite aware his eldest daughter could be headstrong and impetuous; but he'd never thought her callous or sly. Today he'd had the shocking, shaming proof she was. He felt as incapable of speech now as he had when first apprised of the situation by his wife some hours ago. But speak of it he must...

As the young man detached himself from his group of friends, Edgar was again struck by his impressive, muscular figure, yet he moved with such a graceful stride. He automatically took the outstretched hand, letting the firm fingers warm his. He found himself clinging to them, rather than returning the salute as his host might have expected.

'Now, what will you drink? Cognac? Champagne?' The sincere welcome mellowing the lilting Irish brogue simply accented Edgar's pain.

'You managed to slip away for an hour...' Connor Flinte chuckled conspiratorially as he selected a goblet for the man he could tomorrow call father.

Edgar, incredibly, found himself nodding, a half-frown half-smile contorting his features in a travesty of chummy conspiracy as he watched champagne froth towards the rim of an exquisitely chased flute. Yes, he'd managed to slip away for an hour. No, he had not. There was no further need to furtively retreat from beneath his wife's feet as she fussed over last-minute plans and insisted he stay close in case needed. There was no more need for plans. He now had any amount of time to spend with his friends. For six months past, he'd felt proud to class this man as such...and more. After today, would Major Connor Flinte ever want to pass the time of day with him again?

Mr Edgar Meredith was a man with four daughters and an aching yen for a boy. Mrs Meredith said enough was enough. To her relief, and his dismay, nature now backed her in that. What a handsome and welcome addition to his family Connor would have made. Edgar was already mourning the loss of his son. The warmth in the room seemed suddenly unbearable.

'I'd no idea there'd be so many happy fellows commiserating on me last night of freedom.' Connor grinned, an indolent hand indicating the boisterous guests, including his drunken stepbrother, cluttering his cosy drawing room. The wry humour and fine wine were still mellowing his tongue, but the bright blue gaze was sharp, seeking to adhere to Edgar's evasive brown eyes.

Mr Meredith simply nodded, passed a hand over his jaw before reflexively putting the silver chalice to his lips. Suddenly aware how awfully inappropriate it would be to drink, he replaced it on the sideboard so abruptly it skated away an inch or so. With a feat of courage Edgar forced himself to look up.

For a moment their eyes held and then relief swamped Edgar. He knew! He knew and was prepared to make it easy for him. There would be no need to scrabble for useless excuses to attempt to justify and mitigate his daughter's outrageous behaviour. There was little comfort to be drawn from the reprieve or acknowledging his cowardice. 'I'm sorry. I'm…so very sorry…' The words quivered, suspended in silence, as raucous laughter eddied about them.

Connor steered him brusquely towards a cool corner of the room, far from the roaring fire, the roaring drunks toasting his marriage.

'Why?'

Edgar swayed his head, wincing beneath that single, spat syllable as though it had been a tirade of abuse. 'I don't know… She's obstinate…headstrong…' he offered feebly. Then quickly added, 'I've not had an opportunity to speak to her or chastise her. When I returned from Windrush she had already absconded to York…'

A choking sound smothered further words. The bleak laughter terminated in an oath and a hand tore into ebony hair. 'York? She's run as far as that? Sweet *Jaazus,*' seeped out through scraping white teeth.

'An aunt…she has an aunt who lives there. My wife's sister…' Edgar Meredith informed him quickly, hesitantly. 'We had no idea of it, I swear. Mrs Meredith is distraught. She can hardly stand unaided. Had I the slightest notion she'd do this… In nineteen years I've never laid a finger on her in anger, and God knows there have been times when she's tempted me with her wilfulness and impudence. But had I known she'd now act so mean, I'd have taken a lash to her sides years since.'

The dark head snapped down; blue-flame eyes seared Edgar's face. 'Don't say that…' The caution was sweetly persuasive, gutturally thick and Connor's white teeth were infinitesimally bared.

Edgar closed his weary eyes and licked his parched lips. He made a monumental effort to control his shivering and match the self-possession of his host. 'I'll deal with the formalities, of course, inform the guests, Reverend Dean and so on. As the bride's father…the renegade bride's father…I must shoulder the guilt, the shame and the responsibility….'

'She said nothing to *anyone*? Has she eloped with a secret lover?'

Edgar recognised the frustration coarsening his interrogator's voice and inwardly cringed. How could he recount the pathetic excuses Rachel had left behind her? How could he tell this handsome, personable cavalry officer, who had been decorated several times for valour, that Rachel had jilted him on the eve of their wedding because she had a fancy for a more charismatic and exciting consort? He could barely admit to himself that his eldest daughter and heir to his estate was shallow, inconsiderate and lacking in filial duty, and couldn't see the good in a gentleman because she was dazzled by the peacock dandies she giggled with.

'Is she travelling alone?'

'With her sister, Isabel. My wife and Isabel tried to reason with her. Isabel was for staying behind, so disgusted was she by her sister's deceit. They've always been close; if anyone could have stayed her, I would have chosen Isabel. My wife had sense enough to insist Isabel accompany her rather than risk further outrage by letting her travel alone. By the time I arrived at Beaulieu Gardens they were five hours on the road to their aunt Florence. My time has been better served in attempting to contain the disaster as best I can than following her. She would have known that. She would have calculated on her chastisement being of less importance to me than my duty to you and my family's honour. My Rachel has ever been a beautiful schemer.' He breathed raggedly through white, trembling lips. 'But such merciless plotting is too much. I'll never forgive her for this! In all my life I've never felt so useless or…so angry…or so utterly bereft…'

'Quite…' Connor said.

Chapter One

'Do you not miss having a husband and children of your own, Rachel?'

'I've told you, I'm happy enough to share your Paul…'

'No! Be serious about it,' Lucinda chided on a chuckle. 'Are you ever regretful at having turned down that Mr Featherstone?'

Rachel looked mystified for a moment, her pale brow puckered in concentration. 'Oh, him!' she suddenly exploded on a laugh, having finally placed the last man who had offered for her. That, she realised, had been the basis of his attraction at the time. She had been persuaded—not without foundation as it turned out—that he might be the last eligible man to present himself. And he had seemed well enough: he had a decent head of auburn hair and his own teeth, and wasn't a widower so there wasn't a danger of having his mewling offspring tipped into her lap. But within a month of their engagement being made public, Rachel had realised she wasn't that desperate to attain connubial status after all.

Aware that her friend was awaiting a reply, she dismissed him with a laugh. 'Heavens, no! He was a duellist and a gambler and not very proficient at either. He nigh on had a hand sliced clean off in a sword fight over some Covent Garden nun, and his pockets were to let too often for my liking. I suspect he bargained on having Windrush to refill them at some time.'

'Well, what about that other gentleman? The one who walked with a limp and the aid of a silver-topped stick, but had the face of an Adonis...'

'It's odd you should mention Philip Moncur,' Rachel said on a frown, recalling that particular admirer. 'A month or so ago he sent me some poetry, despite the fact I'd not heard from him for three or more years...since our engagement was broken.'

'How flattering he should remember your fondness for Wordsworth and Keats.'

'Well, if he did remember, he chose to ignore it, and sent me some drivel he'd penned himself—a quatrain that lauded my ethereal radiance and classical serenity. When I ignored that, it was followed by an ode in which he compared me to a marble statue: bleak and beautiful to behold and in need of the sultry sun of his adoration to fire me...'

Lucinda pressed her lips together to stifle a laugh. 'I'd say he's angling to see you in one of Madame Bouillon's togas.'

'I'd say he's angling to see me out of it. Silly man! Why does he not just send over details of his proposition?'

'Rachel! You surely wouldn't consider...well...such an offer?'

'Why not? I think marriage is highly overrated. Being a kept woman has its benefits...money and freedom, to name but two.'

'Well, for goodness' sake! And I would have sworn you would never say or do anything else to shock me!' Lucinda giggled nervously. 'Don't tell June those theories; you know she hangs on your every word deeming it sensible advice. I'd hate *her* to flee at the last minute in a...' Her voice trailed away and she grimaced apology.

'Panic....' Rachel finished the sentence for her, apparently undisturbed by her friend's tactless allusion to her aborted first engagement. But then no one ever referred to *that* episode, under any circumstances. So Rachel simply said, 'Oh, June's different,' whilst fanning her face and throwing back her head to let a breeze beneath the strands of fair hair sticking to her damp neck. 'I can hardly have misgivings about June's match; after all, it took me three whole months to bring it about...'

'About the same time it took you to pair Paul with me,' Lucinda said quietly.

'Yes...I suppose it was about the same.' Rachel cocked her head in mock thoughtfulness. 'My trouble is I'm too selfless. What I should have done was conspired to keep one of those fine fellows for myself.' She sighed theatrically. 'Now I'm on the shelf. I'm reduced to receiving ditties from very poor poets.'

Lucinda chuckled. 'I think Moncur is very Byronesque! Quite gorgeous, in fact, and sensitively cerebral too.'

They sat in amicable quiet for a few moments, watching passing heat-hazy scenery and a procession of flagging promenading ladies. Gauzy muslin shifts were everywhere as were pretty parasols tilting at the hot sun.

'That first gentleman, Rachel...the Irish major...'

'Who?' Rachel snapped, as though annoyed at her friend for picking up the threads of that abandoned conversation. 'Oh, him.' She sighed, bored yet conciliatory. 'That was so long ago, Lucy, I can barely recall how he looks…'

'Well, take a glance to your left and refresh your memory,' Lucinda archly advised.

Rachel did look, quickly, curiously, with a disbelieving smile curving her full, soft lips. It set in stone.

She had often wondered how she would feel if she ever did see him again. After six years, it seemed increasingly unlikely that their paths would cross, especially as she no longer visited London town more than once a year, in the Season, for a short shopping sojourn with her mother and sisters and to see her friend Lucinda. It was only preparations for June's wedding that had brought her family to the metropolis this week.

She had often wondered, too, as the years passed: if a chance meeting occurred, how would he look, how would she look and whether time would make either or both fail to recognise the other. In any case, it was idle trivia and, as such, soon dismissed from her sensible head. The staggering reality was now thrust upon her: just a glimpse of Major Connor Flinte's dark, rugged profile was enough to stir such melancholy memories. Her heart seemed to pause with her breathing; her eyelids drooped in anguish. 'Oh, Isabel…I wish you were here…' she whispered in a ragged little voice.

Lucinda heard the whimper and darted an anxious look her way. 'It's probably not him. I'm sorry. 'Twas a stupid thing to say. That gentleman looks to be too young. The Major must now be in his thirties… He's probably paunchy and greying…and in Ireland…'

'It's him,' Rachel rebutted remotely. Oh, it was him.

She'd known him instantly, yet believed she had forgotten his face. Though he was some distance away, she was sure she could see his gentian eyes; detect a soft Irish brogue on the warm air.

She blinked, took in more of the situation. He was driving a precarious-looking high-flyer and by his side, barely reaching his shoulder, was a dainty female companion looking cool and elegant in sherbet-lemon muslin. The woman's face was hidden from view by a parasol twirling sideways, protecting her face from the afternoon sun low in the western sky. Just a wisp of hair as black as his own could be seen straying beneath her pansy-trimmed straw bonnet.

'I believe that's Signora Laviola with him,' Lucinda said. 'Yes, it is,' she confirmed excitedly as the woman swung her head playfully to one side, as though hiding her coy expression from her laughing companion.

'Don't stare so, Lucinda,' Rachel begged. 'He might turn and see us.'

'He looks to be too engrossed with the sultry songbird,' Lucinda noted. 'So does Lord Harley. See, over there in that curricle with those other goggling fools. The latest gossip is that the lovely Laviola was about to agree to Harley's protection when she dropped him like a stone in favour of a wealthier lover…' Her confidence trailed into belated, tactful silence.

Abruptly, Rachel sat back in the landau's comfy squabs, pulled her own bonnet and parasol askew so it allowed the sun at her complexion but shielded her face from idle glances from the left. 'What *is* blocking the road?' she muttered impatiently, bobbing about to see up ahead. Although some distance apart, the landau and the high-flyer were practically neck and neck and at a standstill, for every conceivable type of conveyance seemed to be, of a sudden, jamming the narrow street.

Lucinda began darting about, too, desperate to get a better look at the Italian soprano who had been in London but a few months, yet had set tongues wagging the moment she arrived. The *signora* was the toast of the *ton*: she had the voice of an angel and a heavenly body every devil wanted in his bed...so Dorothy Draper had told her. Lucinda wondered if her husband, Paul, figured amongst the knaves. She resolved to ask him...perhaps tomorrow, when she felt less fat and homely. She craned her neck more determinedly, but was thwarted in seeing much at all by a hackney cab on the left-hand side that had locked wheels with a brewer's dray. The jarvey had attempted to insinuate an uneasy path between the dray and a coal cart and was now well and truly wedged. No doubt he had been keen to deliver his fare to his destination on time and get a nice tip. Had he managed the manoeuvre it would have been a miracle and money well earned; the narrow street was now choking with carriages and the babble of frustrated people keen to get about their business.

Agitated by the increasing likelihood of a glossy ebony head turning her way to investigate the jarvey's raucous complaints—which seemed to drown out everyone else's—Rachel jumped up to discover what was causing the bottleneck. Her straining senses just caught a few guttural expletives and a wafting aroma of pulped apples. Their cloying aroma hung heavy on the hot air as she watched a costermonger airing his grievances to a listless beagle with much pointing and gesticulating at his upset barrow and spoiled fruit.

The altercation to one side of her, between the jarvey and the young brewer, redrew her attention as they began swapping increasingly inventive insults. The passenger in the hackney then poked his powdered periwig through the window of the cab and made an extremely common gesture at the coalman, who had felt entitled to add his two penn'orth to the raging debate on road manners on account of his bent spokes.

Rachel gave her driver's sleeve a tug. 'Can you not turn this thing about, Ralph?' she begged vainly, for she knew already such a manoeuvre was nigh on impossible in such a crush.

'T'ain't as simple as that, Miss Rachel, or I'd a bin gorn long since. Ladies shouldn't hafta listen ta such tawk.' This observation was accompanied by a baleful glare at the lad on the dray and a censorial shake of the head at the judicial-looking crimped head.

'What is it to you? Eh?' demanded the perspiring face beneath the wig on noting Ralph's disgusted demeanour.

'Ladies present,' Ralph intoned with a nod at his passengers.

'Magistrate present,' the man countered with a grim smirk. 'And I've a good nose for a no-good knave…'

'I'm persuaded…' Ralph muttered beneath his breath.

The magistrate continued tapping his sizeable, greasy proboscis. His mean little eyes swivelled about then he stabbed a finger at the brewer. 'I scent a fiddler. I don't recall that name on your cart, or you, from the Brewster Sessions. I've a mind to see your liquor licence.' It was a wild aim that hit a bull's-eye.

The young man glared at Ralph. 'Now see wot yer done. Couldn't keep yer beak out an' now yer've set the beak on me!'

'Don't dare tawk to me in that there tone o' voice,'

Ralph bellowed, and within a moment was off his perch and on to the dusty cobbles. His temper rendered him deaf to Rachel's hissed orders for him to immediately remount and get them home. Whipping off his smart driver's coat and hat, he shoved starched cotton sleeves towards his elbows.

With an agile spring, the young brewer was soon off his dray and confronting him. Having prepared their palms with spittle, there ensued a pugilistic ritual where they bobbed and swayed whilst circling a circumspect yard apart. Just as Ralph took a stance on his bowed legs and dared to draw off a proper punch, his fist was stopped mid-flight by a large, powerful hand.

'Is there a problem?'

Rachel had not seen anyone approach: she had been preoccupied with priming her weapon; if necessary, she was prepared to prevent Ralph being laid low by braining his youthful opponent with her rolled umbrella. Lucinda's swift intake of breath had Rachel instinctively forcing open the parasol with jittery fingers and tilting it over her face. The soft Irish drawl had already given her a fair warning of who the newcomer might be and as a result her heart was hammering at an alarming rate.

Ralph made a show of belligerently flexing his recently released fingers. 'Lucky you 'appened by, sir. I'd 'ave decked 'im toot sweet an' no mistake.'

The coalman, atop his cart, had been leaning forward in rapt anticipation. Now he flopped back, folded his arms, and expressed his disappointment at the aborted bout with some weird facial contortions. He denied Ralph his optimism regarding the outcome by sucking his teeth and shaking his head.

The magistrate welcomed the arbitrator by waving

an indolent hand through the cab window. He knew an affluent, influential gentleman when he spotted one and liked to foster any such acquaintance. 'These two ruffians...' a finger indicated the coalman and the brewer '...are aggressive fellows taking fun from impeding me in my lawful business. I'm due in sessions...' he extricated his pocket watch '...damme...some ten minutes since.' And this fellow—' he nodded so sharply at Ralph his wig slid over his eyes '—is determined to be as insolent and offensive as may be. I'll see the lot of 'em flogged and fined for disorderly conduct and obstructing a Justice of the Peace.' The periwig was straightened with a satisfied flourish.

'That's not fair! And not true, either!' Unable to listen to the wild exaggerations, Rachel emerged from behind her parasol, which she shut with a snap. With a deep breath she raised her golden head.

The distinguished gentleman with jet-black hair and a devastating likeness to her erstwhile fiancé was so close to the side of the landau she could have reached out and touched him. Bravely she skimmed nonchalant sky-blue eyes over his strong familiar features. *It's not him: I don't recall him being quite so tall or so dark,* was one welcome and coherent thought which emerged from the jumble in her mind. Her eyes sped on to glare at his worship.

The magistrate was gawping in disbelief that this pretty little madam had made such bold accusations, or that they could possibly be directed at himself.

'If you had waited your turn in the queue instead of attempting to barge ahead, the carriage wheels would not have tangled. We would now all be going peaceably about our business,' Rachel reasoned hotly, leaving his worship in no doubt he was the target of her denunciation.

The magistrate's jowls sunk to his chest before he recovered composure and set them wobbling with a determined twitch of his head. 'My dear young woman.' His tone dripped condescension. 'Have you any idea just *who* you are talking to? *Who* you are accusing of that grave sin: bearing false witness?' His smooth tone conveyed he knew exactly who *he* was talking to and he was not impressed: she was one of those blue-stockings with milky liberal views and no proper respect for the authority of a superior male.

'But *I* know who you are,' a congenial mellow voice interjected. 'Arthur Goodwin, Esquire, isn't it now? I believe I recognise you from Mrs Crawford's little soi-rée last week...or is it that I'm about to bear false witness...?'

Arthur Goodwin, Esquire, suddenly lost the puffed-up demeanour he had adopted when this fine-looking gentleman claimed his acquaintance and instead looked exceedingly wary. 'Indeed,' he croaked. 'I...er...I... might have been there...I don't seem to recall you.'

'I'm not offended...'

Arthur's eyes swivelled at the irony in the accented remark. That particular evening, at that particular lady's bacchanalian extravaganza, he couldn't have re-called his own name, he'd been so foxed. He'd barely remembered to retrieve his breeches from the mattress of the adolescent minx who'd serviced him before wending his way home. 'Pray remind me who you are, sir?' he burbled in a jolly tone.

'Devane...Lord Devane. Strange that we meet again

so soon. How is Mrs Goodwin? You mentioned she was suffering, as I recall.'

'Indeed…I might have said so…' Arthur squeaked, already fearful of the peal he'd be rung by his good lady should she get wind of his regular visits to Mrs Crawford's to discover if new young girls were taken on. Should the virtuous lady come to hear that he'd been known to curse her as a frigid, scab-faced slut when in his cups… Like a timid snail, his head retracted into the safety of the cab.

Samuel Smith, the young man who had been driving the dray, was ready with a covert wink of sheer admiration as his saviour looked his way. It was followed by a nod of gratitude.

'Care to help with this wheel of yours?' Connor responded drily, a tip of his dark head indicating the buckled rim.

Sam immediately set to.

'Have *you* a spare minute to lend a hand?' Connor enquired with a look at the coalman.

The slump-shouldered merchant jerked out of the trance brought on by the fascinating proceedings, realising he'd forgotten about his final delivery, lumped on the back of his cart.

The jarvey gamely pitched in too and, like the other men, speculatively eyed this handsome gentry cove with such a quiet, commanding way about him.

Sam Smith found himself pondering his lordship's motives for getting involved at all; which brought him to sliding glances at the beautiful blonde woman in the top-notch landau. His Nibs seemed particularly interested in her; although she seemed determined to look every place possible but at him. Which was odd, considering her friend couldn't take her curious eyes off him.

But it had been the fair lady who'd championed them. Usually the Quality didn't know the trades existed...until they needed a hasty ride or a fire in the grate, or their cellar stocked on the cheap. But she'd spoken up for three menials for no more reason than that the pompous toad of a beak hadn't been right nor fair... But then he'd heard tell of his worship Arthur Goodwin and already knew he never was...

Ralph bent knowledgeably over the warped axle, testing its weight, ready to assist the men with the repairs. Rachel discreetly beckoned him, with frantic fingers, desperate to be heading home. There were many dark, heart-rending memories being stirred by the sudden appearance of this man who resembled Connor Flinte so exactly, and she wanted to be alone to decide if she were brave enough today to pick them over.

The traffic was again moving freely. In the distance the costermonger could just be glimpsed towing his cart and at intervals gesturing obscenities at those vehicles whose passengers were still irritated enough at the delay to chivvy him as they passed. The only other stationary vehicles left in the street were Lord Devane's phaeton and Lord Harley's curricle, which had now managed to manoeuvre a path to the phaeton and its pretty passenger.

Surreptitiously, Rachel observed the Italian woman who was acting the coquette with three raucous dandies. However diligently she flirted, she was managing to keep a vigilant dark eye on her absent companion. Rachel hadn't noticed Lord Devane look back at *her* once.

Lord Devane? Rachel rolled the name around in her

mind. From what she recalled, he sounded like Major
Flinte when he spoke, he looked like him when she
allowed her eyes to flit to his rugged visage…but the
name was new to her. Was the man too…?

'Let us be heading home, Ralph,' tumbled from her
lips whilst her mind investigated the absurd possibility
that there might be two such striking-looking Irish gentlemen, and a case of mistaken identity. She knew he
had a stepbrother of about the same age, but remembered that Jason Davenport had fair hair and, being of
different parentage, naturally looked quite different.

Having been lax earlier, Ralph made amends by immediately doing his mistress's bidding. He launched
himself into the driver's seat with a sprightliness that
mocked his bowed legs and advanced years.

Lord Devane strolled over, seeming to accidentally
arrest their departure by catching the bridle of the nearest grey in order to fondle its ears. The mare turned its
head willingly into the deft caress. 'We've not had a
chance to exchange a few words…' The casual address
was at odds with the sharp blue eyes minutely examining Rachel's features.

With an amount of pique, Rachel realised that if it
was Major Flinte, she had been a little arrogant in assuming *he* would know who *she* was. There was no
discernible recognition in his eyes, just the steady attention of a man appraising an attractive woman. And
she knew she was deemed pretty. Her parents told her
so, Lucinda told her so, her mirror reflected their views.

Gentlemen who didn't know her at all sought intro-
ductions; gentlemen who *did* know of her, and her history of failed romances, still sought to charm her,
vainly confident that they could be the one to turn the
tables on her and break her heart. She found it faintly

amusing that they believed her in the dark over their designs or their motives. She had heard the gossip that sums of money had been wagered in the past on who would successfully woo and win her, then unceremoniously ditch *her* in a very public way.

So, when in London, she allowed a few stupid fellows to come calling and take her for a drive in Hyde Park at the fashionable hour; she encouraged them to visit her parents' box at the opera or theatre. Just as gossip was fomenting over what seemed to be a particular attachment between herself and a town dandy, she would scupper it by snubbing him forthwith, thus reinforcing her reputation as a callous little tease. She had no regrets; and she had no conscience over it, she told herself, apart from the very mundane one of never having profited herself from a little flutter on the outcome of the gentlemen's puerile games.

The horses snickered, jolting her to the present. Her eyes flicked up, met a narrowed blue stare fringed by the longest lashes. Something turbulent…frustrating inside her stilled, became calm.

Oh, it's him…and he knows me; he thinks he knows what I'm brooding on too. He knows nothing of how I really feel. Do I know how he feels? Is he still angry at me? Still bitter and resentful at having been publicly humiliated? It must have been awful for him…so humbling… There's nothing in his face…no emotion at all. Why is he passing himself off as a lord? Simply to impress that weasel of a judge?

If so, the ploy had worked. The hackney carrying Arthur Goodwin to court passed close by on wobbly wheels, and the magistrate's face appeared at the window. A tentative, conspiratorial smile flickered at Lord Devane before he was borne away.

The dray and coal cart soon followed the hackney. His lordship inclined his dark head in acknowledgement of their waves and shouted farewells.

'*Noblesse oblige,*' Rachel muttered sourly beneath her breath. It mattered little whether he was now a real aristocrat or afflicted by delusions of grandeur, he was simply Major Flinte to her and thus she need not fret over offending him. That, in all its terrible effect, was already achieved... 'Remove your hand, please, so we might leave,' she instructed coolly.

Lucinda, who had been quietly watching the tense, wordless interaction between the couple, spluttered out, 'I am Mrs Saunders, Lucinda Saunders. I am very grateful for your assistance, my lord. It could have ended badly had you not intervened. Thankfully, all has turned out well...' A meaningful look then slid to her friend, inviting Rachel to take up the conversation.

'And you are...?' a soft voice prompted.

Rachel swung her head about, looked levelly at him. 'Oh, I am...very grateful for your assistance, too, sir. And you are...about to be so good as to immediately step aside so that I might get along home.' Rachel tapped Ralph's arm and settled back into the squabs.

Ralph looked abashed. He looked at their Good Samaritan, he looked at his churlish mistress. He settled on looking off into middle distance. The horses remained idle.

'Shall I tell you what I think you are?'

Rachel felt the cheek turned to him prickle, her heart slowly thud. 'You obviously have time to waste, sir. I have none; but if you must accost me, please make it quick, for I am getting quite impatient.' She flicked her golden head, gazing past his broad shoulders encased in finest taupe material. 'As is your carriage companion. I believe she is trying to attract your attention.' Her flitting eyes had alighted on an olive-skinned visage peering at them over a sherbet-pale shoulder. The Italian woman was practically bouncing on the seat as she shifted back and forth in irritation, and her head turned every few seconds to stare at them. The diva had certainly lost her air of cool sophistication along with her trio of admirers: Lord Harley's curricle was just turning left at the top of the street.

Connor Flinte seemed little interested in his phaeton or its passenger. Just an idle glance arrowed that way and he seemed no more inclined to rush off than before. In fact, he waited until Rachel looked at him again before replying, 'You want me to be quick? Are you sure? It's been so long, too…' The hard smile that followed that soft speech sent Rachel's pulse pounding. 'Very well. What I think you are…is little changed, Miss Meredith. That's my initial opinion.' He gave a small, lopsided smile while watching a few of his fingers smooth a languid path along the landau's glossy coachwork. Deep blue eyes mocked her beneath heavy eyelids. 'And that's fortunate for me. But pretty disastrous for you…' he added in a voice as sweet as honey. Then he was walking back towards his phaeton. He'd taken up the ribbons and soothed the signora's ruffled feathers by the time Rachel gathered sense enough to choke at Ralph,

'Home, please! Now!'

Chapter Two

He will not ruin what is left of my day, Rachel vowed silently as she banished persistently intrusive thoughts of Major Flinte from her mind and walked arm-in-arm with Sylvie along the carpeted corridor to find their sister June.

Truce! No baskets or garlands, Rachel had told her little sister moments before, with a rueful smile. Earlier in the day they had argued over their bridesmaids' bouquets and, in doing so, upset June, soon to be a bride. Now Rachel felt eager to restore harmony. 'A posy of gardenias dotted with laurel leaves and trailing ivy…that's a fair compromise, don't you think?'

Sylvie gazed up at her eldest sister with large, luminous eyes the colour of violent storm clouds. 'It sounds…tolerable, I suppose,' she sighed. Her cheeky lack of enthusiasm was belied by the wordless hug of thanks she gave her big sister. 'William is arrived to dine. He is terribly good looking, isn't he? I should have liked to marry him if only he would have waited a while and not fallen in love with June. Will you find someone like William for me, Rachel? Perhaps a bit taller, with dark hair instead of fair, and longer sideburns, and no freckles. I'm not sure I like freckles on a man, even just that little bit William has across his nose. I'm not sure I like them on a woman, either. Noreen doesn't like hers; she puts lemon juice on her face to try and whiten them, you know.'

Rachel smiled while her slender fingers combed through Sylvie's platinum curls. Once let loose, they rebounded immediately into supple coils. 'You, my love, will probably have no trouble in finding just the right man, and without any help from me when the time comes. I shall be approaching my dotage, you know, when you hit your prime, and probably be resigned to knitting, not matchmaking. I can see it now,' Rachel sighed. 'Seven years hence, you will be the bane of our poor papa's life and breaking the hearts of gallants with careless abandon.'

'Like you do now, you mean?' Sylvie innocently chirped up. She'd heard that her elder sister was called a nasty flirt. In fact, since she was six years old and the awful thing happened to Isabel, she'd grown used to overhearing whispers about Rachel's heartless treatment of gentlemen.

As no one ever told her much, still stupidly believing her a baby, she'd learned to glean snippets of interesting news by loitering out of sight when Noreen and her sister, Madcap Mary, were in a confab. She'd learned of Rachel's poor reputation that way, and of June's proposal from Mr William Pemberton. She'd looked suitably surprised, though, when her mother told her a few days later she was to have a brother-in-law.

The Shaughnessy sisters would pick things over while polishing silver in the back parlour or making the beds. Noreen did most of the picking and her blockhead sister most of the nodding. But every so often Madcap might bark out her own rough idea on what's to do in the Meredith household. And sometimes, Sylvie thought, it wasn't as daft as it ought to be...

'No, please don't follow my example...' A throbbing solemnity to Rachel's words made Sylvie snap out of her reverie and angle a curious look up at her.

'I expect we might find the lovebirds in here.' Rachel abruptly pushed open the door to their little library.

Their sister June and her charming fiancé, William Pemberton, were nowhere to be seen. But the room *was* occupied: by her parents, seated either side of the table. So earnestly were they conversing across its leather top that it was a moment before they realised they were not alone. Both Mr and Mrs Meredith looked startled and a little discomfited at the sight of two of their beautiful daughters joining them.

Sylvie broke free of Rachel's sisterly clasp and ran, in a rustle of georgette and an unusual fit of demonstrative affection, to hug her papa. Edgar Meredith patted at his little daughter's white hands, clasped round his neck.

Rachel, cursed with a heightened perception of other people's moods—especially her parents'—felt her stomach flutter in anticipation. 'Is anything the matter? Has Madame Bouillon tendered yet more outrageous suggestions for our costumes next month?' The modiste making their wedding finery had lately been tendering increasingly bizarre designs for their approval. 'Never fear, I can deal with her, you know.'

Her papa sketched a smile. 'I've never doubted that, my dear. I took your good advice, Rachel. I hid well away until she was gone. No feathers and fronds for me…'

Rachel's exquisite powder-blue eyes skimmed the desk top. 'Has the post been while I was out?' she asked, noting the letter that seemed to lie portentously between her papa's squarish hands. The palms were flattened on the leather as though he might at any minute shove himself back from the table.

'No…not the post. This was hand-delivered by a servant. It's simply a reply to a wedding invitation,' Gloria Meredith volunteered in a tone that was far too airily dismissive to properly erase her eldest daughter's apprehension. Every aspect of June's marriage preparations was treated very seriously.

Rachel sat in a chair by the hearth. It was not lit as the day was still warm enough to make the idea of a fire positively unwelcome. Instinctively she inclined towards the grate, recalling that earlier, as she had been on the point of setting off in the landau to go to Charing Cross with Lucinda, a smartly rigged servant had been on his way up the steps of their town house. She had supposed the errand that brought him was something to do with her papa's city affairs. As she believed all wedding invitations issued months ago and all expected replies long since received, she would never have guessed the true nature of his call.

Sylvie wandered away to an open casement and playfully hung herself over the sill. Stretching to a shrub just below, she proceeded to bat at a branch laden with lilac heads. A pleasing, delicate scent spread into the room on the sultry dusky air. Rachel frowned at the disturbance, for there was a disquieting atmosphere within the room her straining senses could detect but not quite fathom. 'Well, don't keep me in suspense,' she lightly chided. 'Who is this late-invited guest? A celebrity we must have? Or are we simply making up numbers? Have there been some recent cancellations? Whose company are we now to be graced with at Windrush?'

After a pregnant pause, in which her parents' eyes clashed, then skittered in opposite directions, her papa said with a sigh, 'It's from the Earl of Devane. It's a refusal, or should I say, his lordship declines, with thanks, our kind invitation, for naturally he is too well-mannered to simply reject us. It is obvious he has given the occasion no real thought: he has responded far too quickly for that.'

'The Earl of Devane?' Rachel breathed, the shock of hearing that name again so soon quelling her feelings of indignation at the family snub. '*Lord* Devane?' Rachel repeated in a voice of strengthening incredulity.

'Yes,' her father confirmed with a significant look at his wife. 'You sound as though you know his lordship…'

'*Do I?*' Rachel demanded in return.

'You…you spoke as though the name sounded familiar to you, my dear,' her papa ventured.

'That's because I spoke this afternoon to a man styling himself so.'

'You did? *Where?*' her parents chorused in surprise, unsure now whether to look glad or aghast on learning this news.

'The meeting was on the highway, brought about by a little carriage accident,' Rachel informed them, jumping to her feet. 'No; not the landau.' She mistook her papa's obvious consternation on hearing this news as a reasonable anxiety over damage to his new coach rather than to his eldest daughter.

'What *is* going on? Lord Devane is Connor Flinte, or I'm very much mistaken. What has he done? Bought himself a title with his army severance pay?' she scoffed.

'Nothing so vulgar, my dear,' her father corrected in a tone of mild reproof, as a paternal eye checked her over for any sign of physical injury. 'He has simply taken up his birthright. His Irish grandfather, on his mother's side, has recently died and the Major has inherited his earldom. The succession was gazetted. He is quite entitled to style himself Lord Devane.'

Whilst digesting this startling news, Rachel's thoughts scampered ahead. She flicked an accusing finger at the parchment laying on the leather-topped table. 'What…what do you mean, invitation? You surely *would* not…*have* not…invited him to June's wedding after all that went on?' She fell silent, chewing her lip. All that *went on* had been of her doing. *He* was blameless, as her parents, especially her father, had reiterated time and again in absolute despair just after that awful episode. 'Why on earth would you ask him to attend when it is likely that his appearance would excite every kind of speculation and spiteful probing? People are bound to again ask unanswerable questions about what happened to Isabel and…and—' She broke off, unable to say more, her burning eyes covered by a cool, pale hand.

'We don't talk of Isabel, you know that,' her white-faced mother faintly chided with a searching look at her youngest daughter. Sylvie appeared to be in her own little world with her chin resting on her clasped hands as she gazed out into a beautiful early evening.

'He declines.' Edgar quickly changed subject in a tone laden with profound disappointment. 'We have

Lord Devane's refusal within a few hours of the invitation being issued. I think that tells us all we need to know. He was his usual polite and dignified self when I gave it him. And he will doubtless continue to be civil. But he has no intention of accepting the olive branch your mama and I have bravely extended. Our intention was to put paid to any residual bad feeling, and in a way that was private, and yet acceptably public too. What better way for us to collaborate in showing the world that all is forgiven and forgotten, than to join together in celebrating a wedding? What more fitting occasion than June's marriage to William? They are two of the mildest-mannered, most inoffensive people anyone is ever likely to encounter...' After a dejected sigh he continued, 'Connor's co-operation in this would have laid the scandal permanently to rest. But we have had our olive branch immediately returned to us, in perfect order, of course.' One of Edgar Meredith's fingers absently touched the crisp parchment in front of him. 'I believe I knew all along what his answer would be and I cannot blame him...'

'No, you never could do that...' Rachel said with quiet, bitter censure.

'There was nothing he did that I could arraign. He behaved impeccably even under direst duress,' her father whipped back with uncommon force and volume. His eyes fixed on his daughter and his withered lips strained thinner. 'With what should I have charged him? Being too perfect a gentlemen? Being too lacking in greed and self-interest? The contracts were signed, the wedding a little over twelve hours away; he might have successfully sued for breach of promise and taken your dowry, you know. He held it in his power to shame and ruin us all. It would have done me no favours in the city to have contested such a controversial case. And your reputation, miss, would have never recovered from being dragged through such mire. Instead, he took unwarranted humiliation on himself and spared you. He suffered unwarranted financial losses and spared me. The Major was greatly out-of-pocket from his own expenses, yet refused any recompense I offered. I even had to insist he take back your betrothal ring! He wanted nothing, not even that to which he was perfectly entitled!'

Gloria Meredith shot up from the table as her husband's voice quavered with barely suppressed pain and anger. An unsteady hand was held out cautioning Edgar, the other extended, palm up, appealing to her white-faced eldest daughter. 'Enough! Let's not quarrel. How silly this has all been. I believe it was a foolish thing to do, my dear,' she tentatively put to her husband. 'Our intentions were good: healing rifts and finally putting the tragedy behind us is what we wanted. Yet, in truth, it is achieving nought but breaking open the scar. The Major…Lord Devane,' she corrected herself on a tiny, forced smile, 'manages to act decorously at all times, yet we find ourselves unable to do ought but bicker amongst ourselves. Let's not make him out too much of the hero in this.'

'Yes, let's not.' Rachel clipped out coldly. For a moment or two she and her father faced each other in a hostile, combative silence that was eventually brought to a close when the library door was opened.

June and William entered, laughing. After a few paces, they hesitated, their similar expressions frozen into mask-like smiles, as they both sensed the tension within the room. Recovering her composure, June, who was barely five feet in height but supple as a sapling, threaded her tiny hand through her fiancé's brawny arm, and bravely proceeded to haul his tall, sturdy frame into the library, a sunny smile re-animating her sweet, heart-shaped countenance.

'Ah, there you are, June; come in...come in!' Mrs Meredith greeted them with such a wealth of welcome and gratitude in her voice, her third daughter might have recently returned from overseas instead of across the street where she and William had been visiting friendly neighbours. 'How are you, William?' she demanded. 'It will be good to see your parents at their *musicale* later this week. It's a while since I spoke to them. Your mama and I must catch up on how preparations proceed for the big day...' In her haste to say something, anything, to ease the atmosphere, Gloria had forgotten that she disliked her daughter's prospective mother-in-law. Since their betrothal, she had gained the impression that Pamela Pemberton deemed June way below her son's social station, and that she fully expected any preparations made by the Merediths for William's wedding would be found sadly lacking in grandeur.

Thankfully, William's sincere devotion to his betrothed proved he was at odds with his mother. He worshipped the ground that June tripped upon, treating her with affectionate reverence, and on visiting Windrush, venue of their marriage, he had been delighted with the place, claiming that, in all things, he was a very fortunate man.

And indeed he was. By anyone's standards, June was exceedingly fine in looks and character; and no expense had been spared in ensuring the wedding celebration would befit the union of two wealthy families. It would be a day to remember. Rachel and everyone had said so…and so it must be…

Besides, why accept the role of underdog? Mr Meredith could boast a city salary comparable to, if not slightly in excess of, Alexander Pemberton's income from his law practice. Thus Gloria was of a mind that the Pembertons had nothing to feel superior about. Perhaps Pamela *could* lay claim to a distant ducal connection, but it was so far removed as to be utterly worthless. With a wry, private smile, Gloria recalled her sweet Rachel saucily airing that opinion direct to Pamela when they were sitting out a set at the Winthrops' midsummer ball last year.

In fact, bearing in mind how her eldest daughter had contrived to put Pamela firmly in her place, *and* bring about a proper introduction between June and that woman's son on the very same occasion, it was a miracle that her schemes to matchmake the pair had been such an outstanding success. June and William were deeply in love, there would be a grand wedding and nothing must spoil their joyous occasion. Gloria was as determined on that score as was her eldest daughter.

Gloria slid a glance at Rachel; it skipped to Edgar. Father and daughter had retreated, still bristling, to opposite sides of the room, ostentatiously far apart. Yet in many ways they were so close. Both stubborn, protective of people they cared about and apt to act rashly or on impulse. Yet they were also at times ready with very sensible opinions. It was just a shame that they rarely accepted such common-sense advice themselves when it was offered.

A little smile touched Gloria's lips as she watched her husband making an effort to appear calm and convivial as he chatted to William about the new bay hunter he had that week purchased. For all William's upright, amenable nature, she knew he would never come close to replacing the marvellous son who had slipped so suddenly through Edgar's acquisitive fingers six years ago. What worried Gloria was that her husband had never fully accepted that particular relationship was lost to him...And he must...

Her grey eyes traversed to Rachel. In profile she looked quite breathtakingly lovely as she rested her golden head on the casement frame and gazed off over the cloud-darkling lawns. In such a demure, alluring pose it was hard to conceive she couldn't have any man she set her heart on. But, to Gloria's infinite regret, she couldn't now bring to mind any gentleman who seemed to pay serious attentions towards her eldest daughter. For a year or more, since Rachel turned twenty-four, she had accepted that her first-born was likely to remain a spinster, not only because gentlemen were wary of her reputation but because she herself would opt to keep that status.

It was unfair; other women had daughters with squints and buck teeth who had married well. She had a girl blessed with the serene, classical beauty that painters and poets swooned over and strove to capture with their craft, yet still she remained unloved by any but her family. Who would believe that beneath those honed, fragile bones lay a steely will, or that her cool, fair looks concealed a bold and fiery temperament. And then there was Isabel...dear, sweet Isabel, lost to her so young before she had had a chance of making a good match...Gloria felt her eyes fill with tears. She mustn't think of Isabel...not now. She had another daughter to concentrate on. June was just as worthy of her attention as were Rachel and Sylvie, even though, bless her, she never seemed to demand or require it as did the others…

Approaching the open window where Rachel and Sylvie stood together, Gloria automatically tidied the curtains billowing in a balmy breeze. Sylvie suddenly leaned out over the sill again, snapped off a twig of lilac and, separating the cluster of blooms, presented one to her sister and the other to her mama. Then, careless of her clothes or modesty, she hoisted herself in a white flash of ruffled drawers and petticoats right over the ledge and slipped away into the garden.

'Oh, that girl!' Gloria muttered ruefully. 'Truth to tell, there are days when I wonder if she is a girl at all. She's the greatest tomboy of the four of you and I thought you were never to be beaten on that score. Do you remember your tree-house and that collection of crawlies you kept?' Gloria gave a delicate shudder. 'You had quite a menagerie, as I recall: insects, amphibians from the pond, and that grass snake. Poor Isabel was frightened witless by that enormous furry caterpillar you put in her bed…' Her mother's voice cracked and she rapidly blinked her eyes.

Rachel bowed her head, letting the powdery perfumed petals of Sylvie's gift brush her face. 'Poor Isabel,' she softly echoed. 'Poor Papa, too,' she added in a wry tone. 'He has ever been disappointed with me, hasn't he? He would have preferred it if I had been born a boy, I know. Then I might have collected beasts to my heart's content and had Windrush as my inheritance to his heart's content.'

'All fathers yearn for a son and heir, Rachel,' her mother responded mildly. 'It's the way of the world.'

'It's why he wanted me so soon married, isn't it? To

get his son at last. I was but nineteen,' she reminded her mother in a raw voice.

'Not so very young, my dear,' Gloria rebutted. 'I was a month short of my eighteenth birthday when I married your papa. I was a month short of my nineteenth birthday when you were born...'

'That was then! I feel differently. Six years ago I wasn't ready to be anyone's wife!'

'You said you were, Rachel. No one coerced you to accept Connor's proposal, certainly not the man himself. You insisted that you were in love. Your papa needed to know that before he accepted Connor's suit. Your happiness was paramount. Perhaps I mistake my guess, but I would have said, at first, you were very much in love with your fiancé...'

'I was wrong. I made a mistake when still a teenager, yet I must pay and pay.'

'That's not true, Rachel,' Gloria soothed with a catch to her voice and a glance at her husband. 'You cannot honestly say that we have persecuted you over this, can you?'

'Besides, Papa has his son now,' Rachel said, humbled by her mother's gentle honesty. 'William is a fine man; quite the perfect addition to any family.'

'The lilac will be finished when June is married.' Gloria changed the subject after a significant pause, cupping the fragrant floret in her hand. 'Such a pity: the chapel always looks so picturesque when the bushes are in full bloom by the lych-gate.'

'The roses will be out and the lilies...and the jasmine and sweet peas...' Rachel smiled faintly. 'The gardens will look splendid...everything will be splendid.'

Rachel knew that her mother needed reassurance on

much more than the estate's variety of horticulture. But she hadn't overstated the wonderful show of flowers they could expect next month. If anyone knew Windrush and its natural attributes, Rachel did. She was cognisant with the entire estate: from dry stone wall to chimney stack, from lilac bush to lily pond. Every one of its two hundred acres was familiar, dear to her. And, unusually, despite being female, one day it would be hers. As eldest child it was her inheritance.

'I don't want to pry, my dear, but was Connor…did he…?'

Rachel gave a choke of laughter. 'Yes, mama, he did recognise me and, yes, I believe he has an axe to grind, although for the moment he keeps it suitably sheathed. To be fair, he behaved very well…impeccably, as Papa would put it. He came to our assistance, actually, and but for his intervention we might even now be stranded in Charing Cross, watching brave Ralph doing battle with a brewer…' She gave her mother a concise account of what had occurred, and the people involved. Finally she added, 'It's odd; yesterday, I would have sworn I could not have accurately described how he looks after all this time. Yet I recognised him straight away; the moment Lucinda pointed him out…' Tiny lilac buds were absently nipped away with her nails and dropped through the window on to the dry earth below.

'What did he say to you? What did you say to him? You weren't rude, Rachel, were you? Your papa would be furious if he thought you had again been mean to that man.'

'Of course not.' Rachel reassured her on a faint laugh, feeling her insides squirm at the fib. In truth, she *was* remorseful over her behaviour. Lord Devane was a stranger now and he had given her no real cause to be surly. The lilac head was ferociously denuded, then tossed away. 'He said…well, not much actually. He just mentioned he thought me little changed…'

The cadence of his Irish drawl had been imprinted on her mind ever since: *You're little changed, Miss Meredith, and that's fortunate for me and pretty disastrous for you…*

A sense of deep foreboding had assailed her thereafter as she'd watched him stroll so casually away. His words had been carefully chosen for effect, she knew, and should not be too carefully attended, yet she had constantly picked them over for hidden meaning. During their carriage ride home, Lucinda had said that she'd certainly detected sarcasm in his comment, but nothing more sinister. In fact, she'd admitted to finding his humour rather droll and appealing, which had earned her a scowl from Rachel.

But Rachel had felt reassured by Lucinda's objective opinion, and by the time she reached Beaulieu Gardens had decided that Lord Devane's remarks were intended to be crushing rather than threatening. He had been ironically giving thanks for having escaped marriage to a woman who was still, as he saw it, sadly lacking in the basic graces. Had she given a fig how he took to her after six years, she might have felt mortified…but she didn't, so she wasn't…

As her reflection subsided, Rachel became conscious of her mother's steady gaze. Casually, she resumed recounting the details of this afternoon's events. 'Then Lord Devane departed in his phaeton with a female companion. Lucinda believes the woman is an Italian opera singer who is allegedly all the rage and very popular with the gentlemen. I imagine they are…are in a liaison: she seemed keen for him to rejoin her, and to witness her flirting with a few macaronis who were dawdling about. Anyway,' Rachel concluded on a smile, 'I am quite glad now that we did happen upon each other. After six years, the dreaded meeting has come and gone…and good riddance. And I'm sure his lordship feels the same way. Whatever Papa says, I am glad the Earl of Devane had the good sense and manners to reject the wedding invitation and stay well away. He obviously deems it best not to socialise with us and I, for one, do not feel we shall be deprived of his company. Quite the reverse.'

'It sounds as though his lady friend might have been Maria Laviola…'

'Yes, I think that's the name that Lucinda mentioned.'

Gloria Meredith seemed about to add something, but a winsome smile closed her dropped jaw, not further conversation. The news that Signora Laviola was to be guest of honour at the Pembertons' *musicale* planned for later in the week might, on reflection, be best kept to herself.

She patted affectionately at her eldest daughter's arm while pondering that if the fêted diva was Devane's mistress, then he would probably deign to attend that evening. If Rachel knew, she might possibly make excuses to stay away. Gloria didn't want that. Her eldest daughter's unusual absence from their family party might stir more spiteful speculation than would her appearance at the same venue as the man she had once callously jilted. Rachel was right: the dreaded reunion was over with. It was now time for all concerned to treat the affair as old news and render the gossips disappointed. With another little pat at Rachel's arm she approached June and William, determined to try and prise out of her prospective son-in-law a few details about his mother's chosen outfit for the nuptials.

Chapter Three

He was glad he still had that effect on her, Connor thought as he watched Rachel Meredith blush. Even when they'd been engaged, she would colour prettily at the sight of him. In his youthful arrogance, he'd liked to imagine it was in pleasure. His cynical smile strengthened, causing her to sharply turn her head. Now he knew differently. She'd blushed then, as she did now, because his presence disconcerted her and she wanted one or other of them to be elsewhere. A mean achievement, to be sure; nevertheless, a part of him was satisfied knowing something was the same: she wasn't entirely indifferent to him.

Under cover of a laughing conversation with his stepbrother, he leisurely repositioned himself so he could discreetly study her. His eyes skimmed her sylph-like silhouette, sheathed in opalescent blue silk. Was she presenting him with her best side? he wryly wondered, as his eyes lingered on her perfect profile. Her golden ringlets looked artfully arranged, the column of her long neck beneath the burnished coils of hair resembled flawless alabaster. Quite a goddess, he reflected ironically, then winced. It was too much truth for comfort. Earlier this week he'd seen her at close quarters and he'd not managed to stop thinking of her since. Grudgingly, he'd had to admit to himself that, even though approaching twenty-six, she was certainly as lovely as she ever had been. Now she was on her feet, with her figure properly displayed, she was revealed to be as alluring and desirable as the nineteen-year old temptress who'd enslaved him. If anything, her shape looked lusciously fuller.

And God knew she had tempted him, behaving like a novice Jezebel while he had behaved like a eunuch, who also acquiesced to act blind, deaf and dumb. He'd not been unaware six years ago that the bold teasing glances from her big blue eyes were not exclusively his privilege. Louche gallants who preyed on and pandered to the vanity of responsive females had been similarly enticed by his beloved. Those gentlemen had relished seeing him suffer in silence whilst his future wife playfully acted the coquette and treated him like a risible fool.

He was cognisant with beau monde etiquette: a lady—especially one whose reputation was protected by a formal relationship—was permitted to have her circle of admirers. He knew, too, that a display of jealousy by a partner was seen as unnecessary and vulgar. Even so, there had been times when polite society mores put his teeth on edge, when his patience and endurance had been strained to the limit. On one particular occasion at Vauxhall Gardens, Rachel's blatant flirting with a dandified fop he was known to detest had engendered such mischievous gossip as couldn't be ignored. He'd been on the point of dragging her into the nearest thicket, to teach her a lesson in prudent behaviour around aroused men, when she'd smiled at him as though no one else mattered.

So he'd let her be, even though knowing there was little more implied than that she'd mastered the art of defusing his ire and keeping him tame. He had been in love with her, and curbing his temper, his male needs and acting in the way he thought she'd wanted had become second nature. How wrong he'd been. She hadn't ever wanted him at all. For her, it had all been some sort of childish game she had decided to play on her terms...only her terms, or he paid a forfeit.

Of their own volition his eyes were straying to her body again. He watched her sense his scrutiny, become flustered beneath his roving eyes. She half-turned towards him as though she might challenge his covert observation with a steely glare. Instead, she put a hand to her face; it cupped a rosy cheek, then fussed at her hair before she deliberately presented him with her graceful back.

A very sardonic smile slanted his sensual lips; the provocative little madam with come-hither eyes was gone. Perhaps in the interim a man with a shorter fuse than he had treated her to a much-needed lesson in modesty and respectful behaviour. He'd heard she'd aborted other betrothals over the years and now was considered on the shelf; not primarily because of her age, for her inheritance was a tempting lure, but because she was branded a heartless tease who might make ridiculous any man who dared approach her.

She certainly exuded an air of tranquil detachment in her frost-blue gown and, though he couldn't compare them now her back was turned, he knew the shade matched her large, icy eyes.

Since the moment he'd caught sight of her looking

cool and content, chatting to her friend in her landau, he'd wanted to upset her equilibrium. Yet, strangely, when she'd been hemmed in on all sides by belligerent men, he'd been only a moment or two entertained by her predicament before he'd found himself stepping in to help. And why he'd made that stupid remark on taking his leave, he'd no idea. Simply to unsettle her, he supposed.

And now he had the urge to do it again. He wanted to strip her of hauteur and deliberately make her hurt the way she had deliberately hurt him. He wanted to be her nemesis. And that was curious. Six years ago he'd congratulated himself—others had, too—on coping admirably with the loss and humiliation of being jilted. Then he'd forgotten her. He'd fought a war, made enemies, made friends, made money—he'd even made love once or twice in amongst the numerous couplings he'd enjoyed. Now, because his lost fiancée looked beautiful and unmarked by any of it, he was consciously acknowledging his need for revenge.

He dropped his eyes from her, quelling a twinge of self-disgust, and indicated to his brother they should move. Making polite responses to the many greetings received en route, he allowed Jason to steer him slowly through the people thronging the Pembertons' hallway. Eventually they'd picked a path to a dual stairway that marched in symmetrical twisting sweeps to the reception rooms above. Through the din of a hundred conversations, Connor could detect instruments being tuned in readiness for tonight's concert. As he mounted the first step, the discordant medley became more distinct because the cacophony in the hallway no longer buffered the sound. Instinctively he knew the lull in conversations was significant to him and he glanced up.

His mistress was gliding down the stairs towards him in a pure white gown dotted here and there with scarlet rosebuds. It had been artfully designed to display an alluring décolletage while the gossamer folds of the skirt hinted at the exotic skin beneath.

Some considerate soul had thought to open every door and window the house possessed to try and expel the heavy heat that refused to disperse at dusk. A welcome, tepid breeze had been flickering the candle flames and cooling the brows of stuffily attired gentlemen. Now it reversed its effect: a sudden gusting draught got beneath the gauze of Maria's skirt and made it billow as high as her shapely nude knees. Countless cravats were suddenly being loosened from inflamed throats and a collective male sigh whispered about the vestibule. Some ladies, recognising the signs and girding their loins for a little amatory skirmish later, cursed the dratted woman.

Connor just caught Maria's low, amused chuckle, but she adopted a bashful mien whilst restraining the fine material taut across her lissom thighs.

In absolute silence she continued her descent towards him while he watched her from beneath lazy lids. Idly he wondered whether he'd be the one paying handsomely for the indecent scrap giving pleasure to so many. His secretary had presented him with a stack of bills for his perusal that morning. A good amount seemed to be from milliners or modistes who claimed to have turned out yards of lady's finery in his name.

Maria's sultry gaze was roving his face and she smiled an intimate, exclusive welcome before her sloe eyes condescended to drop to the waiting, watching assembly. Her small chin tilted proudly, sending a ripple of thick black ringlets over her bare shoulders.

Rachel, in common with everyone else, was viewing the explicitly sensual display with an absorbed fascination. The atmosphere seemed to crackle with a shocking excitement. She found it impossible to look away, as Maria Laviola triumphantly joined the Earl of Devane on the wide, wine-red step. The *signora* then melted so close to him it seemed his broad, black-jacketed torso was emerging from a tousled white sheet. A small hand was slipped possessively through his arm before Maria turned to greet the gentleman accompanying the Earl. With an inaudible murmur of recognition, Rachel identified him as his stepbrother, Jason Davenport. The soprano's sable curls bounced prettily as she went on tip-toe to whisper in her lover's ear. Then her lips were hovering close to Jason's fair hair as a little intimate conversation was bestowed on him, too.

The woman was revelling in the role of femme fatale, Rachel realised. She adored the undivided attention it brought her, whilst pretending to be unaware of it. And now, having theatrically sketched her territory to the ladies present, she was apparently satisfied. She slipped an olive-skinned hand through the crook of one arm of each of her companions and the trio proceeded slowly up the snake of stairway.

As they neared the top, Rachel came to her senses and jerked her head away from the sight of the two tall, urbane gentlemen and the dainty, voluptuous woman swaying sinuously between them. It was only then she became aware that a number of people with long memories and malice on their minds were now openly staring at her. While she had been observing the man who had once been her fiancé with his mistress—and she was quite aware now, as was everyone, that the woman held that position in his life—she had been, in turn, eagerly watched. Her reaction to that rousing little tableau had doubtless been part of the entertainment, for tomorrow, in their clubs and drawing rooms, they could leisurely dissect it, embellish it, read in to it what they would.

Her sister's prospective mother-in-law was standing close by with Lady Winthrop. The tubby Baroness was slyly regarding her. So was Pamela Pemberton, who seemed equally amused. Much to her chagrin, Rachel could feel betraying blood seeping into her cheeks, confirming their suspicions over her sensitivity to the scene.

The woman is a spiteful bitch, Rachel realised with a pang of pity for her sweet sister's plight. That depressing thought was joined by another: her guilt at having a hand in inextricably linking June's future to Pamela's. She'd been the one to introduce June to William before she fully comprehended what an old besom was his mother. Thank heavens William was nothing like her in looks or character! He seemed to favour his father. Alexander Pemberton had always seemed to Rachel to be a kind and civil man with a pleasanter countenance than his sharp-featured wife possessed and none of her airs and graces.

Rachel succeeded in wiping the smirks from their faces by forcing a serene smile. With a hissed instruction for June to prepare for action, she linked arms with her younger sister and went to do battle.

Without preamble or even a greeting for her son's future wife, Pamela launched into, 'We were just saying, Miss Meredith, was that not the Irish gentleman you once were—?'

'Oh, well spotted, Mrs Pemberton! How very clever of you to recall it all from so many years ago. La, but I had almost forgot about it myself. How odd that such a trifle has intrigued you for the duration. Yes, it is indeed the gentlemen I refused to marry. And how nice it is to feel comforted by one's youthful conduct. I swear at the time, for a day or so at least, I *was* in two minds…'

Lady Winthrop smiled thinly, and faux surprise sent her sooty eyebrows soaring into her chalky forehead. 'I find that hard to believe, Miss Meredith. 'Tis indeed strange that an unwed lady, her débût far behind her, should congratulate herself on having rejected such an eligible catch. Why, above half of the debutantes at Almack's on Wednesday could speak of nothing but Lord Devane and how best to hook his attention. The remainder were already spoken for and looking quite put out. I own I grew mighty tired of hearing young ladies lisping his praises.' Her sparse lashes fluttered at the ceiling, her voice chanted in a squeaky pitch, 'How handsome he is, how charming he is, how rich he is…'

'How unavailable he is…' Rachel descanted.

Lady Winthrop's gaze relinquished the plaster cherubs to stab at her.

'His lordship looks to be well catered for in the romance stakes, wouldn't you say?' Rachel explained innocently.

Pamela Pemberton snickered. 'I think the young ladies my friend spoke of might insist on a more… *regular* relationship with the Earl than perhaps he presently enjoys with Signora Laviola.'

'Oh, I have it on good authority it is a very…regular relationship that the Earl enjoys with Signora Laviola,' Rachel whipped back, squeezing comfortingly at her sister's arm as she heard June choke in embarrassment. She was edging dangerously close to being outrageously coarse. Well-bred ladies, even those with their débût far behind them, did not talk so indelicately. She wasn't sure she cared how that affected *her*. It was damage to her family's reputation, and especially June's, with her marriage imminent, that made her employ a little control and caution. This, after all, was a member of her sister's new family…however horrendous the idea.

Mrs Pemberton glanced uneasily about as though pondering the wisdom of continuing to be party to such rough banter. June was then on the receiving end of one of her glares as though she, the only person present to have contributed nothing, was guilty of something.

As June flushed miserably beneath that spiteful, silent censure, Rachel bridled and became more determined to squarely take the blame. 'Actually, I have a little related *on dit* to share…' she whispered, then deliberately paused and inclined her head conspiratorially. The older women exchanged a glance, then, too intrigued to care of vulgarity, moved their gross turbans closer to the sleek golden ringlets. 'I understand that it is with great regularity that his lordship…attends the *signora's* recitals. He is not known to have missed even one.' She smiled as the disappointed women recoiled in unison. Their rouged lips became more corrugated as they straightened their necks.

Actually, Rachel understood nothing of the sort. She hadn't the faintest notion whether his lordship listened to his mistress sing or not. Nor did she care a jot either way. What did vastly annoy her was that she'd come here unaware what was in store for her. Had she known, she would as lief have spent the evening locked in a library with nothing to read but Philip Moncur's poetry. As it was she couldn't even retreat home to that task. If she cried off, pleading illness, it would only agitate more gossip. There was nothing to be done but endure this evening as best she could.

'Well, I dare say your parents don't find the whole matter as amusing as you seem to, miss,' the childless Baroness primly lectured. 'Four daughters to settle is no joke. I know I should not like it above half if a younger girl of mine were married before the eldest were off the shelf.'

'It is as well then that you will never be so troubled, ma'am,' Rachel said sweetly, pointedly.

'Indeed, no, I should not like it either,' Pamela interjected shrilly as she noticed her friend's ruddy countenance boiling at that jibe. 'Although now, of course, I believe I'm right in saying there are but three Meredith girls. For poor Isabel is gone…and what a terrible to-do that must have been for your poor mother. I can't imagine such private grief…'

'Indeed…and that's why it's best not to speak of it. Especially on such a public occasion as this.' The masculine voice was unyielding and held more than a hint of cold disgust.

Pamela's complexion pinked beneath her powder as she looked at her only child. She adored him and was chary of his scolding over her love to gossip, although as she impressed on him, time and again, there was no harm done, for no malice was involved… To reinforce this, she gave her beloved boy a sugary smile; he returned her one that bled further colour into her cheeks.

June's relief at the sight of him was almost audible, and, with a tender smile, he drew his willing fiancée close to his side.

'And, of course, I was mistaken,' Pamela self-reprimanded with a jovial hand flap. 'La, I forgot to say that June is settled by soon marrying into our family…and very welcome…which just leaves Miss Rachel and little Miss Sylvie at home. And several years, I'd say, to that youngster's come-out by the look of her. Although, when last I saw her, I thought, My! isn't she growing tall! And so pretty! Quite a heart-breaker in the making, to be sure…' Aware that perhaps that was an unwise observation, taking into account Miss Rachel's history, she ceased her chatter and fiddled with her thin ringlets.

'I'm sure you're right, ma'am,' Rachel sighed, enjoying the woman's discomfit. 'And no remedy for it; I believe it's a family trait.'

Pamela stabbed a fierce look at her tormentor, then swivelled her eyes about, seeking an escape route. 'Why, June, I think I see your mother over there,' she burst out. 'I must just go and speak with her over essentials…the wedding, you know…' With a meaningful nod at Lady Winthrop, the two matrons were hurrying gladly away.

'I'd like to say she means nothing by it,' William offered quietly, 'but I'm not sure how honest a statement it would be.'

'Well, we must give her the benefit of the doubt,' June said gamely. 'I believe she sincerely finds Sylvie pretty.'

'And do you believe that she sincerely welcomes you to our family?'

June looked flustered, her eyelashes aflutter, as she strove for a diplomatic answer.

'You are sincerely welcomed by me, with all my heart, my love.'

'I know,' his fiancée whispered, her glistening hazel eyes clinging adoringly to his face.

'Well…' Rachel said, feeling exceedingly contented yet also intrusive, 'I think I'll just go and seek out Lucinda and Paul. I know they arrived some while ago—before we did—I saw their carriage stopped at the curb as we drew up outside.' With a few backward steps she happily turned away. She knew that neither her sister nor William were really conscious of her poor excuse to discreetly depart. Their eyes, their thoughts, were with each other.

It was easy now to negotiate a path through the assembly: just a few groups of people, absorbed in their private conversations, were about the flagged hallway. Most of the guests had already moved to the music room on the first floor, or were on the stairs, en route. Rachel scoured the colourful mass of bodies, garish as exotically plumed birds soaring beneath a glaring light. Halfway up, on the left-hand side, she spied her parents, with their hostess. The woman's turban was almost horizontal as she craned her neck to see past her father to talk to her mother. Inwardly Rachel smiled. Mrs Pemberton was apparently all amiability now she had taken a set-down from her son. William obviously knew how to deal with his mother. He was a fine gentleman…a wonderful gentleman. Rachel was once more pleased to acknowledge her sister's good fortune and accept praise for having a hand in it.

About to start up the stairs herself, for she could hear the fluting opening bars of a melody, she gave one last peer about the emptying vestibule for her friends. As a group of men moved away from where they had been lounging against the wall, she located Lucinda and Paul Saunders just behind. She ignored the dandies ogling her and, tilting her chin, set off to join them. Before she was halfway there, her pace was faltering. On closer inspection, they, too, had the look of people who would prefer to be alone. Lucinda was coyly angling her dark eyes up to her husband's face with a very fond expression animating her countenance. Paul seemed oblivious to all but his wife's ardent attention. Slowly he raised a single finger to caress one of her flushed cheeks.

Rachel took two swift steps backwards, desperate not to be noticed by the couple. Swishing about, she diverted out of sight back to the stairs. She hesitated, a solitary figure on the bottom step, the melodic air drifting down doing nothing to lift her sudden melancholy. Her long slender fingers began sliding agitatedly over the slippery polished banister while she attempted to quell a tightening in her chest. Horrified, she realised that she might cry. That absurd notion prompted her to instead stop a laugh behind an unsteady hand.

How could she feel lonely with her family and friends close by? she impatiently rebuked herself. She had every reason to feel elated. Her best friend was *enceinte* and in love, and her dear sister June would soon be married to the nicest gentleman of anyone's acquaintance. The hurting lump in her throat seemed undiminished by thus bolstering her spirits. Blinking her eyes, she swallowed, gripped the handrail and took a determined step up. After two more she felt better, recovered enough to part her damp lashes. There was no shame in entering a room unaccompanied by friend or relative. It was only an odd circumstance that she should be on her own. She drew a shivery, steadying breath, bravely shaking back her hair that gleamed beneath a thousand flames like spun gold, and looked up.

The ensuing gasp was involuntary and quite audible. Dismay held her momentarily spellbound, then, with a clumsy bob, she was sidling sideways on the damson carpet to grab at the opposite banister. Gripping it as though it might save her life, she again began to mount the stairs whilst, with blurred eyes, she minutely examined William's ancestors, marching off up the wall. Peripheral vision kept her aware that a pair of muscular black-clad legs, a step or two above her, were keeping pace with her escape. Then, as though irritated with climbing stairs backwards, he crossed the tread. He came so close she stopped, desperately smearing away tears with her fingers while studying an especially fearsome-looking warrior glowering at her from beneath a visor.

'Shall we get this over with?'

'I beg your pardon.'

'I said…shall we get this over with?'

'I heard the words, sir, it's the meaning that escapes me.'

Realising that speaking to a gilt-framed portrait might seem strange, she abruptly spun about on the wide stair, and rested her back against the banister. She looked boldly, challengingly at him through spiky wet lashes. He was handsome, she had to admit. And very imposing. Quite frighteningly so. She didn't recall, six years ago, ever having felt intimidated by him. Now she did. Or perhaps she just felt stupid…for crying for no reason. But then she wouldn't cry now. Not in front of him. He wouldn't know, anyway…it didn't show…

A corner of his mouth tilted her a smile, while his very blue eyes lingered on her face. He was still watching her when his head flicked, indicating the top of the stairs. 'There are above a hundred people here tonight who are anxious for an incident to gossip over tomorrow. They'd like it to concern you and me.'

'Well, they shall have to settle for a gossip over you and your...your friend who sings very well, I'm told. I should like to listen to her,' Rachel announced briskly and, gathering her skirt in one hand, she renewed her flight up the stairs. Before she'd achieved three steps, her way was barred by a dark arm fastening on the polished mahogany a mere inch in front of her bosom. She seemed to sway dangerously backwards on the spot.

'Be sensible, Miss Meredith. It need take only five or ten minutes; a little polite conversation, a smile or two...perhaps we might even manage to dance together and really confound them.'

Rachel swallowed, then pivoted back to face him. It was sensible advice. Even in her agitation she knew that. They would never be left alone; speculation as to the one's high or low regard for the other would always prevail until the matter was finally laid to rest by a display of indifference.

What had she to lose by making an appearance of casually chatting to this man she had once callously jilted on the eve of their wedding? She moistened her full soft lips. 'I believe my father was kind enough to present you with the opportunity to quash rumours of any lingering bitterness between us...by attending my sister's wedding next month.'

'That's next month. This is now. Why wait so long?'

'Why, indeed?' Rachel rejoined softly after a long

pause. For an awful moment she thought he might make no more of it and go. But his expression suddenly softened from an impassive study into a smile. In a move that seemed oddly conciliatory to Rachel, he stepped down to join her on her lower step rather than expecting her to rise to meet him. His bow might have been a little mocking, though, she supposed, as he held out an arm. It was the least she could expect. After a tiny hesitation her long, elegant fingers hovered on his sleeve, and for the first time in six years she allowed Connor Flinte to escort her to polite society at play.

Chapter Four

The first people Rachel noticed as they walked in silence into the music room were her parents. Through a chink in a curtain of stirring bodies she saw that her mother was facing her, her father was presenting his solid squat back to the entrance. And Mrs Pemberton was, it seemed, still their good friend.

Rachel observed the moment that her mother caught sight of them: she abruptly ceased talking. After a stupefied second, Mrs Meredith's neat little jaw sagged further, making her appear a deal more dull and double-chinned than she actually was. Her expression, so severely altered, prompted Pamela Pemberton to inquisitively crane her neck about to locate what was so astonishing. Fortunately, the human shutter was already closing. Rachel was grateful for being spared her hostess's immediate attention. But it would come. Oh, it would certainly come.

Her father, of course, was oblivious to it all, for he was not attending to the ladies' chatter, but to his own. Despite standing with his wife, Edgar Meredith was actually conversing with a man in another group. Positioned like bookends, rigid-backed and with hands in pockets, they were talking with their chins jutting parallel to their shoulders, eyes darting up and down to the ceiling while they jigged from foot to foot. Edgar's interlocutor seemed equally bored with the company, even though the ladies in his circle looked considerably younger and rather glamorous. It was a moment before she realised that the man was in fact her father's brother-in-law. It was a long time since she had seen Nathaniel Chamberlain and she barely recognised him. Never a handsome man, in the interim he had become quite podgy and quite bald.

Nathaniel was married to her papa's sister, Phyllis, who had refused to have anything to do with her brother, or his family, since Rachel scandalously jilted Connor. Phyllis had been quite happy to bask in the glory of having been the one to bring together her niece and the son of one of her acquaintances. For Phyllis and Lady Davenport had once moved in the same circle. Rachel wondered, as she had many times before over the years, if they still did...

As Rachel peeked at her papa and his brother-in-law, she was stabbed with an ache of remorse: it was because of her jilting the man beside her that these once good friends must make conversation in such a clandestine fashion.

It had been at one of the Chamberlains' mediocre little dances that Rachel, then nineteen years old, had first been introduced to the handsome young Major. In common with the other young debutantes present, she had found him wonderfully attractive with his glossy black hair and sapphire eyes and that soft southern Irish brogue that so swooningly honeyed his tone. When he singled her out for particular attention that evening, she had been unbelievably flattered and so pleased. Not least because so many of her peers could barely contain their bitter-eyed envy. Yes; she had to admit that, at nineteen, beating her rivals to him had considerably boosted Major Connor Flinte's appeal.

Determinedly, she looked about, took in her surroundings. At present she was a bystander to the action; soon she would be its nervous protagonist. Her senses seemed heightened in anticipation of that time as she absorbed all manner of minor detail from the threshold of the plush, aromatic room. Verbena and lavender from cologne, and spice from perfumes and buffet foods mingled in the sultry air, infiltrating her nostrils like incense.

On a small raised dais Signora Laviola had been idly shuffling sheets of music in her hands, presumably in readiness to start her performance. Rachel noticed that Lord Harley and one of his cronies were loitering about the foot of the stage, like faithful puppies. Sporadically a rewarding smile was tossed their way. One such flashing look from the diva darted directly from her lapdogs to her lover. Rachel watched the flash of recognition narrow Maria's eyes. Probably she remembered her from their brief exchange of glances in Charing Cross during the rumpus with the vehicles locking wheels. Rachel sensed the dark almond eyes slide over her. The woman's suspicion was quite legitimate; twice this week the *signora* had watched the Earl pay her obvious attention. She met the hostile appraisal challengingly for a second or two, then with a toss of butter-coloured curls turned her head.

And that was just the start! It seemed that everywhere she then looked she was subjected to a shrewd scrutiny.

Ruefully, she wished that, on the stairs moments ago,

she had declined to take part in this singular scheme to secure them both a quiet life. And it had only been moments ago, despite the fact she felt as though she'd hesitated here for hours instead of minutes. A spurious show of concord no longer seemed such a good idea at all!

Pamela Pemberton's eyes had finally homed in on their quarry, resulting in a comically astonished grimace. That was the final straw! Rachel's façade of composure crumbled. An irrepressible choke of laughter had her quivering helplessly against her escort.

Connor looked down at her, then angled his raven head to see her demurely averted face shielding a tortured expression. She heard him swear softly in relief, then drawl, 'For a moment there I thought you were crying again. What's so funny it's transformed tears to laughter?'

His unwanted perception was exactly what Rachel needed. Her hysteria was immediately stifled. She put up her chin; indeed, it lifted so high her eyes skimmed the ceiling before flitting over a sea of watching faces. Some people she recognised and knew would recall the scandal; others, fairly new to the social scene, had simply sensed the atmosphere engendered by their appearance and had grasped something gossip-worthy was afoot. Yet she managed to reply coolly, 'I'm not...I wasn't ever crying. You're mistaken, sir, I'm afraid.'

'Fine. You've not been crying. Let's not bicker and dispel the myth too soon.' With a sideways look, he added mildly, 'We've been well and truly spotted, so try not to look quite so downcast. We're aiming for harmony...carefree...remember? Now, do you want to join your parents?'

'No! Not quite yet, sir, if you don't mind.' The first

word was barked; in mitigation, the others emerged in such a meek whisper he had to stoop to hear them. Rachel cleared her throat and endeavoured to think of something else to say, so that she could converse in a properly modulated tone and prove she was quite able. Then she caught sight of her papa…and his wide smile…and his wink!

A small involuntary groan escaped her and her eye-lids dropped in exasperated embarrassment. Oh, she knew how much her father liked this man…had always liked this man. She might very soon be on the receiving end of any amount of his unsubtle praise and innuendo. That horrifying realisation made her blurt gruffly, 'Might we sit over there? Just for a few moments, if you please, sir?' She indicated a quiet alcove by staring pointedly at it. If they headed that way they need pass very few people, yet it wasn't quite a retreat either.

As Connor steered her towards the small table and a few chairs set adjacent to the door, Rachel was aware that their progress was being closely monitored by sharp eyes and sibilant voices.

Rachel settled gratefully into the chair her escort po-litely pulled out for her. She thanked him as, noncha-lantly, he rested a hand the colour of mahogany on its rosewood rail.

'Well, let's start with the weather,' Connor drawled in his easy, Irish tone.

To an observer, his expression must have looked pleasantly bland; only Rachel understood the ironic amusement in the blue between his thick black lashes.

'Now, would you say it was hotter today than yes-terday? Do you think it might rain later this week?' He looked off into the middle distance, for all the world adopting the idle attitude of a man doing his duty by a female acquaintance. With a ghost of a smile, he murmured to a burnished crown of golden hair, 'By the time we get to the likelihood of a storm brewing, I imagine our hostess might be upon us. She looks to have already covered some ground there. Several lordly folk have been skirted about en route.'

'Perhaps she momentarily finds you so much more diverting, my lord…being new to the ranks.'

Connor idly examined his nails, then spoke to them. 'That sounds pretty much like sour grapes, Rachel. Now, does the fact that I'm an earl bother you?'

'Nothing about you *bothers* me, my lord. Why on earth would it?' Rachel shot back honey-voiced, yet the emphasis on his formal title dripped rebuff. She'd not given him leave to be so familiar and use her given name.

He seemed unaffected by the reproof and laughed. 'Oh, I don't know… Perhaps now I've risen in the ranks I imagined there might be certain things you regret…'

Rachel's sugary smile turned coy. Slowly her face lifted to his, mock enquiry winging her eyebrows. Pretty blue eyes peeped up at him through a nest of silky brunette lashes. It was a charming pose…but a wasted effort: his attention was elsewhere. Without taking a proper look to verify her suspicions, Rachel immediately identified the reason behind his steady, discreet regard for the opposite end of the room. She had twice before this evening been an unwilling witness to a smouldering-eyed man, captivated by his lady-love. She even knew when his mistress was satisfied with his wordless reassurance, for he remembered her again, and the trifling little charade in which they were co-starring.

'Don't look so tense, Rachel...Miss Meredith,' he corrected himself with studied solemnity. 'People will think I'm keeping you here with a concealed weapon pointing hard at you.'

On immediate reflection his words seemed to disproportionately amuse him. He choked a private laugh at the ceiling, which only served to make Rachel feel increasingly wretched. But it was her own behaviour that disturbed her the most. With a flash of insight she realised she had been on the point of mimicking the behaviour she had seen her sister and her friend use. Unbelievably, she had wanted to flirt with a man who had every right to despise her. Naturally, he'd been oblivious to her scheme. Had his boredom been feigned, as a deliberate snub, it would have been easier to bear, but he'd simply been distracted, far more partial to his present love than his past.

At nineteen, she had managed to twine a respected Major in the Hussars about her little finger. For months he had danced obediently to her tune...whichever she demanded be played. Now he ignored her! For a few vital seconds she'd hovered on the brink of desiring a little rapport with him...and he had ignored her! And why should he not? And why should she care? Or feel humbled?

But she did.

People never ignored her; especially not men. She might not be liked very much, but she was never overlooked. A knot of angry humiliation was writhing in her, threatening to eject her from the chair and propel her, childlike, to find her parents. But she mustn't run away, not just yet, for through the blinding heat of her indignation she realised that Pamela Pemberton was indeed hovering very close.

For appearances' sake the woman was exchanging a few perfunctory sentences with each new group she happened upon in the meandering course of her beeline towards them. Once she joined them, others would, too. Then any further opportunity to talk privately with this man would be unlikely. Tomorrow she and her mother and sisters were returning to Windrush with their wedding clothes, to begin earnest preparations for June's nuptials. Her papa was following a day or two later when he had concluded his business in the City.

Lord Devane might soon repair to his Irish estates. Save for odd, remote chance, she would never again set eyes on him. Suddenly it was imperative that before they parted, they talk properly. She wanted to conduct herself in a way that gained his full attention, if not his respect. So far she had acted like a silly, wistful girl: first wallowing in maudlin self-pity on the stairs, then making a clumsy attempt to act the coquette. She might have been a gauche miss, fresh from the schoolroom, instead of a woman in her twenty-sixth year, who had once…no, three times…been engaged to be married.

She glanced up, unwittingly catching Mrs Pemberton's beady eye. Panic-stricken, she willed their hostess to remain where she was, just long enough for her to…quickly apologise. There was no easy way and no time to delay. It was so simple, so focused now. Their betrothal; his devotion, her destructiveness; the whole messy business of the jilting, needed to be resurrected simply to properly lay it to rest.

Pamela's shrill voice, just a yard away, launched her into hasty, quiet speech.

'You are quite correct, sir. I do have regrets; perhaps the greatest of which is that owning to it has taken so long. But first I must stress that your elevation to the peerage has not prompted what I am about to admit. I'm sorry for having behaved badly towards you. Not only six years ago, but more recently. I was rude to you when you helped me on the road the other day. And there was no reason for it. I could claim mitigating circumstances, such as shock at the surprise encounter, but it really wouldn't do. There was no excuse. Accordingly, I understand why you said what you did in retaliation to my lack of manners, and what you meant by it. Indeed, I can only agree that you made a lucky escape six years ago, even if perhaps it didn't seem so to you at the time. We would not have suited...' She swallowed, polished her nails furiously with her thumb, aware that she indeed now had his unwavering attention despite the fact her eyes never relinquished her lap. 'So, thank you for preventing Ralph being hurt. He is far too old to be fighting with younger men. I rung him a peal about that when we arrived home. I was also glad you gave that beastly magistrate a set-down. He has no right to hold such a position, for he did exaggerate what occurred to the point of falsehood... Why, hello, Mrs Pemberton. Lord Devane and I were just saying how unconscionably hot and humid it has been this week. We believe a storm must be brewing.'

Rachel plucked from her reticule a dainty fan. It was snapped open with a wrist-flick and she proceeded to sway the lace before her flushed complexion.

She couldn't look at him although she desperately wanted to gauge his reaction to her concise, blurted apology. Was he amused by it? Disgusted that the part that greatly required her remorse had barely been touched upon? Possibly he was now indifferent to any mention of it. It was so very long overdue, after all.

The most she could claim was that he'd been taken aback by her impromptu dialogue. Naturally, after six silent years, he'd not have deemed her estimable enough for repentance. It was too little too late and was scant consolation for the pain and humiliation he'd once had to endure. But it was better than nothing. And it was all he would get. She felt remarkably calm; release sighed through her, as though a burden she'd been unaware she was carrying had been lifted from her, leaving just the ghost of Isabel to haunt her memory…

Quietly, Rachel listened to Pamela Pemberton effusively welcoming her eligible male guest while in her mind she obliquely registered the other peers present and concluded that, yes, her former fiancé was the most eminent; Pamela's oleaginous gushing was merited and to be expected.

She knew the woman's eyes constantly scoured her face, hoping for a noteworthy, stray reaction, so Rachel continued to neutrally admire her bright and brash surroundings from behind the gossamer tool cooling her complexion. Another few minutes and it would be appropriate to move on and join her parents. Just another few minutes and she would be free…

'Now, I must accuse you, my dear, of being a naughty little tease this evening. I think some other people hereabouts might describe you thus too…' Shrewdly guessing at Rachel's thoughts of escape, Pamela had said something calculated to keep her fixed firmly in her seat.

With her ego still fragile and unable to believe the woman would so blatantly challenge her, Rachel's fan trembled to a halt and she stammered, 'I…I beg your pardon?'

Pamela triumphantly eyed the scarlet staining Rachel's ivory cheeks. If the little madam thought she could get away with embarrassing her in front of her beloved boy and the baroness, she had a lesson for her. She wasn't a woman to be trifled with in her own home!

So much for her smug bravado at having once jilted this eligible gentleman! It seemed she had nevertheless taken pains to worm her way again to his side. Perhaps the fact that he now had an earldom and a larger fortune had some bearing on her sly change of heart!

Pamela thought she didn't deserve another chance at him, and neither should she get it. The Winthrops' niece, Barbara, was keen on getting him to pay his addresses, and he had seemed quite taken with her at her parents' card evening. But then he did dispense that Irish charm quite liberally and impartially... Obviously he had forgot just how much of a fool this young woman had once made him appear. It wasn't so very long ago she'd left him the laughing stock of the *haut ton*. Now, with such impeccable credentials, no one dared smile in his direction, unless he smiled their way first.

Impressing upon him his welcome seemed vital; so did discrediting this artful baggage. 'Handsome bachelors are so very well received at any gathering,' Pamela simpered. 'So I'm trusting you to give the lie, my lord, to Miss Meredith's earlier declaration. If true, it will break so many ladies' hearts.' She fluttered a look at him from beneath her sparse lashes, then inclined towards him conspiratorially, her veined hand hovering on one of his immaculate dark sleeves. 'Miss Meredith tells us that you are already spoken for! *Unavailable, and well catered for in the romance stakes*,

I believe she said.' She paused for effect, slyly relishing Rachel's increasing consternation.

Contained fury at having her mischief misinterpreted and publicised, especially to this man, had turned Rachel's complexion brick-red.

'Is this young lady privy to your secrets? Is there a lady so fortunate? Or must we simply scold Miss Meredith for being such a constant tease…?'

Connor laughed: a choke of sound that combined disapproval with genuine humour. For a moment he stared off into space as though he was marshalling his wits for a response. Then, ignoring his hostess, he gave Rachel's hot confusion a long cool look. Her fan whizzed furiously in front of her face and her attention seemed to be attached to a plaster cornucopia embellishing the wall above her head.

'I'm flattered by your compliments, Mrs Pemberton, and the strength of your interest in my personal affairs. What can I say, other than perhaps your congratulations are called for? Convey them to Miss Meredith…' He paused until Rachel slid a startled sideways look at him. Mrs Pemberton's drop-jawed dismay went unnoticed by him. 'It seems she has been ludicrously successful in teasing you over…nothing at all.' With a glint firing his eyes that made Rachel's stomach squirm, he executed a curt bow, took a step back, and turned to go.

Pamela, having been scorned twice in an hour by gentlemen with whom she'd striven to ingratiate herself, became desperate not to let him go on such an inharmonious note. 'So you think a storm is brewing then, my lord?' she squeaked, on a wide-eyed grin that quite obviously forgave him his snub.

'I don't see how it can be avoided,' he returned with

smooth emphasis. Fleetingly his sardonic eyes skimmed Rachel before he was gone.

'I had a nice chat with your mother...'

Rachel stabbed a look at the woman with eyes like ice shards. How dare she address her so convivially! The bitch was actually trying to be amiable and brush aside the fact she'd been so spiteful only moments ago. She'd attempted to insult her; shame her and make her out to be angling for the Earl's attention. Not only that; she'd hinted to the man himself that she'd been boasting of hooking him! It was outrageous! Not once had she tried to deliberately put herself in his way! Quite the reverse! A sudden, awful thought struck her. Did *he* believe she was fishing for his attention? That she'd schemed at loitering forlornly on the stairs tonight simply to lure him into approaching her? Was that why he'd said she might harbour regrets now he'd risen in the ranks? Did that final look he gave her sum up his contempt for her belated apology because he thought it had been prompted by her mercenary golddigging? The mortification made her choke furiously, 'A *nice chat*? With *my mother*?' She twisted a bitter smile. 'I'm amazed! That's far more than you deserve from any of the Merediths this evening. It's certainly far more than you shall get from *me*! If you'll excuse me...'

The aria suited her pure, golden voice very well, Rachel thought. The soprano knew her forté. Not a murmur could be heard from the rows of occupied chairs arranged in a semi-circle about the base of the stage. This final piece was clearly demonstrating the fine range of her voice as it built towards a high sweet crescendo.

The fact that the Earl of Devane didn't appear to be

amongst the adoring admirers present in the foremost row of chairs facing the dais had not seemed to affect the diva's performance. Her tortured expressions, her theatrical mannerisms were quite naturally perfect. Rachel had to admit, the lady *was* very talented.

Sam Smith stood on the pavement and looked up at the brightly lit first-floor casements. Finely dressed ladies and gentlemen were drifting in and out of view, providing a fascinating glimpse of untold luxury as they nibbled at fancies or sipped from crystal or china. All the men looked rich and important; all the ladies looked glittery and beautiful. Then he saw her, the most beautiful one of all, wafting into view, laughing and relaxed with that woman she'd been with last time he saw her. She raised a glass to her lips and fire sparked off its rim. Her golden curls and pearl-pale complexion were indeed a sight for sore eyes, he thought, as a hand went to his bruised face. He winced as it touched his distended eye-socket and came away blood-stained.

The lady *was* present; with luck, the gentleman would be too. He'd seen the way Lord Devane looked at her and guessed the man might be where she was.

He'd been on his way past, with his sister, in search of lodgings for the night, when he'd noticed that elderly cove who'd wanted to fight him earlier in the week. From his vantage point, in the bushes, Sam slid him a crafty look from his good eye. There he was, sitting snooty atop a different fine rig, keeping his distance from the other coach drivers who, bored with the wait, were passing time by playing dice on the cobbles. It didn't take a lot of brains to work out that the throng of coaches lining the street, the idle servants, and the blazing windows in one big house meant that Quality was having a ball.

On a crazy whim he'd decided to stop; for he had nothing left to lose, and his little sister, Annie, had so very much to lose if he didn't look after her. So now he was waiting, for how long he knew not. It seemed as though he'd already skulked in the shadows for an hour or more. But he was prepared to wait; till dawn if need be. He must keep his nerve and speak to the man. What could Lord Devane say? Only 'no'…

Chapter Five

Jason Davenport glanced up from his cards and his eyes glittered contempt at the foppish newcomers.

'Come…sit down, Harley,' Connor drawled amiably.

Benjamin Harley sauntered closer to the baize-topped table, mean eyes narrowed, fleshy lips curled sullenly. He flipped open a bejewelled snuff box, nipped himself a snort, then after a cough and a cosy with his chums sniggered, 'You surely don't think I'd indulge in a hand with *you*, do you? Last I heard, you'd thrashed the whole regiment at faro.'

Connor casually shuffled the cards in his hands. 'And that worries you does it? That I'll win?'

'No. It worries me that you'll make sure I lose…'

The ensuing silence seemed interminable. There were several gentlemen loitering in the room, close to the wide, open doors that led onto the terrace, indulging in a little discreet smoking, or tippling out of sight of their wives' critical vigilance.

'Are you saying that I cheat?'

'It's hard to credit you never lose…'

'Be more specific...' Connor insisted in his silky Irish way.

'What is this talk of cheating?' a woman's accented voice purred into the tense atmosphere. Maria Laviola swished forward like a fresh breeze in her wintry white gown with berry-red adornment. A languid hand sheathed in a scarlet glove flopped onto Connor's broad shoulder.

'You sang like an angel, my dear,' Harley enthused on cue, keen to distract interest from his resentful outburst.

The compliment was immediately added to by other men in the room, eager to jolly the atmosphere and also show the soprano their appreciation.

'Are you to perform again this evening?' Harley demanded.

'Not here...perhaps elsewhere...later...' A sultry glance slid Connor's way and he reacted with a privately amused smile.

Fanning her pretty face with lacy fingers, she moaned, 'It is so terribly warm this evening.'

'Poor old Devane, doesn't deem it so.' Harley smirked. 'I'll wager he's still feeling a chill.'

'How so?'

'We must blame Miss Meredith; I believe that lady has quite froze him out...once again.'

Peter Waverley, a good drinking chum of Benjamin Harley's, unwisely let go of the chair back he was using as a prop, to stifle a guffaw with a feeble hand. Immediately, Jason's chair was scraped backwards from the table as though he would physically remonstrate with the reeling popinjay.

Connor shrugged an apathetic response, while curling hard fingers over bunched muscle below his brother's sleeve.

'Is there room for a few more?'

Edgar Meredith entered the room, smiling, with his brother-in-law, Nathaniel Chamberlain a circumspect yard or two behind him. Nathaniel took a cautious peer about for his wife, Phyllis, in case she spied him and chided him later over consorting with *undesirables* as she classed the whole Meredith clan.

'Dammit!' Nathaniel muttered beneath his breath. Edgar seemed on reasonable terms with the Earl of Devane: they were about to sit and have a drink and a game of cards together! If Connor Flinte bore no grudges, and he was the injured party, he saw no reason why his wife still should feel indignant over it all, simply because she'd once set up the match between Connor and Rachel.

'Here, take my place,' Connor coolly offered Edgar Meredith on standing up. A tanned hand brushed baize, scooping his winnings and idly pocketing them. With a lethal stare at Benjamin Harley, Jason grabbed his few coins and was soon following his brother towards the small terrace.

Nathaniel Chamberlain looked askance at Edgar. Obviously he was mistaken about the Earl and his equable attitude towards past slights. Edgar looked excruciatingly uncomfortable, as did their host, Alexander Pemberton. All present guessed the reason for Lord Devane's departure was Edgar's arrival. Nathaniel sensed his brother-in-law's pain and winced inwardly. He knew Edgar had always felt a deep affection for the Major and now desired at least a little harmony with him.

'You're bored. I knew you would be. We should have gone to Mrs Crawford's…'

'No, I'm not bored. Quite the reverse. I'm intrigued,' Connor absently admitted as he strolled, with Jason in tow, on to the tiled balcony. Loosening his cravat from his warm neck, he unravelled the blue silk, then wound it slowly, thoughtfully about a broad palm. Still pre-occupied, he carelessly stuffed it into a pocket of his jacket, thereby ruining its stylish lines to a degree that was sure to have given his tailor an attack. He gazed down at his blanching knuckles gripping the fancy ironwork of the balustrade and his thoughts returned to Rachel…Miss Meredith, a laughing exhalation reminded him.

What the hell was she about? He'd observed more emotion in her in this one evening than he ever recalled her revealing in four months of courtship. And as he was pretty sure the show was contrived for his benefit, he refused to be touched by it. He'd watched her nervousness, her tears, her embarrassment; he'd even seen her looking ashamed and contrite…before she'd looked murderous when their hostess had so obviously set out to expose and humiliate her. Oddly, he'd not rejoiced in that; he'd felt disgusted by Pamela Pemberton's gloating spite, and hoped that had been obvious to them both.

Six years ago, when Edgar Meredith had broken the news to him on his stag night that he'd been jilted, he'd expected from Rachel at least an apologetic note in the days and weeks that followed. Nothing came. Not even a few lines of non-committal explanation. Her lack of communication spoke volumes: nothing was needed from her for he was not worth the bother. It was enough that her father should deal with the trifling affair. It should have been so easy to hate her, yet he couldn't. And in the vacuum that had filled those weeks prior to returning to the Peninsula and the carnage of Salamanca, the numbness pervading him hadn't been totally attributable to the amount of alcohol he'd consumed. She'd left him insensate, drained...

Now, he'd long regained his faculties, and decided that Miss Meredith was old enough and fully deserving of a little tardy retribution. But she'd read him like a book; she'd set about acting forlorn in the hope of drawing him in to draw his teeth.

At one time, seeing her discomposed might have eased his own anguish. It might have cheered him. Not now. Now he didn't want her humble and nervous. But he did want her. And in view of all that had gone before, he didn't see why he shouldn't have her. She owed him... And if redress meant using her vulnerability to his advantage, so be it. And he knew he could, if he wanted. Considering he had, six years ago, rarely permitted himself to kiss or touch her, it was odd that he knew he could seduce her...tonight, if he chose.

'Intrigued? Over what?' Jason suddenly sliced through his brooding thoughts.

'Oh, this and that...'

'Oh, this and that...' Jason mimicked sarcastically. 'Hell and high water, Con! She nigh on crucified you! Made you look like a bloody fool!' his stepbrother burst out. With an exclamation of sheer disbelief he stormed, 'You're ripe to let her try again, aren't you? Are you mad? Have you not yet learned that she's a callous bitch? She's got a reputation as a constant tease, you know.'

Connor tipped his head up at the starry night, letting the tepid night air beneath his loosened collar. 'Yes, I know. I knew even before our hostess was good enough to spell it out this evening. Of course I knew...' he muttered to himself.

'Moncur seems to be prowling about her again, like a lovelorn swain,' Jason snapped. 'Watch and learn. A pony says he'll be limping away again soon, tail between his legs.'

'Not a lot else he can do,' Connor drawled facetiously. He swore savagely, ashamed of the mean jibe at the man's lameness. 'Do you think he's after a second chance, too?' Aware just how much that unguarded comment revealed, not only to his brother but to himself, a weary hand scrubbed across his lean, shady jaw. A grunt of laughter sounded behind it. 'You're right; we should have gone to Mrs Crawford's...'

Jason made a move as though he was ready to act, albeit belatedly, on that sensible idea.

'But I'd like to know what Edgar Meredith is about,' Connor suddenly remarked with a complete change of tone and direction as he sauntered away along the paving. 'He's a deal too often keeping me company. Everywhere I go, he materialises. If I'm at Watier's, he's dining there. If I'm due at Gentleman Jackson's, he's already training when I arrive. Jaazus, the man's too old. He must have gained his half-century two or three years since, and he's carrying too much weight. A day or so ago I thought he might collapse with a seizure, he was trying so hard to spar convincingly. He's been shadowing me most of this evening... Not that I dislike the man, but he's beginning to make me nervous.'

'Well, that's a good sign,' Jason retorted with acid irony. 'The man's got four daughters to despatch. Are you sure you don't know why he's stalking the Earl of

Devane of Wolverton Manor and its hundred thousand acres, creditably maintained by fifty thousand a year? Heavens! You're too modest, Con.'

'He has *three* daughters to marry off…and one of those will soon be wed. One is not yet old enough to be out…'

'Which, *quelle surprise*, leaves just the most difficult to shift: the eldest, who once you rather liked.'

'That's history…' Connor leaned on the rail and stared off over lunar-limed lawns. He was well aware of Jason's sardonic gaze on him, and for some reason, refused to meet it. 'Isabel would have been about twenty-three years old now,' he murmured, hoping to deflect his brother's cruel eyes.

Jason obliged him by turning about, and adopting Connor's pose, leaned his forearms on the iron balustrade. He cleared his throat. 'Terrible business, that… Influenza, wasn't it, as I recall?'

'Scarletina. There was an epidemic in York. Rachel wasn't to know, of course. They arrived at their aunt's unexpectedly. Had they had fair warning… No one in their right mind would have gone into the city had they realised.'

'Are you sure at the time she *was* compos mentis?' At a withering look from Connor he shrugged. 'I wouldn't be the first to say only a self-absorbed dimwit would act in the way she did.'

'She was young…nineteen…'

'Her sister was two years younger, but by all accounts decades more mature. I heard that the sister didn't want to go. I heard she was so disgusted with Rachel, she opted to stay behind. There can't be one moment of one day when, self-absorbed dimwit or not, she doesn't wish she'd let Isabel do just that.'

'It wasn't Rachel's doing. It was their mother who insisted they travel together…'

Jason let out a breath with a sorry shake of his head. 'So Mrs Meredith shares the burden of guilt…' He looked at his brother's profile carved against a backdrop of velvet night sky. 'That's the most you've ever talked to me of that episode, Con. I reckon that's significant.'

'Sure it is…' Connor drawled with a lop-sided smile at the heavy, milky moon. 'It means it's time to go.'

Sam Smith shrank back into the laurel bush as the double doors opened and a clump of people spilled out of the brightly lit aperture and drifted down the steep stone steps. He could just detect mingling words and laughter in amongst the melody that had been liberated from the house to waft on the balmy night air.

Cursing the poor lighting, he tiptoed out and followed a way behind to try and firmly establish the man's identity before he accosted him. He was a tall and broad-built fellow who moved with supple strides, even with the clinging woman hampering his pace. If he was wrong, copping a shiner to match the one he already had would be the least of his worries.

The couple were heading towards a chipper coach, and suddenly its carriage lantern shed a beam full upon the gentleman's face sloping his raw-boned cheeks into angular planes and putting a gloss on his raven hair. Sam relaxed. It was him. He glanced at the woman but her features were concealed by a demure pose and the wide brim of a fancy bonnet. Only black curls luxuriant about her shoulders hinted at her dusky beauty. Perhaps it was his little sister, Sam heartened himself, she shared his colouring…

Connor's right hand went automatically to the silver stiletto, a fairly permanent fixture in his pocket and, for some reason as his fingers caressed its silky hilt, he recalled Rachel and what he'd said earlier about pointing a concealed weapon at her. Exasperated, because he couldn't, even now, get her out of his mind, yet amused, too, by the ambiguous truth in those words, he turned to confront the man. One sight of his adversary made Connor give in to the farce of the situation…and the whole evening; he burst out laughing.

Sam Smith jumped in the air in fright and held up his hands. 'I'm not a dipper, honest. I just wanted to talk to you, my lord,' he rattled off shrilly.

Connor drew a deep calming breath, blew out his cheeks and took a pace towards the bedraggled youth. He squinted at him closely. 'And you are?' he asked, although he suspected, beneath that bloody bruise that had swollen one side of his thin visage, that he might look oddly familiar. He had a height and wiry build that was memorable; it was also inconsistent with the beating he'd taken and his cowed manner.

'The name's Smith…Sam Smith. You was good enough to give a hand to fix my wheel earlier in the week. Only it ain't my cart no more…not that it ever was mine exactly…alhough it was my job to make deliveries for my guv'nor…only now he ain't my guv'nor…'

Sam took a humble step back and bowed his head. 'Please don't send me off, my lord,' he implored. 'At least not afore you've heard me out. I'm well and truly run aground but I ain't a thief and I ain't after charity, neither, if that's what you're thinking…'

'What's up, Con?' a drink-roughened voice called.

Connor speared a look over his shoulder at Jason as

he meandered towards them. His brother signalled tipsily at his coachman to wait as the man took up the reins.

'Nothing I can't deal with,' Connor told him succinctly. 'Mr Smith and I became acquainted earlier in the week.' He inclined his head close to his mistress's hat brim and murmured a few reassuring words about visiting later. 'Would you take Maria home for me, Jason?'

Jason looked surprised, then delighted as the privilege penetrated fully into his brandy-befuddled brain. Immediately he proffered an arm to the lady. 'Are you sure you don't need assistance?' he asked dutifully, in the tone of voice that let Connor know he'd be severely disappointed, should the answer come in the affirmative.

'I think I can manage,' Connor returned drily with a glance at the quaking youth. Whether Sam Smith was palsied from pain or fright was hard to gauge. He certainly shouldn't have felt cold in the sweltering atmosphere, and he certainly wouldn't pose a threat to anyone in his present condition.

Maria's exasperation at the turn of events was evident in her sulky, protracted sigh. Although she remained silent, she sent Sam Smith a poisonous look as she passed by on Jason's arm.

A few minutes later, after Connor had observed his brother's phaeton turn the corner, and he had been proved correct in thinking the Pembertons might arrange for a constable to be in the vicinity tonight, he turned his attention to Sam Smith. The youth was still warily watching the beagle's back.

'If I find you're wasting my time, I'm likely to be seriously displeased...'

Connor watched Sam with a minimum of curiosity as he beckoned at some bushes. For some reason he felt beyond surprise as a young woman slipped out between laurel branches and hurried with a lithe grace towards them.

'This is Annie...my sister. She's fourteen...'

Connor looked from the girl's burnished crown of auburn hair to the boy's battered face. Suddenly the puzzle slid effortlessly into place and he was again on the point of humourless mirth when a wave of righteous anger surged through him. Far from trying to rob him, Sam Smith was trying to sell him his sister, and by the looks of things, he wasn't the first uninterested punter he'd approached that evening.

A large fist chucked under the boy's chin, forcing his bloodshot eyes to meet blazing blue. 'Did I look as though I lacked female company tonight, or did I look as though I was well catered for in that respect?'

Rachel again! He was using words that reminded him of his blasted past love! Past fiancée, he amended in his mind. She was his past, yet he seemed determined to keep her in the present. He was employing phrases she'd said...allegedly said...about him. His ire increased. His fingers forked over the lad's jaw, tightened until he howled.

''Snot like that, m'lord. Honest. She's me sister, not a pro, an' I'm the direct opposite to her pimp. 'S why me face took a clubbin'. I was tryin' to protect her...'

Connor released him with a savage flick. After a steadying stare into space, he gave Sam a grim glare. The girl remained stock-still, unmoved by any of it, with downbent head and hands clasped behind her back. She looked plainly and comfortably attired, certainly not in the manner of a prostitute, but not waif-like either.

'What in God's name is all this about?' Connor blasted through gritted teeth, his accent thickened by bottling his anger.

In response, the boy simply took a pace towards his sister and, putting a gentle hand beneath her chin, raised her head.

Connor stared. For some reason Sam's simple action was entirely appropriate and very illuminating. No more was necessary. His sister, Annie, had an uncanny, startling beauty which seemed more exquisite for being compared to her brother's unlovely physiognomy. Her skin tone looked parchment white, her eyes as black as polished jet and, as Connor watched, Sam pulled the ribbon from her hair and it tumbled in a waterfall of luxuriant waves over her shoulders. She simply stared up blankly at him.

'I can't do it no more. I can't keep her safe. Every cove we meet wants a piece of her…even them as should know better. 'Specially them as should know better…'

Connor watched the lad's bloodshot eyes sheen with tears. 'Now I've got no work an' no place to stay. How long will it be afore Annie's on the streets…really on the streets?'

'Who hit you?' Connor couldn't think of anything else to say for a moment.

'Me uncle, Nobby.'

'Your *uncle* wanted your sister?'

'No! He just wanted to hit me 'cos that slimy toad wanted a barrow load of geneva or he'd make us trouble. It was that jarvey's fault. Couldn't keep his trap shut, could he? He let on to that bent beak who I was.

He knew me; sometimes we have a mug o' porter in the Jolly Farmer where the hackneys congregate. He let on who was me guv'nor, too… Me uncle were right narked. Now I lost me job and me squat. Annie used to cook and clean so Nobbie let her stay, too.'

After a moment reflecting, sorting and sifting information, Connor summarised, 'I take it Arthur Goodwin, Esquire, is a Trading Justice who wanted his cellar stocked with free gin in return for issuing you with a liquor licence at the Brewster Sessions.'

'At first that's what he wanted. Then he saw Annie…'

Connor looked at the girl, looked at her brother. He closed his eyes. 'Where are your parents?'

'Dead. Pa died years since from the lung disease; Ma from the gin just last Michaelmas…'

'What are you expecting me to do about any of this?' Connor asked quite gently…too gently, he minutes later thought.

'I trust you. You didn't need to help us out the other day… You've a good heart…you're not like Quality—' Hurriedly, he expounded, 'That is, you seem decent…'

Connor shifted restlessly, cut off Sam's praises with a sardonic laugh. 'What do you want?'

'I want you to take her in.' There was a pride and dignity behind the youth's audacious demand. Even when Connor quirked an expressive eyebrow at him he didn't waver. 'She's not bright, but she's a good girl. She can cook, clean, sew. She used to dress me auntie's hair right nice afore she got the chills and turned up her toes. Perhaps one of your ladies might like…' He cleared his throat at a quizzical look from Connor.

'That is…you might know of a lady who needs a good maid…'

Connor smiled to himself. Such ladies—even respectable ones—were hardly likely to take in such a young beauty and present themselves with problems keeping her out of sight of roving-eyed amorous husbands or lovers. 'I take it you've tried domestic agencies?'

Sam smiled bleakly. 'Oh, yes. Annie's been in fine houses…with fine masters. Like I said…it's especially them as should know better that she has to fear. She's chaste still, but I ain't sure how we managed it. She started in Beaumont Street and stayed just a day. Sir Percy Monk thought she might make a pretty playmate for his son. She's got a right set of talons on her, I'll give her that,' he added with a limp grin. 'Marked the blighter good and proper.'

Connor pursed his lips; he knew the boy, and his vicious, licentious reputation. He was sixteen years old and no better than his lecherous sire.

'I want you to take her in,' Sam repeated in a quavering voice. 'Arthur Goodwin won't dare cross you. He's afraid of you. But he'll hound me and Annie. He said as much. He said he wants her and he won't give up…'

Connor put a hand to his forehead and rubbed, cursing inwardly for ever having left home this evening. He hadn't come here to listen to his mistress sing. She was wont to warble in the throes of passion and that was more than enough for him. He'd come here because he knew Rachel would be attending; she'd lured him to her side, just as she had on the road earlier in the week. But for that fateful incident with the crush of carriages, he wouldn't now be stuck in this farcical quandary. It was her fault! A weak smile acknowledged his irrationality. With a sigh he asked, 'And you? What are you intending to do?'

Sam Smith swiped a brash hand across his nose, shrugged. 'Oh, I'll get by. Always do. I can duck and dive...or work in a stable. I'm a good groom...been apprenticed,' he added with a flicker of optimism dampening his bravado.

Connor found the laugh got stuck in his throat. He looked up at his coachman, gazing off diplomatically into the night. His current groom, having retreated from holding the door, to his place at the back of the carriage when his master struck up conversation, just swivelled his eyes skywards. Connor opened the carriage door himself and merely jerked his head at the interior.

Wordlessly, the girl clambered in, unaided.

'How did you know I'd be here?' he asked Sam, hoping to curb the boy's silent streaming tears with conversation.

'I saw your lady...up at the window...' Sam snivelled, smearing his face with a dirty palm, his auburn head jerking back at the brightly lit casement.

'Oh...not this one, not the one who left with the other gentleman...' Sam looked anxiously at him through red eyes, as though frightened the miracle might slip away with a stupid word. His cheeks dripped rusty water again. 'I meant your blonde lady as was kind on the road. You seemed to like her...so when I saw her here I thought...' He snuffled a laugh, cuffed his mouth. 'I thought she were right brave to give that Arthur Goodwin a dressing-down. His ugly mug were a picture...'

Connor laughed, too. But for a different reason. Out of the mouths of babes... 'Oh, that *my* lady,' was all he said.

Chapter Six

'I'll match your call and raise you this…'

Benjamin Harley tried to freeze a betraying smile as the fistful of fifty-pound notes was waved at him. With a dramatic flinging open of his fingers, the man let loose the money and it fluttered down to settle on a cushion of similar paper already littering the baize. Quickly Lord Harley looked away lest he inadvertently exposed his steadily mounting excitement. He slanted a stare at Edgar Meredith across the cards he held fanned in a languid hand. Carefully, very carefully, he lowered them from possible prying eyes and placed them face down on the baize. He couldn't remember the last time he'd been lucky enough to hold such a promising set of pictures. His eyes slid to the pot, calculated note denominations by their visible edges; the mountain of sovereigns that had been early antes, he didn't bother counting…there were too many.

An hour and a half ago, eight men had started this game of cards and their bets had amassed into a very tidy sum. A very tidy sum, indeed. Two players had already folded; two had adopted the studied thought-fulness that betrayed a bluff; one was looking exceedingly nervous. And one was looking exceedingly foxed. And he held a full house; the winning hand…he was sure. He was thus determined to keep his wits about him. Resolutely, he pushed away a few inches his half-full brandy balloon in a move that was sure to have routed a weaker set of men.

'It's getting too rich for me,' Nathaniel Chamberlain muttered with a sorry look at the cash that once had been his, now tucked away beneath the tipsy pyramid in the centre of the table. Neatly, he cupped his hand of cards, but didn't yet discard them. Leaning at an angle to cosy with his brother-in-law, slumped in the next chair, he hissed low and vehement, 'And if you've any sense left, Meredith, you'll follow my lead.'

'Fesch me a drink,' Edgar slurred at him, and held out his empty whisky glass.

'Don't be a fool!' Alexander Pemberton added his own cautions to Nathaniel's. He stooped on creaky knees until his mouth was close to the top of Edgar's thinning pate. Earnestly he gritted, 'Listen to what your brother-in-law is telling you. It's time to admit defeat. Cut your losses now…'

'Everyone wan's to give me a'vise. I doan need a'vise. I need a drink.'

'I'll buy you a drink.'

Edgar swayed his head at the soft Gaelic drawl. He frowned across a shoulder at a pair of black trousers. His bleary vision climbed past a figured-silk waistcoat in pearl grey, resplendent beneath the lapels of a char-coal, superfine tail-coat. His neck angled awkwardly so he could take in a perfectly folded cravat crowned by high, white collar points. Eventually he blinked at a face of dark, stern beauty. 'Why…look whooze ar-rived,' he crowed. ''S the Irishman. His lor'ship's low-ering hisself to talk to me tonigh'. See, everyone…' He flapped a hand about. 'See, the dashing Major's here in the Palm House an' is condashending to talk to me. So you're talking to me 's'evening, are you? I'm honoured, milor'. Woan play cards with me though, will you? Frightened I'll cheat, are you?' He started to giggle. 'He's chary o' me cheating…' He slunk sideways in his chair and elbowed Nathaniel in the ribs. 'Thinks I'll shteal his money…' he hissed in a stage whisper. As though just remembering that the object of his scorn had offered to get him a drink, he contorted himself about again, and stuck out his empty glass at the Earl of Devane's hip.

Benjamin Harley curled a lip in amusement and slid a sideways look at his chum, Peter Waverley. Peter had been busily examining Edgar's last bid. He held up five fingers to Benjamin, denoting the additional hundreds of pounds he needed to stay in the game.

Harley's humour turned greedy. His mind was again on the pot…and securing it as soon as maybe. 'Shall we continue, Meredith? I've better sport than this awaiting me this evening. And she's far easier on the eye…and wallet than you are when drunk…' He managed a weak grin, for he was fretting to get play again underway before Meredith passed out or upset the table. Either way he might lose out if the game were called void. Quickly he matched Edgar's last bet and, dithering over whether to stick, or up the ante, allowed avarice to overrule his need to bring the game to a speedy conclusion. He raised the stake by scribbling a promissory note for one thousand pounds. His eyebrows elevated meaningfully at Edgar; he then included the other men still playing in the challenging look.

Edgar fished in a pocket, then delved deep in the

other. He tried his breast pocket. The gentlemen sitting around the table watched anxiously.

'I didn't say I wouldn't play cards with you,' came mildly, yet audibly, from behind him.

Edgar continued digging for gold. A handkerchief was tossed idly on to the table, a silver snuff-box followed in a clatter, then spectacles skidded away to wink candlelight. 'You didn't shay anything at all to me, ash I ric'ricall. Avoided me like I shtank, ash I ric'ricall. If you're not too grand and fash… fashdidious, si…sit down, then.' Edgar wobbled his head at Nathaniel's seat and hiccoughed again. Annoyed with the sudden spate of spasms rocking his chest, he ceased talking and gulped in a lungful of air. Steadily he began swelling about the neck and elevating in his chair.

'Aye, take my place…please,' Nathaniel said. He scraped his chair back from the table, shaking his head at Edgar. 'I'll not make excuses to Gloria for you, y'know. You'll not cry off apologising for this lunacy yourself…' Noticing his brother-in-law was becoming horribly florid and pop-eyed, he thumped him on the back.

Edgar exploded, shrunk into his seat then hiccoughed and swore. He waved a disgruntled hand at his brother-in-law, scattering a stack of sovereigns in the process. 'Fine' me something to scribble with,' he directed him rudely. 'An' mine' your own business…' He turned to Alexander Pemberton. 'Did I ask him to make m'excuses? Alibi for me only the once…only once ever has he done that…'

'Have you got something to say?' Connor quietly drawled at Lord Harley. He stuck a cheroot in his mouth and lit it. Having settled himself in Nathaniel's chair, he lay back in it, long legs stretching out lazily to the central pedestal. Blue eyes raised, gazing at the furious-faced man through a haze of slate smoke, whilst Edgar, beside him, continued to mumble and hiccough and pull out his pocket linings in search of some cash.

'It ain't in the rules. You want to play, Devane, wait till this game's done.'

'Anybody got any objections to me buying Chamberlain out and playing now?' Connor asked the few men seated about the table who were still in the game.

'None at all,' Toby Forster declared with a grin. 'Too deep for me in any case,' he explained. Having folded his hand, he lay back in his chair with an air of someone relishing future proceedings. His friend, Frank Vernon, looked at him lounging at ease, looked at his cards, then, with a hopeless groan, pitched them in too.

'Just the three of us, then,' Connor told Benjamin Harley and, withdrawing the cigar from between his teeth, he placed it carefully on the pewter ashtray.

Lord Harley's face turned a dull red, then the blood drained from his complexion as slowly the full implications of this subtle manoeuvre sunk in. His frustration erupted in a muttered imprecation forced through his set teeth.

Connor smiled, amused. His eyes remained cold. 'Come, don't fret, Benjamin,' he drawled silkily, while watching Edgar scratching script in black ink on to the white parchment that his brother-in-law had brought him. With a flourish the pledge was signed, the quill was lobbed back in the direction of the standish and Edgar flopped back in his chair. Connor's vivid blue gaze was still riveted on the parchment as he mocked Harley. 'I'm sure your lady friend will wait…unless, of course, she's sober now and remembers you…'

'I shall send an express to Beaulieu Gardens. Yes, I've decided, that's definitely what I shall do.'

Rachel sighed. She had heard these declarations a score or more times in as many hours. 'Send it then, Mama,' she agreed in defeat.

It had been two days since a violent storm subsided, having lasted a day and a night, before rumbling on its way. Still her father had not returned to Windrush, neither had he sent word of what occasioned his delay. He was only a few days' overdue and she had explained away his non-appearance and the lack of a messenger arriving with a note as being, in all probability, due to the hostile elements preventing anyone travelling north out of London.

Old Ralph had innocently contradicted that comforting train of thought. On their first venture out in the carriage along the sludgy track to the village of Staunton to pay a visit to friends, he'd cheerfully asserted that the folk of Cambridgeshire be best battening down the hatches next. The tumultuous weather was not heading south to London but blowing north-west. And, over the years, Ralph had proved himself to have an instinct for these things. He could smell snow in the air, see frost in hard bright night skies, feel a mist in his bones… Yet, still Rachel persevered with telling her mother that London might now be under siege from the weather.

In truth, she *was* feeling an odd twinge of apprehension over her papa's whereabouts. Not that she feared for his safety, but she knew that sometimes, when in all-male company for too long, he allowed himself to be distracted by a carafe or two of fine burgundy…or brandy…or suchlike. But he was not often *very* drunk. Just once or twice had she seen her papa drowning in his cups…and it had been an alarming and degrading sight. She could quite clearly recall being appalled at the way alcohol could ravage a seemly gentleman and render him a witless wreck.

Rachel bowed her head towards the semi-circle of sunshine silks on the carpet. With a sniff she pushed all else but June's wedding to the back of her mind. A finger hovered first over a butter-coloured hank and then moved to one of a lemon hue. Plucking up the richer thread, she passed it to Madcap Mary.

'M'um.'

Rachel acknowledged the servant's grunt of thanks with a quiet, 'That needlework looks beautiful, Mary.' She ran a finger over the delicate gold filigree loops that were forming about the hem of a snowy damask napkin. Her praises were sincere; her admiration the more pronounced for owning her own skill with a needle and thread was amateurish in the extreme. The fact that this oafish-looking young woman could produce something so exquisitely fine filled her with a sort of joyous amazement.

'M'um. Thank you, m'm.'

Rachel watched a pleased flush tint colour into the servant's sallow complexion and Mary anchored a floppy strand of copper hair back behind an ear with a finger as thick as a sausage.

Rachel heard her small, childlike sigh of content-ment as she settled her shapeless bulk back into the armchair and her fingers flew even faster. Rachel placed a few more hanks of the same shade on the stack of pristine linen that lay folded neatly on the chair arm.

Standing up, she walked off to the window and gazed immediately in the direction of the sentinel horse chestnut trees that marched off up the driveway. The pleasant vista was absent of a human presence; then Ralph's son, Pip, their general handyman, appeared from behind a bush. He was backing slowly on to the main track whilst methodically raking shingle. Rachel sighed and accorded her mama an idle glance. She had settled enough from fretting over her husband to concentrate on composing a list of viands required for the weekend.

In the hope of keeping her mother distracted from thoughts of her father, Rachel ventured that a haunch of lamb or a goose might make a nice change from veal or beef...

'Your papa is not so keen on fatty meats as he was: they're too rich for his digestion now he is grown older. Oh, I must write a note and send it with Ralph straight away to the post carrier. I swear some ill is befallen him...'

'I think, Mama, you ought abandon that idea,' Rachel said with an incipient smile. Spinning away from the window, she sped, dimity skirts in fists, to the door. Having yanked it open she spun about and apprised her startled mother, 'Papa is just appeared at the bend in the road.'

'What on earth can it be?' June whispered, her hazel eyes round with worry in her small, heart-shaped face. 'Why is Mother so distressed, do you think?'

'It is nought... She is probably just chiding him over his tardiness,' Rachel said with an unconvincing little laugh. She slid a look at Sylvie; even their youngest sister, who was wont to let family squabbles fly over her pretty head, looked subdued and a mite anxious as the commotion emanating from the library carried on unabated.

Another shriek, this time of a timbre that could only be described as despair, shivered the house. It had June immediately out of her chair. At the door, she hesitated, wringing her hands together, then looked agitatedly at Rachel. 'Perhaps we *should* go and see…'

'No…' Rachel said quietly, aware of Sylvie's clinging eyes on her, too. 'Whatever it is we will know soon enough. Let Papa have his say, in private. We will know soon enough,' she repeated gravely.

Her father had been home not yet an hour. Instead of the smiling dapper Papa she had been expecting to welcome over Windrush's threshold, a man she barely recognised had shuffled wearily in, looking as though he had not enjoyed a wash or a shave for some days. His dishevelled appearance was nothing, though, to the moody cast of his features, or the droop of his posture. He looked as though a burden of cares weighed upon his shoulders.

With barely a coherent greeting for his eldest daughter, he had slowly rid himself of the encumbrances of rumpled cloaks and hat, then cut off her questions with, 'Let me speak to your mother first, my dear. Time enough to deal with you later…'

And so Rachel, out of astonishment, had complied with that. But still the haunting sight of that grey-faced man, bristly of chin, and jaundiced of eye, dragging past her into the bosom of their house, set her stomach in knots. Something bad had happened and an inherent sense told her that somehow it affected her more than the others. More even than their hysterical mama…

A short while ago she had been reflecting on the last time she had seen her papa drunk. It had been six years ago. The same amount of time since she had listened to her mother's grief-stricken cries resounding through the house when she learned the news of dearest Isabel. Rachel felt lead settle in her stomach. Some tragedy of similar magnitude had occurred to overset her mother to such a degree and put her papa so out of countenance. Part of her wanted to run to her room and put a pillow over her head to shut out the terror as she had done years before. But then she had been but nineteen. Now she was stronger, more mature and hiding would not do. No, hiding would not do, at all. She needed to know what disaster she must now face. On a sigh of capitulation she sombrely left the room with her two younger sisters, pale and silent as spectres, drifting in her wake.

'You do not seem shocked, Rachel. Or not as shocked as I imagined you would be,' Edgar Meredith ventured, shattering the still silence in the room. 'I own I was worried you might scold your old papa.' The notion seemed to leave his humour unimpaired.

Rachel raised her ice-blue eyes to his face. His weak, appealing smile faded and he visibly flinched beneath that fleeting, freezing stare. Then his eldest daughter's contempt was turned on the crumbling embers in the grate.

Edgar hurrumphed deep in his throat, rubbed at his grey, bristly chin. He pushed himself from his armchair, and began pacing the room with an attempt at a jaunty step. 'I said to your mama it is no momentous disaster. And I can see that my sensible girls are in accord with their papa's calm and reasonable view,' he continued, happily regarding the three solemn young ladies perching awkwardly on the very edges of their chairs in Windrush's impressive library. No one looked at him, not even little Sylvie. Her head was bent towards her fingers clasped in her lap while her slippered heels beat backwards against the base of the chair, one after the other, one after the other, in relentless rhythm, until suddenly her mother shrieked, 'For God's sake stop that, Sylvie, I implore you! My nerves…'

As his wife quickly turned her face away to the wall again to shield from sight her red-rimmed, puffy eyes, Edgar resumed quickly, 'Yes; no momentous disaster. We are not poor. We are not ruined. We simply must relocate and revise our plans a little. In fact, those wedding guests who are presently in town and have made it clear they are loath to miss out on the other highlights of the Season by journeying to stay for some days in Hertfordshire will be relieved…nay, delighted by the change of venue. The Winthrops' ball might not, after all, clash with June's dates. Beaulieu Gardens is appointed well enough to receive any amount of eminent guests, and is so centrally positioned for everyone…'

'Then we must rejoice, must we not, that we shall, after all, not incommode any of them.' Rachel's slow, stinging sarcasm cut off any more of her papa's persuasion. Stiffly she pushed out of her chair, clasped white-knuckled fingers in front of her, in a pose that could have been mistaken for humble. 'Tell me again, Papa… Yes, please do repeat, very precisely, what you have done, for I find I cannot quite comprehend that anyone…*anyone*…but especially not a fond father and devoted husband would act in so…so selfish, so stupid, so irresponsible a way as to have jeopardised…'

'Don't *dare* give me that insubordination, miss!' Edgar roared into his daughter's audacious tirade, making his wife grip the chair arms and blink rapidly at the wall. June's head bowed almost to her lap to hide her glistening eyes. 'I shall do as I wish with my own property, when I wish, without being lectured on the subject by a female who has no right to ever challenge my behaviour…'

'I have every right. It was mine! By birth it was *mine*!' Rachel breathed in a raw, choking voice. 'You have gambled away what was lawfully mine.'

Edgar approached her, bristling defensively beneath her rage and disgust. Their heights were almost equal, so to impress on her his superiority he expanded his chest on a deep breath and jutted his chin. 'No, miss…it is…*was*…mine,' he corrected in a clipped tone. 'It is *mine* until the day I die; thereafter is it…was it…*yours*. As you see, I still breathe, and shall continue to do so, despite that fact that I know how very much you desire to choke the life from me.' His mouth tightened as he saw the betraying tide of rosy colour staining his eldest daughter's complexion. His voice quivered with authority and emotion as he resumed, 'I say again, in case you are at all unsure of my meaning, that I shall do as I will with my own chattels. Never shall I beg leave to act from dependants who benefit from the shelter and support I provide. I refuse to be upbraided or nagged…' This was addressed to his wife. 'And I refuse to account to any of you for my gambling or my drinking or for any other masculine pleasures in which I might decide to indulge.'

His wife stabbed at him a reproachful look at that particular dictum which he patently chose to ignore.

'Oh, Papa…you've done it on purpose… You've never forgiven me, have you?'

The statement was ragged with perception yet very quiet and this time Edgar's sallow cheeks regained sanguinity. But his resolve was unimpaired by his eldest daughter's awful accusation. Steadily he continued, 'I say again, we are not poor. We are not ruined. The day any of you is ejected, impoverished, on to the street because of my doing is the day you may berate me for failing in my duty as head of this household. Until that time, if you wish to continue to partake of my protection, I will hear no more of it!' With that parting shot he marched from the room, and with a final flourish banged the door shut as he went.

'I said stop that noise, Sylvie!' Gloria Meredith screeched at her youngest daughter as the sonorous silence was shattered by the rhythmic tattoo of feet again beating time.

Sylvie jumped, quivered in her seat for a moment, then rushed from the room, stifling a sob with a thumb stuck in her mouth.

After a strained silence, Gloria cleared her throat and quavered, 'You should not have spoken to your father in that tone, Rachel. It was very bad of you. I'm not saying he's blameless, but gentlemen will always gamble and will always suffer misfortunes at the tables. Properties have changed hands thus since time immemorial. Your papa has been…unwise and…unlucky, but, as he says, it is not the end of the world.'

'*Unlucky!*' Rachel spat. A grim smile skewed her shapely lips. 'Do you really believe this has anything to do with *luck*?' She stalked off to the window, feeling freezing cold yet consumed with a fiery rage. Her mind was crammed with a million seething thoughts yet she seemed unable to say more because a well of murky despair was stagnating her intelligence. There was still a corner of her consciousness that wanted to believe it a mistake…a joke… But one sweeping glance, encompassing her mother's blotchy countenance and June's slumped, quaking shoulders, deprived her of that possibility. Oh, it was real. Closing her eyes, she forced herself to find coherent speech. Words scattered through her stiff lips in brusque sentences. 'I should say this has been cleverly schemed at. Father's not been unlucky. Losing Windrush is just part of his grand plan. He wants to settle old scores and ease his conscience. It's the fault of that conniving Irish bastard.'

'Rachel!' Gloria Meredith sharply remonstrated, standing up. 'I'll hear no more of this…this talk. You forget yourself and who you speak to and are become coarse and vulgar out of bitterness! You heard what your papa said. The Earl won fair and square. There were witnesses to the whole game. Your uncle Chamberlain was there. So was Mr Pemberton. You have no quarrel with the integrity of those two gentlemen, surely? Your father has stressed he has no grievance with Lord Devane…no accusations to make about the way play went that night…'

Rachel gave a bleak laugh. 'No; he has no accusations to make. But I have. That Irish—' She swallowed, fought to dissipate her bile. 'That Irish major fooled me too. I thought he meant what he said to me at the Pembertons about quietening the gossips and smoothing over past unpleasantness. His intention, of course, is the exact reverse. He has now made us the butt of *beau monde* derision and has certainly taken his revenge on us…me. And my own father has allowed him…conspired with him in it to ease some notion of past indebtedness. I would guess, despite what has occurred, he still likes him, too.' She gazed at her mother with huge, soulful eyes. 'I would guess he still likes him a deal better than he likes me…his own flesh and blood.'

Gloria, arms outstretched, started towards her daughter, but Rachel spun away and avoided her. She pulled a hand across her cheeks, and choked a laugh. 'I think Devane knew very well when he got into that game and realised that my father had no cash with which to bet that, whilst drunk, he might stake Windrush. As you say, Mama, country seats have ever been won and lost on the baize. He knew that this property is my inheritance. He knew that losing it to him would devastate me more than knowing the estate had been accidentally razed to the ground. Since we returned here from London you have asked me several times if Lord Devane and I were now friends and I didn't properly reply. Now I shall. I know without a shadow of a doubt that we are not friends, Mama. In fact, I can confidently state that we are about to become the bitterest of enemies.'

Chapter Seven

'Don't go, Rachel, please. There's no need. I truly don't mind being married in London and I know William won't object. As Papa said, it does have certain advantages for the guests…'

'I don't give a tinker's cuss about the guests, and neither should you! It is to be your day. Yours and William's. Don't you dare write and tell him there is to be any change,' she hastily interjected as the thought occurred to her. 'You shall be married at Windrush, as originally planned. Windrush shall be my inheritance as our ancestors planned. The status quo is to be maintained, that is what I have planned. All will be well again, I promise,' Rachel concluded with a mettlesome smile and a toss of her golden head.

June looked unconvinced so Rachel gave her sister's arm a little encouraging shake. 'Don't look so terrified,' she admonished. 'I'm the one who must soon do battle with the Irish usurper.'

'Don't speak so, Rachel! You know Mama and Papa will be angry if they again hear you cursing his lordship.'

'I wasn't actually swearing, although I'll confess to

being plagued by the desire where he's concerned. An usurper is just a fancy term for a thief...a mean embezzler, which justly describes him.'

'Well, don't let them hear you say that either,' June warned on a grimace, her eyes sliding to the chamber door. 'Papa maintains he isn't dishonest, and won't hear a word doubting his integrity, and Mama agrees with him.'

'Well, she would, wouldn't she?' A scoffing little laugh escaped Rachel. 'Our poor mama is of that downtrodden generation that thinks once a woman is wed she relegates her ideas, her beliefs, even her character beneath her husband's, however biased and bigoted he might be. So, if you intend retaining any degree of independence and identity, within connubial bliss, ponder on our parents' relationship and let it be a salutary lesson to you.' She finished the homily on a humorous look and an exaggerated finger wag.

'Is that wrong, then, Rachel?' June hesitantly queried. 'Wanting to be like Mama? Accepting a wife's role is to be loyal and dutiful and perhaps even subordinate to the man she loves? Is that stupid?'

'No...well, not necessarily...' Rachel muttered with vague impatience, for she had no wish to be seriously lecturing or setting standards in her sister's marriage. 'Anyway, William is a different kind of man to our chauvinistic papa. He is younger...more liberal and progressive in his views on women's dues and their capabilities. He holds no prejudices against the women derogatorily termed blue-stockings by the less intelligent and well read, and I know he supports Elizabeth Fry in her prison reforms for women and children, for we've discussed it before. He's also not unsympathetic to Princess Caroline and the poor woman's plight at the hands of her gross consort.'

'It seems you know more of his politics and beliefs than I do, then,' June said with uncharacteristic tartness. 'For I don't recall *us* ever having such a conversation.'

'That's because, when with you, he is too busy admiring and adoring you to speak of such mundane things,' Rachel soothed, whilst patting down the clothes in her trunk. 'He is a man in love. He wants to entertain and woo his beloved. You, my dear, have inspired an envied, elusive love match. You will have time enough, once the honeymoon is over, to talk of Government policies and the price of bacon. William is a fine man. He cherishes you. You won't be bored, even when being cosy and comfortable together. I like him very much.' Rachel sighed in conclusion.

June twisted a smile. 'And he likes you. At one time I thought perhaps a little too well—' She broke off as Rachel flapped a dismissing hand.

'Get away! I'm far too old for him! I look to be at least four years his senior! He is grateful to me, that is the most of his consideration. And so he ought to be! After all, I bestowed on him the honour of an introduction to my beautiful, sweet sister. You were surrounded by admirers last year during the month we were in London. I swear poor William thought he might be beaten off by one of those distinguished fellows in Life Guard regimentals. You were barely visible at times for a battalion of red coats.'

Piqued by the hint that her beloved looked like a boy, June quickly advised, 'He *is* nearly twenty-four, you know.' She sighed. 'T'was only ever him I wanted, in any case. But I confess to liking the look of a military man.' A sidelong look accompanied, 'I always swooned over the Major in his Hussar's uniform. I know I was only thirteen when he was courting you, but I suppose it won't hurt now to say that I *was* very jealous that you had him. I used to dream that some day…' The disclosure tailed off. Instead she revealed, 'When Connor would visit, expecting you to be home, only to discover you'd gone out with Isabel, I would shamelessly traipse after him, you know. If Papa or Mama were at home they'd try and trap him until you returned. But if Sylvie was in the nursery and no one was about but me, I'd be delighted to have him to myself. I'd falsely promise you'd soon be back and he'd simply smile in that way he has that just tilts a corner of his mouth.' June's lips slanted in an unconscious yet studied approximation of what she was describing. 'Then he'd linger a while, and he'd ask how my lessons went.' Despite receiving no response from her sister, June knew she was stirring Rachel's interest. What she'd always feared was that her beautiful older sister might be amused by her schoolgirl crush on Connor.

June had spent her formative years in her charismatic, headstrong big sister's shadow. The difference in their ages had once prevented her sharing Rachel's glittering social life. She remembered that Rachel and Isabel, born just eighteen months apart, had been inseparable. Even now, with no sibling here between them, getting Rachel's full attention was rare and complimentary. June hadn't once thought this romantic little tale might bond them in a bittersweet reminiscence. Softly she continued, 'There was one occasion he caught me spying on him late at night through the banisters at Beaulieu Gardens.'

Rachel folded the dress in her hands, made neat the edges, before turning to look at June. 'I never knew you ever noticed him like that. You never said.'

'I often wondered why *you* never noticed him like that,' June ventured to say with rare pithiness. 'At thirteen I vowed if I had him, I should never stand him up when he came to take me out. I vowed I would never leave him idling at a loose end in case another young lady caught his eye. But then I was too…naïve…I suppose, to realise that you didn't care if another lady lured him away, for you didn't really love him at all…did you?'

'I wasn't standing him up. I was…I was making him aware I wasn't prepared to be always there… waiting…when he and Papa had nothing better to do with themselves,' escaped Rachel in a hoarse whisper. It was followed immediately by, 'What did he say when he caught you spying on him? Probably told you to go away, I suppose. He never seemed very interested in children…'

'Oh, no, he was kind. He waited till you and the other guests—it was Aunt and Uncle Chamberlain and some other, very grand people who were with you— had gone into the drawing room, then he came over to talk to me. It was as well Mama didn't spot me there, at close to midnight, in my nightgown and bare feet. I expect she'd have had a purple fit.'

'No doubt…' Rachel murmured, but continued begging June with a look for further scraps of the story.

'You'd been to the opera with a Lord and Lady someone or other. I know it was The Magic Flute by Mozart, for Connor gave me the theatre programme and the white rose from his buttonhole. He looked quite magnificent, I thought, with his sleek black hair and that scarlet coat…' June shifted on the bed where she was sitting. 'I still have the programme and I pressed the rose. I don't know why I've kept them so long…*six years*… How odd. Now *I'm* about to be a bride, not you. I'm in love…yet still I have keepsakes from another man.' The peculiarity was stressed by a widening of her honey-coloured eyes. 'I felt sure he would tell you he had given me those momentoes. I thought between yourselves you might have found my daft infatuation amusing.'

'No, he never told me,' Rachel said softly. 'I never knew…' She shook out the gown she had just carefully folded, then refolded it exactly as it had been and smoothed it before placing it into the trunk. With a complete change of tone she laughed. 'It's as well, then, he has since shown himself to be unkind, or we might now all be languishing in thrall to that cheap Irish charm he employs.'

Something in her sister's shrill tone moved June to reassure her. 'No matter that you didn't much care for him, I'm sure he adored *you*, Rachel. I recall how he would look at you. I used to wish that some day someone would look that way at me…'

'Well, now you know better than to be taken in by any such nonsense,' Rachel returned briskly. 'Bovine-eyed regard is simply clear evidence of a beast-brain.'

'I noticed the way he was looking at you when you came in together at the Pembertons' soirée…'

'He played his part well, did he not?' Rachel interrupted busily. 'All smooth solicitude and sophistication. And I never guessed it to be the prelude to his revenge. I feel quite foolish now about that. You see, June, damning proof; he is still a beast…a monster, in fact. And to my chagrin I expect I shall honestly become quite beastly myself as I battle to recover what is rightfully mine…ours. You will be married here in Hertfordshire. There is no doubt of that. Soon I shall return with the deeds to Windrush. There is, indeed, no doubt of that, either!'

From the corner of a blue eye she saw he was still watching her. But Rachel didn't turn about or acknowledge his attention in any way. Instead she thanked Ralph as he helped her up into the travelling chaise. Settling back into the creaky old squabs, she deliberately turned her head away from the bricks and mortar she loved…the house she would soon scheme and battle for.

Since the afternoon in the library earlier in the week when she had learned of her sire's drunken antics, and had had the brazen audacity to take him to task over turning her world upside down, father and daughter had kept their distance—and a glacier of politeness between them—when a chance encounter brought them face to face.

Yesterday morning, at breakfast, when she had announced her intention to travel to London with Noreen Shaughnessy accompanying her, she had read in the glancing look that clashed her parents' eyes that neither believed true the reason she gave for so soon journeying once more to the metropolis. Neither of them had challenged her decision to go; and only her mother commented upon it, pronouncing a slightly faltering hope that she should have a pleasant trip. Not that Rachel had expected them to try and stop her going. She was, after all, a woman approaching her twenty-sixth birthday. Every Michaelmas, for the past six years, she had travelled to Aunt Florence in York. This autumn would be no exception to the rule. Strictly speaking, it was not unusual or improper for her to travel alone with just a sturdy, respectable female servant for company.

On this occasion, because she wouldn't be forced to be a liar by circumstances imposed on her by Devane, she'd every intention of acting on the excuse she gave her parents for her brief sojourn in town. She'd written straight away to Lucinda, and although it was too soon for a reply, she knew her friend would be grateful for her presence, as her little son, Alan, was an energetic child who, Lucinda had fondly moaned, was quite a handful now he was up onto his feet and getting nimble just as she was getting clumsy and retiring more and more to her day bed. When Lucinda had been pregnant with that little boy, Rachel had gone to stay with her friend, for poor Lucinda had suffered debilitating sickness in the first months of her pregnancy. Lucinda's older sister was unable to assist as she was also in an interesting condition and soon due to be delivered of her second child. Paul Saunders had fairly begged Rachel to be an angel and undertake the office of companion and mentor to his wife, for he was anxious that the unremitting bouts of nausea were making her seriously depressed. Rachel, despite being a single lady, was very poignantly acquainted with those twins, pain and joy, that attached themselves so powerfully to pregnancy. She had wanted to be useful and was more than happy to keep her best friend company. Within a month the sickness ceased, Lucinda's spirits lifted, and she sailed serenely through the latter part of her confinement.

Rachel was not yet sure how much she would reveal to her friend about what had really brought her to

London. Obviously the gentlemen's clubs and the ladies' salons would have been abuzz with the news that Lord Devane had taken the Merediths' country estate in a gambling hell. But, as her mother had rightly said, it was not so unusual an occurrence, for fortunes and property to change hands in such places.

That thought redrew Rachel's awareness to the large oblong casement that overlooked the drive and presently framed behind squared panes a slight, solitary figure within its weathered beams. Still she avoided looking directly at him. She had taken up that position herself just a few days ago, and with pitiful innocence, gladly watched her papa galloping home. Never once had she guessed he might bring such awful tidings with him. Now it was his turn to stand sentinel and wait and watch. He, she was sure, knew full well she was going away with the intention of righting the appalling wrong he had done her.

Beside the carriage, Noreen was taking her leave of her sister. With a final pat at Mary's broad back, she gave her a little push and Mary was obediently scuffling back over gravel towards the house. With a trenchant look at her mistress that terminated in a subordinate bob of her fiery head, Noreen was soon settling herself into the seat opposite with her dun cloak neatly pulled about her.

As the vehicle jerked forward Rachel instinctively turned her head, and looked up. Her father raised a hand. Involuntarily she returned the salute, although smiling back was beyond her. And then she'd lost sight of his pathetically gaunt figure as they entered the avenue of magnificent horse chestnuts that straddled the drive with gigantic timber limbs.

Edgar Meredith placed his raised palm flat against

glass and watched as his eldest child slipped from sight into a tunnel of spring fresh greenery. He tilted his weary head and whispered to the ceiling, 'Good luck, my love.'

'I'll wait.'

'Ahem, I don't think that would be wise, Miss… er…Meredith, did you say?

'Yes, I did.'

'Well, Miss Meredith, I have no idea just how long the Earl might be abroad.'

'Is he due to return today?'

'Today, yes. When, I have no idea. I shouldn't wish to alarm you with the news, madam, but yesterday his lordship was out from before midday to beyond midnight.'

'Be assured I am not made timid by the knowledge. May I sit here?'

Rachel indicated the closest high-backed, uncomfortable-looking mahogany seat set against a cream-washed wall. In truth, the thought of loitering for so long was little short of terrifying. But then she doubted she would need to. It was not quite yet the hour to dine. She imagined Lord Devane might reappear to partake of his dinner before he socialised for the evening. The Earl's butler was deliberately being pessimistic in order to move her on. He had the unyielding mien of a man charged solely with the task of preventing undesirables settling anywhere within this august abode. Even in this vast vestibule. But then it was exceedingly imposing, if a trifle austere, with its royal-blue velvet draperies and heavy dark furniture backed against the lofty walls.

Joseph Walsh, the butler, was under the impression

that this woman should be grateful he was even granting her a show of tolerance. He strove to retain the illusion a while longer, lest he might be mistaken in mentally maligning her as an odd eccentric out on an obscure calling, or as a scheming minx out on the make. He'd been in Connor Flinte's employ for some years now. He had travelled with the Earl to Wolverton Manor, his vast estate in Ireland and once, in the role of valet, endured less luxurious accommodation while sharing a bivouac with the Major on the continent, and he didn't recognise her from amongst his master's friends or formal acquaintances. He knew for sure she'd never been welcomed into this house.

You'd need to be a blind man to miss she was a beauty, beneath the smudges, and she was obviously driven by an urgent and stubborn desire to speak to the Earl. Not a promising combination, all things considered. Despite the grime, her attire was of good quality, her manner and speech proclaimed her genteel, and she looked to be some years past her majority…more missionary than mistress material…but then, when he reflected on the hussies that masqueraded as ladies in society, what did a crisp vowel and a nice poke bonnet signify?

Joseph Walsh had, in his career as gentleman's gentleman, held positions with some of the most eminent bachelors the peerage could boast and he was fully cognisant of their self-indulgent pleasures. A few years ago he'd worked for a young viscount who would boldly knock up the household and usher lightskirts into his own residence when foxed and frisky. Most of his noble patrons had thankfully maintained some protocol and been entertained more discreetly by their paramours. But he was able to clearly recall, over twenty years of service, quite a few instances where bold wenches had turned up uninvited on the doorstep with their bellies swollen and their hands out too. Oh, he knew the tricks of that particular trade and the games the Quality played. Thus his eyes, beneath his wiry peppery brows, were professionally dispassionate in their distaste as he looked Miss Meredith over, in particular to detect any loss of a waistline under her cloak.

Rachel bridled beneath his supercilious scrutiny. Had she guessed what really flared those fastidious nostrils, she might have slapped his po-face. She imagined what disgusted him was that ladies usually took more care with their appearance before presenting themselves at this illustrious address with every intention of gaining entry. She was not being seen at her best, she knew. Her hat was dusty, her pelisse hem mud-caked. She was, she admitted to herself, looking distinctly tired and travel-stained.

London and its environs had recently been battered by a wild bombastic storm, so the eloquent pot-man at the Bell at Edmonton had imparted when they had broke their journey on the way into London in order to refresh the horses, as they had on the way out of it barely a week ago. The courtyard at the hostelry had been running with mire that collected in the ruts engineered by the frequent to-ing and fro-ing of numerous carriages. And, careful as she had been to keep her clothes out of the potholes, her boots and hems had become encrusted on the short hop and skip from coach to tavern.

Now, after a lengthy journey, she was arrived at her destination. And she had no idea why she had acted so bizarrely by coming straight here without even repairing to Beaulieu Gardens to wash her face and change her clothes. A nap to refresh her body and mind would also have been of sound benefit before she went on the attack. Now, stranded, in Devane's hallway, with the wind gone from her sails because he was nowhere about to take the full vent of it, she realised it might be best to try and make a dignified retreat and return when better able to cope with the situation.

A smart young footman was lounging by the entrance, still holding wide one side of the double-doors while leering at her. Obviously he expected her to be sent back down the stone steps, possibly assisted by the toe of the haughty butler's boot. She tilted her chin, glared at him with ice-blue eyes and knotted her mouth in violent indignation. It clamped tighter for she was suddenly bedevilled by the vulgar urge to regale these two menials with the news that she had once had the good sense to reject the man they obviously deemed too grand to grant her an audience, even had he been within doors.

Coolly, determinedly she bit her tongue, and gathered her bespattered garments in her tight fists. Keeping the heavy hems clear of the polished wood floor, and skirting the cream and blue oriental rug with a fierce dragon design, she swept to the mahogany chair she had opted for and made use of it. In case that didn't clearly display her intention to sit tight, she untied her bonnet strings, combed out her untidy golden snarls with nervous fingers, then placed the headgear on her lap with an air of absolute finality.

She stared challengingly at the footman by the door until his cocky expression drooped. He swivelled uneasy eyes to his superior. The butler merely jerked his faded sandy head, and at the signal the great door was pushed shut. With a furtive expression of admiration

now on his face, the smartly liveried young footman
was marching off into the deeper recesses of the house.

'Is his lordship expecting you, Miss Meredith?'
Joseph Walsh asked with exceedingly weary courtesy.

'Yes,' Rachel immediately lied. Then with a wry inner smile realised that, of course, it was probably no
lie after all…

Rachel glanced up at the hallway clock and noticed
the time was already five minutes to eight; she calculated that Noreen would by now be unloading at
Beaulieu Gardens. On discovering that Lord Devane
was out, a pre-arranged signal to Ralph, waiting in the
road, had sent their carriage on its way. From a purely
practical point of view, it seemed pointless for them all
to kick their heels in Berkeley Square, awaiting the
arrival of the usurper. Noreen could be usefully em-
ployed in unpacking the trunks, and Ralph in attending
to the horses.

Her servants thought she was addled in the wits, too.
She had seen it in their watchful eyes as she alighted
in front of this magnificent townhouse, looking distinctly the worse for wear yet obstinate that she would
present herself at once.

Noreen had limited her cautions on the wisdom of
so soon making a call to simply clucking her tongue
and muttering, 'Sure, an' you'll be after wanting to see
to y'self first, m'm. Time enough tomorrer to see your
friends.'

'Tomorrow, I shall see my *friends*, Noreen,' Rachel
had told her as she gazed up at the elegant façade of
her foe's residence. *But today, I must see him*, had echoed on silently in her mind.

Ralph had gruffly stated, quite sweetly paternal, she
had thought, that he would call back for her in a hour

so she must then be good and ready to leave. Rachel had soothed his unspoken, oblique worries by saying she forbade any such thing for she was certain she would be offered transport home. In view of the bitter accusations congesting her mind, awaiting to be blasted at his lordship's head, she knew she could expect no such courtesy. But she had the means to purchase a ride home later and hackneys were readily available. It had been early still; just seven-thirty and the evenings so light at this time of the year. It had only fleetingly crossed her mind that it might be pitch dark when she finally got to find her bed at Beaulieu Gardens…

Rachel leaned her heavy head back against the wall, watching through the fanlights over the double doors the silver crescent and trio of spangles placed like fancy patches on midnight-blue velvet. A wispy cloud dimmed their mesmerising shimmering, and with a sigh she looked away from the heavens. Her head fell sideways, loosening yet more golden tresses to drape her cloaked shoulders, and she glanced at the clock. It was a superfluous checking, for each sonorous hour chimed away by the magnificent time-piece in the corner had roused her from her troubled thoughts. Ten-fifteen was the time. Those fifteen minutes had dragged like fifty since last she'd been startled into straightening in her hard, inhospitable chair.

After being presented with a little refreshment at eight-thirty—a glass of lemonade and some cinnamon biscuits—she'd remained ignored in the hall, except for a phlegmatic look from the butler on each hourly vigil that took him to the front door to needlessly check and rattle the locks. Even on collecting her empty plate and tumbler an hour later he'd said nothing to her.

During the lonely quiet with just her thoughts to

keep her company, an unavoidable introspection had produced nothing inspiring. Instead, a disquieting certainty was plaguing her that she had acted with a total lack of sense or maturity after arriving at this illustrious address. Adamant she would not be worsted by servants who had insinuated she was unworthy of their attention, never mind that of the Earl of Devane, she had insisted on forcing upon them her presence and demanding an audience with their master.

Six years ago, when she had been engaged to Connor Flinte, their social standing had been fairly equal. He had been a catch, no doubt; but then so had she, with her beauty, her youth and her heiress status.

Now she was past her prime and the heart of her inheritance was gone; a chasm seemed to yawn between their conditions. How her pride was pricked by knowing it! And by recalling how her adversary had been fawned over at the Pembertons' *musicale*. At thirty, he was more eligible than ever; he was obviously well-liked, not only by her partisan father, but by the fashionable set. His London residence, she could see, had some costly, stately appointments, and his servants were naturally charged to vet his callers. Had she not been feeling so very defensive, she would have accepted that his butler was simply attending to his duty, not taking a personal dislike to her. In fact, as she had not requested refreshment, that was an unexpected kindness on his part.

Grudgingly, she realised she had been treated with more respect than perhaps her petulance allowed. As the hour grew late and it became obvious the master was not returning to dine…or to see his visitor, his manservant could have insisted she leave…but he had not.

More and more, as the minutes dragged on, was she beset by an urge to slink away. Yet she couldn't. For her own peace of mind she must remain where she was. It seemed pointless staying, yet equally ill-advised to leave. If she fled, details of her bold intrusion would be recounted to the master when he arrived home.

Arriving here like a whirlwind, acting like an unkempt harpy, in the hope of impressing on him that she didn't give a fig how she looked for he was not worth the courtesy of a clean dress and a scrubbed complexion, had been the sort of tempestuous conduct that would better befit a child Sylvie's age. She had wasted over two hours that could have been put to such good use. She yawned, let her lids flutter low over her drowsy blue eyes. A bath, a proper meal…a nap. All those alluring comforts she had missed. She could have chosen oblivion for a few hours. She could have opted for the opiate of blessed sleep…

Words were whispering in her brain like malicious ghosts, slowly penetrating her cosy dream, spoiling it. She turned her head fitfully trying to recapture the magic of laughing with Isabel, chatting with Isabel…being with Isabel.

Isabel raised her hands; pale fingers were outstretched to her, teasing, as though they might beckon, not wave farewell as she dreaded. They did neither; she felt a gentle human touch on her cheek, stroking. She was being soothed because her sister would soon be gone again…lost to her and far…far away. The fair oval of Isabel's face, the gleam on her long fawn hair were becoming indistinct…fading, even though Rachel called to her…demanded she stay with a sob cracking her voice.

Rachel sought those hands, wanting the comfort of the embrace, but a redolence of masculine scent, a hard male body, frightened her senses out of their coma. She jerked upright in her seat, then tried to press backwards into it. She stared through misty, sleep-blinded eyes at a man. His dark, frowning face was close to hers and she realised he was squatting close to her chair. Beyond him were fuzzy silhouettes of two other men. She blinked and swallowed, blinked and swallowed, already fearful of the dreadful embarrassment which was building just beyond the blanking residue of her daze. For on the periphery of her mind still tormented the anxieties that had hounded her into sleep. Oh, she was aware that shame was creeping closer to cow her and she closed her eyes tight, hoping to hold it at bay.

When eventually she jabbed a look past Lord Devane, this time she recognised, with a stab of despair, the two other men who were witnessing her distress. The short, elderly butler was quietly talking to a tall, fair-haired man. Jason Davenport was looking at her too. His attention never left her. Rachel felt her stomach coil in to knots and in a sudden panic she tried to rise. Her legs were stiff, awkward from sitting so long, and she grabbed behind for support from the chair as slowly she straightened.

Connor was rising as she did, keeping pace with her, close to her and, as cramp made her sob and stumble, he steadied her with a firm grip on her arms.

His soft Irish accent penetrated her torpor, the first clear words she understood. 'Come, it's time to go home, Rachel…'

'What time is it?' was all she could croak on a sniff in response.

'One-thirty…'

'One-thirty?' she echoed back. 'You're late…so late…' she accused on an indrawn, shivering breath.

'I know…I'm sorry…' he soothed in that honey, silky voice that could so easily have drawn her back to rest.

Without another word he moved her close, an arm about her shoulders absorbing the force of her uncontrollable quaking. He took her over the polished wood floor in a way that barely necessitated her feet touching it. She was aware of the butler going that way too. He opened the door, looked at her with great intent, and then she was into balmy night air and lifted, floating, dreamlike, down the steps.

It seemed the most natural thing in the world, as she was rocking gently in his carriage, that he would shift to sit by her, still keeping her close as she drifted in and out of dozes…resting against his chest.

Chapter Eight

'Will you be after wanting me to pour, Miss Rachel?'

'No...I shall manage. That will be all, thank you, Noreen.'

Noreen Shaughnessy looked at her mistress, then slanted a bold stare from beneath her rusty lashes at the tall, distinguished gentleman lounging at his ease by the mantel. After a low, deferential curtsy that caused tufts of springy hair to escape her neat cap and spoil her view of his handsome self, she withdrew.

Rachel remained facing the closed door for a moment. Of course...someone else who approved of him, and a countrywoman to boot. Her full lips took on a decidedly disapproving skew, before she quickly went to the tea tray Noreen had placed on the morning-room table. 'Thank you for coming so promptly, sir...my lord.' She slipped over the mistake in his address with slick brevity. 'First, I must apologise for requesting your presence so shockingly early in the day, but I thought it seemed sensible, for propriety sake as much as anything, to get this over between us as soon as possible...' Again, her soft, shapely lips pursed; this time in regret at not having more tactfully phrased her preliminaries. After all, her aim *was* to exploit that show of warm indifference that this man had first established between them at the Pembertons'. Time enough in the months that would follow for him to discover just how hostile she really felt. For now she was willing to curb her emotions and prepare the ground for the seeds of her plot. In fact, she was willing to do anything within her power to safeguard June a happy and harmonious wedding day at Windrush. Regaining her inheritance was another matter: a feat she was willing to work towards more slowly and stealthily.

A flitting glance reached his face. As she feared, behind his mild expression lurked faint amusement. He also looked disturbingly impressive. His attire was understated elegance: a gilt-buttoned tail-coat of navy blue, and fawn buckskin breeches that seemed moulded to his powerful physique. A crisp shirt looked spotless; a snowy cravat faultless in its fuss-free folds. Tasselled Hessian boots had obviously provided his valet with hours of toil: the one stubbed lazily on its toe, bridging the other, was reflecting the Greek-key design bordering the carpet. She hadn't before felt inclined to notice that he wore his hair unfashionably long and uncurled: a thick pelt of sable appeared to obscure his collar and weak sunlight, stencilling through the lace curtains, was dusting his head with an ebony patina. Her teeth set a little. So, what if he looked well? He'd ever been an attractive man, there was no need to make so much of it now.

Those startlingly blue eyes were not fully open as he surveyed her, but he didn't have the debilitated air of one deprived of rest. In fact, beneath his languid demeanour, she guessed the Earl of Devane was depressingly alert. Her summons for him to come to Beaulieu Gardens at eleven o'clock this morning—a time when no self-respecting member of the *ton* would be out of bed, let alone out of doors—must have reached him at the dawn-like hour of nine. Yet here he was, arrived on time, looking so immaculately turned out that he must have roused himself to be punctual as soon as Ralph handed in her message at his residence.

Not that *she* was a stranger to a meticulous *toilette*: having yesterday made an utter fool of herself in every way, starting with presenting herself at his home looking for all the world like a sloven, and finishing the fiasco by blubbing like a baby, she had undertaken to be dignity personified today.

Every possible advantage must be hers when receiving him on home ground. So, in contrast to last evening's unkempt brat, she hoped that, this morning, she once more resembled an elegant, mature woman.

Her sprig-muslin morning dress was of demure empire line, yet fitted snugly to her bosom thus endowing her moderate bust with a maximum amount of cleavage. The skirt flared little and a hint of curvaceous hips was revealed beneath barely opaque gauze. Her complexion was white with fatigue, yet she'd forgone rouge; she knew that, oddly, the pallor suited her, as did the bruise-like smudges colouring the translucent hollows beneath her eyes for they accentuated their blue. This morning she had taken pains to appear quite interestingly ethereal and in need of a strong man's care and protection—which was what she'd received from a most unexpected quarter last night. She was willing to play up to the concern he had shown her then. It was hardly surprising he'd pitied her considering the pathetic spectacle she had made of herself. It would have needed to be a callous rogue, indeed, who'd remain unmoved while she snivelled like a lost soul. So, against all odds, she had gained something from the débâcle and learned that even the stormiest cloud might turn up a silver lining.

Not that conquering her chagrin had been easy. Three quite presentable gowns were strewn, screwed up, on her bed upstairs where she had lobbed them in roiling pique. She had been still buttoning this one, finally opted for in a panic, with Noreen hopping and skipping around her, plying the tongs to her hair, when his curricle drew up outside at five minutes to eleven. But the furious preparations had been worthwhile: Rachel was sophisticated enough to understand that a lot of her jilted fiancé's studied impassivity derived from the fact that he was not unmoved by her fragile, womanly charms. And she did mean to charm him into submission…for what else, initially, had she to use? Just a hope he might be tempted to oblige her with a favour because once they'd been just hours away from becoming man and wife…

Aware she had been dithering with cups and saucers whilst all this registered in her mind, Rachel made a brisk show of agitating the tea in the teapot. Immediately the utensil was tilted and the brew was streaming into a cup. In a rather thin voice she hastily enlarged on her previous blunt comment. 'I thought it best for both our sakes that we meet early, before any of our acquaintances might be up and about and spy your vehicle outside. I'd hate to give people further cause to speculate over dealings between the Merediths and the Earl of Devane.'

'I understand…'

'Yes…I thought you would. Cream and sugar?'

'Yes, thank you.'

Wordlessly Rachel concentrated on being a competent hostess. With a final extra drip of cream added to his cup, she was satisfied it looked just so, and carried it towards him. She had barely covered half the distance when she realised she'd been overgenerous and the tremor in her fingers was likely to send a quantity of the beverage slopping into the saucer. She halted with a tut and a frown, and stared dismayed at her hot, wet fingers. 'Oh, how clumsy. I'm sorry. I shall get you another…'

'There's no need—'

'No. I shall pour a fresh one,' Rachel insisted, a hint of obstinacy shrill in her tone. 'It is no trouble. There is still plenty in the pot.' She backed away a pace, the cup held out rigidly in front of her as though she feared she might upset the rest on the way back to the table. Why had she not let Noreen perform this stupid ritual? she silently berated herself.

Although her eyes were riveted on the delicate floral porcelain, she was aware of the moment he relinquished lounging against the mantel. She increased her pace backwards as he advanced, the crockery rattling in her damp hand. Firm fingers coiled about her wrist, making it steady so he could relieve her of what remained of his tea.

She watched a hateful rivulet of orange pekoe tracing a delicate blue vein on the back of her hand while wending its way towards him. He dammed the flow with a dark thumb, then, placing down his cup, dried her skin with a handkerchief idly extracted from a pocket. When the linen had disappeared whence it came, still he held her and still her eyes were fixed to the manacle of brown fingers on her wrist. His closeness, his light administering touch, reminded her, undeniably, of last night. Her complexion lost its appealing pallor to a remorseless surge of blood as she remembered cuddling up quite shamelessly to him in his carriage when he brought her home. But they had spoken little, other than for him to tease out of her the necessary information that, yes, she was staying at Beaulieu Gardens, and, yes, but for servants, she was alone…

From settling herself uninvited in his hallway to plunging into a deep dreamy sleep that necessitated him waking her to eject her, she had behaved outrageously. The awful irony was that she could clearly recall being on the point of making ready to fly away home. But before she could act, Isabel had called to her, as often she did when she was upset and weary and, with her eyes heavy and her heart heavy, she had wanted to go to her…just for a short while.

Heaven only knew what his stepbrother must think of her, having seen her thus. No, that wasn't true. *She* knew exactly what he must think of her. He had never liked her. Now, instead of classing her a shallow little flirt of nineteen, he would brand her a calculating spinster out to filch this noble bachelor's attention from worthier females. Jason Davenport and Mrs Pemberton probably had one solitary thing in common: they both imagined she was desperate to once more insinuate herself into Connor Flinte's good books, and any shameless method would do. And they were right…but not for the reason they thought. 'Thank you for bringing me safely home last night,' she blurted out. 'Also, I owe you an apology and an explanation for my…my bizarre behaviour.'

'I'm sorry you had such a long wait and received such poor hospitality in my absence. I've to speak further to Joseph about that.'

'Joseph? Your butler? No…you must not scold him,' she hastily interjected. 'Considering how…bold and presumptuous I was, it is a wonder he allowed me over the threshold at all. And he served me a little refreshment. I intended at first only tarrying a while in case you returned for your dinner. It is my own fault I stupidly lingered so long, then fell asleep. You weren't to know of my visit, so mustn't feel guilty that you did not appear sooner.'

'You're right. I won't,' he drawled with a silky softness. 'On reflection, it seems only fair that you should have wasted one evening hoping I might come home. I recall several times kicking my heels in this very room waiting for you, even though we'd a prior engagement.'

Rachel swallowed, tentatively rotated her wrist in his grip, hoping to free it. So, his sympathy was as transient as her sophistication this morning. But then she should have known his memory was not so short.

'Why did you do it so often, Rachel?'

'Why did you put up with it so often, Major Flinte?' she hissed back, goaded to ungovernable recklessness by his mild words. She threw back her golden head to clash an icy glare with eyes of cerulean blue. A glint of satisfaction made his eyelids heavy, and was endorsed by a slight tilt to his ruthless lips.

So he wanted her to acknowledge the reasons for his revenge. As if she ever would forget! Well, she had a long memory, too! She wasn't about to play this out on his terms. She was calling the tune. And he would dance to it…as he always had!

'I imagine your servants were suspicious of admitting me to your house because of my bedraggled appearance,' she remarked with admirable fairness as, with an abrupt manipulation, she forcibly liberated her wrist. She went to attend to the vase of full-blown yellow roses in the centre of the table, straightening the stems and collecting loose petals from the polished mahogany.

There was no response to her gracious blame-taking, but she was aware of the blue flame of his regard on her face as she roved the carpet, idly searching for somewhere to dispose of the perfumed debris cupped in her palm. 'I expect you noticed I had mud on my clothes…my hair was everywhere…' she added with a self-deprecating little moue, and a wave of her free hand illustrating how today's sleek coiffure had yesterday escaped its pins to drape her shoulders.

As silence reigned unabated, she realised he was deliberately withholding his participation from a tentative rapprochement, and that by doing so he was successfully eroding her confidence. She needed to quickly bring matters to a head, for she meant what she'd said about not giving any inquisitive individuals cause to tattle over spying the Earl of Devane's carriage outside her address. Once it was known she had been in residence alone, the town tabbies would soon put two and two together and make a salacious scandal. And no whiff of anything untoward must be allowed, by association, to spoil June's good name with her wedding imminent. She tried again. 'I'm sorry to disturb you this morning. I realise that, having kindly escorted me home, there was little of the night left for you to properly rest. I would not have roused you so early had it

not been pressing that I speak to you urgently. I know
you'd rather be abed…'

She got her response, and a hard laugh that chilled
her. 'I don't object to you rousing me, Rachel…but
you're right…I'd rather be in bed…'

Connor's smile was sardonic as he watched her
cease her perambulating. The fistful of bruised petals
were abruptly tossed on to the table. Their powdery
scent permeated the room as she clattered a spoon into
a saucer. Nervously she poured more tea, and immediately sipped at it.

He walked back to the hearth and propped an arm
against it, hoping to God the full extent of just how
well she roused him wasn't obvious. Hoping, too, the
full extent of his coarse vulgarity wasn't obvious either.
But he knew it was. He'd disgusted her and he wasn't
surprised. What did he think he was doing, talking to
her like that? As though she were some auditioning
courtesan? His fingers drummed in irritation against the
white-painted wood beneath them. He was talking to
her like that because a paramour was what he wanted
her to be, and God knew he could be forgiven for con-
fusing the issue. Gently born and still chaste maybe,
but she'd given him every reason to treat her with contempt. He wouldn't, of course; it was as far from his
mind to despise her now as it had been six years ago
when she'd jilted him. Yet she'd acted like the veriest
trollop yesterday. It was hardly surprising his manservant had imagined she might be a cast-off mistress bra-
zenly determined to air a grievance.

He knew exactly what she wanted with him and had
been expecting her. But he'd underestimated her urgency and her audacity, which made him ponder again
that her father must have played his cards close to his

chest on certain aspects of this ridiculous pantomime. She obviously wasn't aware of all that had passed between himself and Meredith. First he was handed a fine estate on a plate and now the same man served him up his daughter. It was all too obvious…too easy; but he was intrigued to find out just how far she would go to get back what she wanted. And how far he would let her go…before he let her go…

His jaw ground in self-loathing. He had a mistress who lavished on him a repertoire of patient, ingenious sensuality; to little proper appreciation, at times. He watched his knuckles rapping out a barely audible tattoo against the wall. In a way he felt sorry that Maria had to work so hard to earn her position in his life.

This icy blonde made his blood boil without even trying. Why was he surprised…annoyed? She'd had that effect on him before. Then she'd been confident of handling him like a pet dog, keeping him tame. And he'd let her have her way because he'd known it was a temporary imbalance of power.

At nineteen, Rachel Meredith had been flighty, petulant and infuriating. She'd also been beautiful, vivacious and steeped in nascent sexuality. And he'd recognised the signs…recognised the erotic prize he'd won. And at twenty-four he had had his masculine priorities: he could be dunned by every merchant in town, his household could disintegrate about his ears while she shopped for stockings, so long as he had Rachel, hot, permissive, in his bed. Then, in moments of lust-free rationality, he recognised that despite her failings, he actually loved her, too. And it wasn't all to do with her alluring body or her alluring dowry. It was just her. Rachel! God, he'd been some kind of besotted fool! But not now. Not ever again.

He could have had his pick of debutantes that year, but he'd chosen her on condition the engagement was short. He had his military commitments to back his stipulation that a wedding be soon arranged. He'd recently increased rank from a captain in the Life Guards to a major in the Hussars. And he was keen to promote his career because, as his wife, her social life, which had seemed so central to her existence, would be controlled by his status. So, in the few months of their betrothal, he'd decided to let her have her head. He'd had every expectation of her soon being his wife…and he could be tolerant of her capricious, childish ways; he'd enough experience with women to feel confident she'd grow up on their wedding night…

Obviously he'd never really known her at all. He'd certainly misjudged her housekeeping skill; by all accounts she ran the Meredith ménage very efficiently. And the sensual heat she'd been fired with at nineteen was nowhere in evidence. Now she stuttered a few awkward phrases because she was determined to be civil, shrank from his touch because she loathed him, and in response he frightened her by acting like a priapic adolescent six years too late. He should have taken her when he had more right and more chance…

Yesterday she'd let him comfort her, but then she'd not had her wits about her. Now she had and he could tell from her rigorous self-discipline that she'd vowed never again to be so defenceless in his presence. He'd witnessed her raw distress and he knew that had simply given her another reason to hate him. Grieving for her sister was private. He'd no business knowing of it. Yet he was glad he did. Not that he relished her pain, but oddly he'd liked being able to salve it. He'd brought her relief… Which brought him full circle, and to won-

dering, acidly, if she'd like to return the favour…especially as he knew she was hovering on the
brink of asking for something.

'I should tell you at once why I arrived at your house
and was discourteously persistent in my desire to speak
to you yesterday…' Rachel rattled off, clattering her
cup and saucer down on the polished mahogany.

'Why bother?' Connor bit over her words, frustration
making him sound boorish. 'Are we going to pretend
that I've no idea why you would come back to London
and urgently want me, less than two weeks after leaving and having been quite indifferent to my existence?
Something perhaps to do with the fact I took your inheritance from your father in a gambling hell?'

Rachel felt stone-cold beneath the toneless blast. But
there it was—the subject was out in the open, at his
instigation, and she must keep it there. 'I wasn't indifferent to your existence. And if I seemed so…well,
acquit me, sir, of blame. It was your idea we should
appear so…careless of the other's presence.' She gave
him a small smile. 'And you were right. It was a clever,
sensible idea; there was no malicious gossip. I thought
we dealt tolerably well together. Aren't you pleased?'

He smiled at his fingers drumming against wood.
'Aren't you pleased?' he mimicked in his soft Irish
accent. 'Now where do I remember that from? You
need to be a little closer when you say it, sweet, and
looking up at me as though you really cared what I
might answer.'

Rachel felt tears of anger burn her eyes. He was
determined to be as obnoxious as possible. 'Actually,
I am back in town, too, to be of service to my friend,
Lucinda Saunders, as she is increasing. Please don't
think my father's misfortunes are all that bring me here.

But now the matter is aired… Yes, I should like to speak about that. I should like to negotiate a short lease on my property so that June might still hold her wedding at Windrush.'

'It's mine.'

'Yes. I should like a short lease, please, to cover the period next month when my sister is to be married.'

He turned slowly, looking at her from beneath his long black lashes. She forced herself to calmly return his stare. She managed a wavering smile, too. 'Why would you need it then? You have your Mayfair townhouse. It is the height of the Season. Few of the aristocracy will be in the country. Your friends and associates will be in London, I'm sure…'

'How do you know who my friends and associates are?'

'I'm sorry…I didn't mean to be presumptuous. I was just pleading my cause.'

'That's right; you're pleading, and I told you, Rachel, you need to come closer to do so if you're hoping to be successful.' His voice sounded like sweetest honey, his eyes resembled a summer sky. His expression was one of callous amusement.

With an attempt at a careless shrug she paced towards him, hoping it wasn't noticeable that her molars were grinding or that her fingers, behind her back, looked gnarled. She halted just before him, cocked her head in a way that she prayed looked arch and knowing. 'There, sir. I am close. I had not realised that now you are older your eyesight and hearing might be failing. Please listen very carefully,' she enunciated crisply, biting off each word to prevent herself coarsely slandering him. 'I am willing to pay you for a short lease on my…your property. The financial inducement

will be worth your while. In fact, I'm willing to negotiate upwards to one hundred pounds—'

'I want a thousand.'

Rachel's powder-blue eyes shot fully open in consternation. 'A *thousand*?'

'Take it or leave it.'

'You know I have nothing like that to give you from
my allowance…'

'You're wasting my time then, this morning, Miss
Meredith, unless you can think of a better inducement
likely to tempt a man lacking morals and basic faculties.'

'I find nothing funny in this,' Rachel forced out
through her gritted white teeth. 'You are intending to
ruin my sister's wedding day. How dare you! The preparations have taken a full eight months! My father had
the grace, the good manners, to issue you with an invitation to the ceremony and yet you are at pains to
ruin everything through your vengeful greed. You do
not even need the rent money, do you? All you want
is revenge. It's me you hate—why make my sister suffer? And she, little fool, once thought herself stupidly
infatuated with you. You played cards with a man who
was drunk. Only the most loathsome individuals gamble for high stakes with either very young or very
drunk men. Yet you did! I don't care that my poor papa
says the rules were adhered to. You're a cheat! A…a
beastly miser… I hope you rot in hell, you detestable
brute…'

'You're still going to need a better inducement than
that, Rachel,' he taunted softly as the tears sparkled on
her lashes and her bosom heaved defiantly against its
flimsy restraint.

Furiously she threw herself at him, her arms raised

as though she would beat at him with her fists. Her hands snaked to his neck, coiled tight…then stilled, as though she was in the throes of a dilemma: whether to clash mouths and attack him with the kiss he seemed determined to torment from her, or grab his throat and choke the life out of him instead. She rested against him, trembling in rage and humiliation, yet oddly comforted as she had been yesterday by the feel of his warm strength against her cool, quaking body.

His hands covered hers, unclasped them from where her nails threatened to puncture his collar. With a sudden jerk, he shoved her back. Immediately she hung her head, hoping to shield the sight of her wet eyes and mutinously contorted features.

'So why did you do it so often, Rachel? Come, tell me…' he needled her, needing her provocation, her participation.

She flung up her head, to reveal her small, white teeth bared. Immediately they commenced savaging her soft lips, then she spat out, 'Because that's what you deserved…because I despised you…because I hated you touching me…kissing me… You disgusted me.'

She flicked her face away a second too late and his mouth caught hers, slick and punishing. She fought to twist her wrists in his grip, but he drew her relentlessly against him until he could fasten both of her hands in one of his behind her back. His free hand trailed her spine, barely touching, cupped her buttocks in a soothing circular stroke before ramming her against his rigid arousal and holding her there. She gasped outrage into his mouth, yet pressed her hips forward. When his fingers tucked inside her bodice and softly brushed at her satiny skin, she held her breath. When a breast was teased free of its demure confinement and his thumb leisurely found a turgid nipple to play with, she moaned her disgust and arched her back, forcing more of her sensitive, throbbing flesh to fill his hand. He obliged her by kneading it with slow artful pressure, and even the hard male laugh that filled her mouth moments before his rapacious tongue couldn't make her stop wanting more.

His mouth suddenly released her bruised aching lips and moved to her ear. 'You despise my touch...I disgust you. Say it now. Then ask me again for that damned house.'

Rachel felt the ice shiver her lower lip, the heat drench her eyes and her head fell forward so that her forehead was resting against his shoulder. 'You're an evil man.'

'I'm a vindictive man.' Gently, with one dark finger, he tilted her face up to his, looked deep into her water-blue eyes before deliberately letting his gaze drop to where her exposed breast still pouted at him. 'And you're the hot wanton I always thought you. If it wasn't for the fact that now I'm older I'm a little bored with fornicating against walls and chairs, I might take the trouble to discover whether Moncur's taught you any worthwhile tricks—'

He easily dodged the small fist that she swung at him, although he guessed that the force with which the mantel clock was swept to the floor meant it was unlikely to resume ticking. Connor stepped over smatterings of glass and internal springs on his way to the door, a choke of laughter breezing back over his shoulder. 'If you're about to need a dustpan and brush, rearrange your clothes before the maid arrives. Heaven forfend that the servants discover too that their mistress is a little trollop.'

'I loathe you,' Rachel whispered while, mortified, she blindly acted on his hateful advice.

'Good,' he said carelessly as he put a hand on the doorknob. 'At least now I feel as though I've gone part way towards deserving it. By the time I've finished with you perhaps we'll be even. Oh…I take it you're soon to journey home?'

Rachel merely jerked her head as a sign of assent.

'When you go, you can do this dastardly miser a favour by saving him the cost of posting a document to your father. Before that gentleman left earlier in the week, from the kindness of my heart and because I have no quarrel with your sister or Pemberton, I granted a dispensation allowing him to retain the property until the first of July. The document's signed and sealed now. You can carry his copy safe home with you.'

Rachel raised her golden head, looking through a mist at his dark saturnine features; her eyes blinked, trying to plumb his for signs of deceit.

He gave her a ruthless smile. 'Don't get to thinking I'm about to be any more sentimental than that, my dear. On the second of July your inheritance goes to auction…to be sold to the highest bidder.'

The door had been closed barely a second before his untasted tea was dripping down the white-painted panels and delicate floral china shards littered the carpet close by.

Maria Laviola lay on her stomach in bed, looking listlessly at Paris fashion plates. Her head twisted to peer over a shoulder as she heard the door slam. An incipient smile curved her lips and her inertia was already dispersing. The journal, which she had idly been flicking through whilst sipping her morning chocolate and nibbling at a little toast, was sent in a flutter of pages on to the floor. She swivelled on to her back. Instinctively her knees bent and her thighs parted. She elevated herself on her elbows, shaking her head to clear her loose black hair from her eyes. She waited, her stomach clenched in an agony of excitement. The familiar sound of masculine boots hitting the stairs two at a time made her drop her head back and smile at the ruched-red bed canopy in pleasure and triumph. She hadn't seen him for two days and two nights and had begun to think…because of what she'd heard about that little hussy…that perhaps there was some truth in such stupid gossip. He was jaded, she knew; but then that was to be expected in men of his exceptional attractiveness and station in life who had been pleasured by women so often. And she knew that such men often tried to whet a sated palate with youth and innocence. But youth and innocence couldn't compete for long with expertise…and over the years she had gained plenty of sensual skill.

She had begun to think that perhaps her days as the Earl of Devane's mistress were already numbered. And she didn't want that…not yet. Not only was he beautifully built, generous and at times an attentive, lusty lover, but he was the most fêted man in the *ton*. Everybody wanted to be with him: quiz him over his army exploits, over the decorations and medals he'd won at Waterloo. They wanted to find out why it was Wellington favoured him over so many others and had made him a senior member of his staff. What did he have to tell about the Iron Duke and his odd, eccentric ways?

Maria knew she was envied because she had him,

by ladies and demi-reps alike. She knew there were plenty angling to oust her and take her place warming his bed in the hope that they might do what she couldn't: warm his heart. Yet he too was envied, because he had her. Doe-eyed young bucks and their sires lusted after her and she was shrewd enough to keep them looking.

She and Connor made a most charismatic couple, she thought. Now, if their relationship was formalised, it wouldn't then matter to her quite so much if he played with any mercenary little *demi-vièrge* to whom he took a fancy.

He plunged into the bedchamber with a cursory word for her young French maid. Immediately Francine was quitting the room with a blush and a whispered, *'Bon matin, milor.'*

It was hardly surprising the girl looked so awkward, Maria thought with a sultry peek at him through her dark lashes. His neckcloth was off and scrunched in a hand and the corded strength of his brown throat was naked to the eye due to the fact that his shirt buttons to mid-chest were already undone.

Maria fell back on to the bed, chuckling delightedly. 'Sometimes, Connor, I wish you could just keep in your clothes long enough for me to appreciate the so-dashing figure you cut. How handsome you look this morning…and so early…' Her dark almond eyes lowered to where his fingers now worked at the buttons on his skintight breeches. And how delectably tight they were, she noted, as the fly gaped. She felt her breath tighten in her throat and she squirmed a little against the bed in anticipation. 'You're up so very nice and early this morning, my lord,' she purred, her eyes still on the magnificent bulge at his groin. Her lips moistened, her bones melted as she realised she had a morning of very little work ahead of her. It wasn't until he stood naked, and his immaculate clothes were balled into one fist in a way that was likely to have given his tailor a fit, prior to them being sent with careless savagery into a corner, that she actually looked properly at his face. There was no time to ask what ailed him...

He came down on her fast, spreading her knees with his and giving her little foreplay before thrusting into her hot, wet welcome. But then she didn't need or want preliminaries. By the time he impaled her she was practically climbing his torso with her vine-like legs, and the growl of triumph and satisfaction that tore from her as he hurtled towards release was feral-like in its huskiness.

She watched him obliquely as he stared up at the ceiling. The ache between her thighs was a delicious, throbbing reminder of what undivided attention he had shown her moments before, of what tender torture might yet be repeated, if she could but make him stay.

Maria trailed a light finger over the hand he had thrown across his eyes. 'You are a tiger this morning, my lord. Where have you been these past two days? Not that I object, since it brings you here so eager to see me.' And that was true, she thought. Let him get his appetite elsewhere if he must; he chose to dine right here, that was gratifyingly obvious.

Connor removed the irritating, tickling finger from his skin and wondered whether he had the energy to get up and go home; he needed to see Jason about keep putting his damned horse and carts in his stable. His stepbrother had now pawned him over two thousand pounds' worth of cattle and carriages to ease his debts.

Not that his rough and prolonged session with Maria

had exhausted him and rendered him lethargic. He'd felt drained the moment he shut the door on Rachel at Beaulieu Gardens. Drat the bitch. Even now, with the thorn in his flesh drawn, he couldn't stop thinking of her.

As though aware that his quiet concentration, his contained irritation, was due to another woman, Maria shaped her mouth in sly determination. Gently, softly, as though not to distract him from his introspection, she straddled him, rocking her hips against his. She lowered herself, tantalising him by keeping her full, honey-tipped breasts swaying close to his face as her mouth descended to lightly touch his. It dotted kisses from his chin to his throat, then her tongue darted to a nub of nipple as she slithered her body lower against his satin-sheathed chest muscles.

He should go back and apologise for being all those things she'd called him, he supposed. He should go back and tell the infuriating ice maiden that, but for a proper kiss, a kind word, he'd sell his own estate before he'd sell hers. And she wasn't as frigid around him as she'd like him to think. God, he wanted her! He knew that now…he knew that too damned well. His breath hissed in through his teeth as Maria's mouth started to work its sly sorcery. His jaw tensed, his torso parted company with the mattress, and so did the fingers of one hand. Automatically they curled against her scalp while the others spread against his eyes. But it wasn't that hard to imagine that the silken crown beneath his palm was golden…

Chapter Nine

Sam Smith loped coltishly along, a tuneless noise whistling out through his touching front teeth. He flicked idle glances at numbers on gateposts, checking them against the bold black scripted direction on the letter he was bearing. The house he was passing had a fancy iron gate with the number sixty-two scrolled on to it in gilt. Number thirty-four was some way yet along this terrace of fine double-fronted villas that comprised Beaulieu Gardens.

His attention was suddenly caught by a familiar face beneath a peaked cap, and he raised a hand to one of his acquaintances who ran errands for one of his master's acquaintances. The page, dressed in maroon uniform, was just entering a grassy oasis enclosed within railings in the middle of the road, to walk his mistress's little Pomeranian dog. Sam eyed the dainty canine on the end of the lead with contemptuous distaste as it skittered over the cobbles. In Sam's opinion, if someone wanted a pet dog, they should have a dog, not a rat. That magnificent Irish wolfhound he'd seen in a picture, hanging in the master's study, now that was a dog. He just wished he could see the beast in the flesh, but it was kept at the master's Irish estate. He'd like more than anything to go there. But he must bide his time, show willing and God willing, the Earl might keep him and Annie on. Then they might soon get to travel with him to Wolverton Manor across the sea. That would keep Annie good and safe from that trading justice and they could start afresh. A new life for them both, that's what Sam wanted. What would they miss? No ma and pa to care for. Both were dead. No sweethearts to hanker after that bound them with invisible cord to their past. All they had was each other…and the Earl of Devane.

When he thought to again check house numbers, he was stopped in his tracks. A rounded female derrière was rocking provocatively in front of him, physically preventing him from carrying out his duty. He leaned a hand against the spear-tipped green railings, a low-lidded look maturing his boyish features as he watched the woman undulate while scrubbing methodical circles on the top step of number thirty-four.

A few more seconds' furious elbow grease to a particularly stubborn spot, and Noreen Shaughnessy sat back on her heels and cuffed her wiry red hair from her eyes. With a puff of exertion, she rested back down on all fours, brush in hand, ready to finish the chore. She hesitated, leaning on the bristles, with her hackles rising. Her humming tailed off and her perspiring face whipped around to peer over her shoulder.

The sight that greeted her made her skin as rubicund as her hair. Despite her embarrassment, oddly what registered immediately in her mind was that blushing hid her freckles.

'Don't yer go rushin' on my account, now,' Sam told her with a certain male insinuation softening his eastend vowels. 'You get it right nice 'n' clean now. I don't mind standing here a while longer and just watching you…'

Noreen scrambled to her feet in a flurry of cap streamers and starched pinafore. The scrubbing brush was pitched with some force back into the pail, splashing the smooth slab. 'Now what might you be meaning by that, you cheeky beggar?' she stormed. 'And look what you've gone and made me do.' With her elbows akimbo, a pugnacious glare was levelled at him, then at her spruce step, awash with dirty water. It was a long time since Noreen had been subjected to this sort of masculine raillery. Her no-nonsense attitude and tendency to lash out with tongue and fists at those as wouldn't take no for an answer, had long since beaten off any amatory interest from the available men at Windrush. She had Mary to consider and none of the coves as tried to insinuate themselves into her affections cared two hoots for her ungainly sister's welfare. And she came with Mary…or she didn't come at all. Now she was annoyed at herself for letting this brash whippersnapper creep up on her and unexpectedly tip her off balance.

She descended a step, sent him a menacing look; undaunted, he grinned wolfishly back. Flustered by his confidence, Noreen considered bounding down the remaining steps to teach his cocky self some respect for his elders. For she was sure she was some years his senior, despite that she was feeling, oddly, like a green girl. She retreated to stand her ground and snapped out, 'Faith, is it a fool you are?' She whipped off her cap and smacked it into shape, then agitatedly shook out her rumpled skirts.

Noreen slid the stripling a sideways look and

guessed he was a servant from a grand house: his smart blue and black livery was of fine cut and cloth. 'Will you be after telling me what you want, then? Apart from your ears boxed, that is…'

'Well, I don't know as I should say…bein' as it's this early in the day, like. You might reckon as I was uncouth.'

Noreen choked and burned; he *was* trying to get up her petticoats.

Sam smiled at her confusion. 'Sorry about the step. Looks like you'll be down there again. Now, if I weren't so busy, I'd give you a hand…perhaps more 'n that…'

'Get away with you! It's none of your sympathy I'm needing—'

'Who is it, Noreen?'

Sam glanced past the plump maid—who seemed on the point of forcing her hot head through her cap, so brutally was she ramming it on to her wiry hair—to see a slender woman framed in the doorway.

Sam recognised her at once. When Joseph Walsh had given him the letter with instructions for immediate delivery, he'd imagined it might be her it was intended for. She was paler, looking a little care-worn since last he'd seen her, but no less beautiful for that. In fact, she looked a fragile goddess, with her proud, solemn features and her golden hair loose on her shoulders, and those enormous eyes the colour of tiny bird eggs. Sam thought she looked the sort of woman you'd need to handle with kid gloves, lest she broke. Or you did. With sudden perceptiveness Sam mused on his master's recent odd moods. That made a subtle smile touch his mouth. Whatever was wrong between them would come right, for never was there a better gentleman in all the world. Path of true love and so on, meandered through Sam's fertile mind as he glanced obliquely at the servant. He climbed two steps and handed her the note to give to her mistress.

He registered that the name of the lady who was plucking at the master's heartstrings was Miss Rachel Meredith. After making her a grave and respectful bow, he was within a trice bowling back along the street. He started to cross the road, hoping to catch up with his friend for a chat as he emerged from the park with the runt of a mutt. Idly he slanted a look back over his shoulder at Miss Rachel Meredith's house and saw the Irish woman staring after him. Cheekily he spun about and nimbly genuflected, before walking on, chuckling.

Noreen, horrified that she'd let him catch her watching him, dropped quickly to her knees, snatched up the scrubbing brush and put it to frantic use.

Rachel frowned at Noreen's florid countenance and then looked at the errand boy idling with a differently liveried page on the opposite side of the street. 'I don't know why, but I thought he seemed familiar,' she remarked, almost to herself.

'He were familiar…too familiar…' Noreen muttered darkly and kept on scouring.

Rachel turned about in the hallway, wondering where she might before have seen the lad. Idly she looked at the letter, wondering if it might be a social invitation. She'd been in town now several days and people were becoming aware of her presence. She and Lucinda had already shared a carriage ride to Hyde Park with little Alan and a trip to the animal menagerie to show him the beasts. This afternoon they were hoping to go to Madame Tussaud's, then, when Alan went home for his tea, on to the fabric warehouses in Pall

Mall, for Lucinda, moaning she was fat, was keen to cheer herself by buying a pretty enveloping shawl.

The seal on the parchment caught her attention. Her heartbeat tripped as she moved the letter closer to confirm it was that of the Earl of Devane. Quickly she turned the note over and recognised the firm sloping script on the other side. She repressed the spontaneous urge to spin about and hurl it viciously into Noreen's bucket of slops by reminding herself that this might at last be the dispensation he had promised she might carry home to Hertfordshire. Immediately she repaired to the morning room to find out if it was.

It wasn't. But it was a social invitation; albeit one that seemed extended with a careless hand. Rachel let the paper drop from her fingers. After taking an agitated turn about the room she picked it up and reread the concise sentences whilst her small white teeth sank grooves into her lower lip.

—I know you want to leave London as soon as possible. So do I. I intend to remove to Ireland at the earliest opportunity. I have preparations underway for a social evening at Berkeley Square this weekend, by way of farewell to my acquaintances, friends and family. If you are still desirous of negotiating a certain business matter before I go, it is convenient for me that I give you an audience then. I have no other free time. I have sent an invitation to your friends, the Saunders. If you decide to attend, I realise it would be best you come suitably accompanied.

Yours, Devane

Rachel chewed faster at her lip. There was no dispensation. He'd been lying all along. But then she'd already guessed as much when the days passed and no document arrived for her to take home. Devane had not made a prior arrangement with her father forfeiting his right to the estate until after the wedding. Had there been such an agreement, her papa would not have kept such monumental news to himself. He would have shared it with them all to soften the blow and ease their shock and distress.

Was her hundred pounds suddenly tempting him? She doubted it. This cavalier invitation—as offhand and take it or leave it as had been his demand for one thousand pounds rent—was simply to impress on her that he now held the upper hand. He could not spare her a moment of his precious time before the event, but he might find a few minutes to bestow on her at his soirée. He was manipulating her, making her dance to his tune, because once she had led him by the nose, dangled him on a string. He'd said, had he not, that by the time he'd finished with her they'd be even…

She crumpled the letter in a hand and let it drop to the table. A surge of aching anger quivered through her, making her feel light-headed. She couldn't again pester him at home over this matter, he knew that. Tempting fate twice and risking a scandal was out of the question with June's wedding imminent. She would comply with his wishes, of course, just as he knew she would. She was already grateful that he might still negotiate a price for a short lease on Windrush. She felt herself lucky that she might yet persuade him not to immediately sell her inheritance. A reprieve was what she needed; just a chance to put into action a scheme to get it back. If that was achieved by appearing humble and pandering to his despotic ego, so be it.

Before such calm philosophy was lost to pride, she went to the small bureau in the corner and found a pen and paper. With a deep breath she sat down, dashed off a polite sentence of thanks and acceptance, sanded and sealed it, all within a few minutes. Of course she would go, echoed in her mind as she went to find Ralph to deliver it. She'd ignore the humiliation she'd already endured at his hands and perhaps even apologise for the abuse she'd heaped on his head. For there was still a possibility that June could be married at Windrush and until that was gone, she would bend to his will…as he intended she should.

Rachel settled the small boy on her lap and helped him line up his tin soldiers on the table. When they were in passable formation, and before the prancing-horsed cavalry could be assembled, too, Alan knocked the redcoats down with a fat fist. He chuckled and turned a mischievous look on her.

'Oh, dear! How unfortunate! An entire infantry regiment has been wiped out,' Rachel said sorrowfully. 'And not a bullet fired or a battle fought! What *will* the Iron Duke say to that calamity? No medals for you, my young man!'

The boy cackled and clambered from her lap. On sturdy three-year-old legs he scampered away to find something else in his toy box with which to beset her armchair.

'I'm sure Paul and I have only been invited as we're your friends. Paul thinks it's because of this new business arrangement he has with the Earl.'

'I'm sure it's Paul who is right,' Rachel lied kindly, not wanting Lucinda to know her own thoughts on the subject: that Devane had simply invited them to act as her chaperons.

'As soon as I got the card this morning I was dying to know whether you had an invitation, and whether you would accept.'

Rachel quickly sipped from her teacup before little Alan returned and knocked it flying from her fingers. She hoped no hint of irony was discernible in her voice as she added, 'Of course I shall attend. Despite what's gone on in the past between the Merediths and Devane, there's no hardship in being civil.'

No hardship! reverberated like the beat of a drum in her brain. Sometimes she felt as though the effort of pretending she had no quarrel with the blackguard would be the finish of her sanity. Not least because she felt so alone now. She needed someone to confide in. She wanted to openly tell her friend that she hated the damnable man; not only because he had pilfered her estate, her inheritance, but because he was determined to shame and humiliate her, too. If not in public, then most definitely in private. She still burned with mortification from the hateful way he had treated her. Yet when she thought of it, the ache that assailed her sometimes crept from her throbbing head to make tender her breasts or stir her insides to a feverish heat…and then she loathed him even more.

But it was another reason entirely that kept her lips sealed. By slandering the Earl she would put Lucinda in an awkward position, perhaps even divide her loyalties. Her husband was chief partner of Saunders and Scott, attorneys at law and marine insurance specialists. And that firm had successfully secured a contract to administer an amount of the Earl of Devane's shipping affairs. Lucinda had discovered from her husband just

last night that the contract had been won and this morning had recounted to Rachel some of the background
to the work.

The late Earl of Devane had left his grandson not
only his Irish estates and his noble title, but a brace of
rotting merchantmen in dry dock that needed extensive
refitting. Paul had doubted a firm as young as his would
be chosen. But Saunders and Scott had received a di-
rective to estimate whether repairing the creaky hulks
was a commercially viable undertaking. As Rachel had
listened, dismayed, to Lucinda recounting how valuable a client Connor Flinte was, and how his patronage
should bring prestige and other rich noblemen to her
husband's partnership, she had brooded that Devane
was intentionally stealing away every ally she had. And
already they were scarce…

'I must say, Rachel,' Lucinda said softly, 'you seem
to be taking the loss of Windrush very calmly. Perhaps
losing the safety net of that estate is the little push you
need to keep you from embracing the life of an old
maid. Or a kept woman! How could you say that that
day?' she scolded. 'I told Paul and he thought it funny.
He says you have a wicked sense of humour.'

Rachel dragged her thoughts to her friend and
frowned her confusion.

'You must remember the occasion. We were in your
father's new landau on that terribly hot afternoon. You
said you'd as soon Moncur sent over his proposition
as his proposal. We saw Connor,' she reminded. 'It was
that day when the apple cart turned over and the carriages got in a crush. Then that beast of a magistrate
told Ralph off, and the young lad driving the brewer's
dray…'

Rachel, who had been helping Alan pull his train

across the carpet, suddenly looked up. The brewer. That young man who had delivered Devane's letter had been the man driving the damaged dray. She had thought she'd probably spied the liveried page somewhere about his house in Berkeley Square. In fact, she recalled him now, dressed anything but smartly, preparing to hit her driver Ralph! And now Devane had him in his employ!

'Your papa is still hale and hearty, is he not? You might never want Windrush at all. If married, you would live with your husband at his home. Paul says perhaps Windrush might have become a burden on you at some time—because of the cost of its upkeep and so on. He says perhaps the Earl has, oddly, done you a favour in taking it off your hands...'

'I hope he never says as much to me,' Rachel remarked sweetly. She gave her friend a smile. 'I've no intention of marrying, no doubt if I'd been a boy my inheritance might have been taken far more seriously...by everyone.'

Lucinda looked apologetic. 'I didn't mean to trivialise it, Rachel. And Paul would be horrified if he thought you deemed we were doing so. I just thought, as you seem, so...so resigned to things...'

'I'm doing my best to be philosophical about it all,' Rachel said tightly. 'There's little else at the moment to be had but wretched wisdom in Windrush's stead.'

Lucinda gave her friend a penetrating look, searching for the sarcasm she knew would be lurking in her lucid blue eyes. Intending to mollify her, she added, 'Paul said that it was clear your father held no grudge against the Earl for winning that game. They were seen in White's together the following day, even though your papa had a dreadful hangover. Paul thinks Mr

Meredith was relieved Connor won Windrush and not that weasel Lord Harley. He was in the game too. He came close to taking the pot instead, you know.'

'No. I didn't know,' Rachel admitted on a sigh.

'Your father has taken it philosophically, too…'

'Obviously a family boon, then.' Rachel regimented the infantry on the table. The smart black-coated Hussars she swept to the floor, making the little boy laugh.

So it was to be a glittering affair, then, Rachel noted sourly as she allowed Paul Saunders to help her from the carriage and they joined the queue of fashionable ladies and gentlemen sedately ascending the stone steps to gain entrance to the Earl of Devane's mansion.

Paul offered both Rachel and his wife an elegant arm each as their turn arrived to step over the threshold. Immediately, Rachel spied the salt-and-pepper hued head of Joseph, the butler, overseeing the lordly proceedings. A warmth needled her cheeks. It was impossible not to recall the spectacle she had made of herself the last time she was here. She smoothed her silk skirt and fiddled with a sinuous coil of sleek golden hair, whilst she repressed her annoyance at feeling intimidated by a servant. Had she imagined she might sneak in without the butler seeing her? How ridiculous! Still, a niggling hope lingered that the man might not recognise her.

Her other persona, that shabby spinster with a fit of the sullens, was nowhere in evidence this evening. She had paid particular attention to her choice of gown tonight; the cut was elegant and ladylike, something perhaps her mother might have worn. But for all its sedate style, the steel-blue colour was a perfect foil for her golden-blonde looks and accentuated her eyes. She had used a little carmine to define her full lips and warm her cheeks and a little soot to darken her lashes. When Noreen stepped back to regard the full effect of her handiwork, having just twined a rope of lustrous pearls into her hair, the frank admiration in the maid's face had made Rachel flash her a warm smile.

'Sure, an' you look good enough to eat, m'm,' the maid had boldly opined as she put away the accoutrements that had brought about Rachel's transformation into that delectable lady.

A faint smile tipped Rachel's lips at the memory, and at the realisation that she and Noreen were settling into quite a comfortable relationship whilst here, alone, in London. Her smile faded as she noticed that Joseph Walsh had not only spotted her, but recognised her. Their eyes held for a moment, then, to her surprise, the butler accorded her an especially deep and respectful bow. He approached them and, waving away a footman who had sprung to attention as his superior approached, Joseph personally ushered her party the length of the colonnaded hallway. At the foot of the stairs he instructed them to proceed to the function rooms above.

When they were about halfway up the magnificent staircase, Lucinda had conquered her awe enough to engage Rachel in conversation, across her husband's immaculate waistcoat. 'This is the most splendid house I believe I have ever set foot in.' Her shining dark eyes skipped over the blue velvet draperies, the profusion of gilt and marble, the blaze of glittering crystal. Ornate wall sconces and the stupendous central chandelier sparked a diamond fire that competed, gallantly, with a fabulous collection of precious jewels shimmering on pearly female skin. 'Isn't it exciting. I hope I don't look too plain and fat, Rachel,' Lucinda mouthed to her friend so as not to disclose her insecurities to her *soigné* husband. Her new lace stole was draped carefully about her rounded abdomen.

'You look absolutely fine,' Rachel softly encouraged. At the top of the stairs, she added more audibly, 'And, indeed, it is exciting.'

Oh, God, it's far too exciting! raced through her mind as she felt her insides squirm and panic pricked her mind. For the first time, she felt the craven urge to let go of Paul's arm and creep away, unseen, into a corner. Her darting gaze had just alighted on their host and hostess greeting people, and she didn't know why she was so shocked and dismayed to be brought face to face with this particular couple. Perhaps it was because they had always treated her with kindness and respect. Perhaps because acknowledging it, even six years later, made her feel guilty.

Connor Flinte was nowhere in sight; it was his mother and stepfather welcoming guests to this refined soirée. Well, what had she expected? That the Earl of Devane might install his mistress in his drawing room to take on the office of hostess? Much as she despised him, she didn't think even *he* would stoop so low as to stand that baggage by his side with her light skirt blowing about her ears while he greeted the Duke of Wellington. And she had heard that that worthy was due to attend at some point during the evening. But then, if gossip were to be believed of the Duke's lusty appetite for a certain sort of female, it was probably precisely the sort of titillating sight that the old goat would relish.

They were barely a yard or two away now, and Rachel's eyes focused again on the tall brunette. Her

complexion and shoulders were milk-pale, and perfectly complemented by a daringly low-cut gown of
crimson satin. Lady Davenport looked absolutely strik-
ing, and, like her son, seemed little older than she had
six years ago. A casual glance from the woman's tawny
eyes flicked along the snaking file of guests.
Immediately they pulled back to Rachel and registered
surprise. Then she was again graciously attending to
the stout lady and gentlemen in conversation with her
spouse.

Rachel tilted her chin. Why be humble or timid? She
might *feel* as though she was here on sufferance; actually she was here by their son's request.

No doubt, when they discovered just why he had
invited her, they would think how very decent and
obliging he was being: sparing the woman who had
once publicly humiliated him a moment or two of his
time before he quit the country. And if they, like everyone else present, privately relished her ultimate humbling…her family's ultimate humbling, she supposed
they of all people had a legitimate entitlement to it.

She clenched her fists, then wiped moist palms on
to her skirts. If she could be a million miles away, she
would be. He knew that. He knew how hard it was for
her to continue with this pantomime of good manners
between them. He must have known how excruciating
it would be for her to face his parents. He obviously
couldn't care less how it affected her, but he ought to
have spared them this very public ordeal. Lady
Davenport had looked surprised to see her, but probably would feign ignorance of her identity. It would be
appropriate after such a long time…

'Miss Meredith, isn't it?'

The lilting accent was wrenchingly familiar. With a

deep, steadying breath Rachel dipped her head in assent and curtsied politely.

Rosemary Davenport took one of Rachel's trembling hands in hers, then turned to her husband, who was greeting Paul and Lucinda Saunders. 'You remember Miss Meredith, don't you, my dear?'

It seemed to Rachel that Sir Joshua frowned down his patrician nose at her in a frighteningly haughty manner. His son grows ever more like him, she thought, recoiling from the memory of Jason Davenport peering at her, from his lofty height, with cold calculation.

'Demme! I don't think I do, m'dear,' Sir Joshua eventually said, dragging his eyes from the beautiful woman flushing beneath his emotionless appraisal. 'Who is she, then?' His features took on an engaging animation as he turned a bright, enquiring look on his *soigné* wife.

Rosemary Davenport gave her husband's arm a punitive little tap. To Rachel she gave an apologetic little smile. 'I think he's funning…but then his memory isn't what it was,' she gently explained. Her tone of voice, and the pain shadowing her deep hazel eyes, let Rachel know that it was no total jest. Lady Davenport placed an indulgent hand on her absent-minded consort's thin arm, giving it a reassuring squeeze.

Obediently, Sir Joshua raised his quizzing glass and peered again at Rachel.

The grave struggle to place her was clear in his face and was sweetly flattering in its intensity. Rachel felt her defensiveness, her discomfort, melt away. He really had forgotten her. But then, without his wife at his side, she might never have recognised him. Whereas Rosemary looked as attractive and vital as she had six years ago, Sir Joshua was much changed. His hair was now thinning and silver, not fair, and his tall regal frame had lost its musculature and looked to be gaunt beneath his fine clothes. As the wordless scrutiny continued, she realised that quite a few people close by were avid spectators to this little exchange between herself and the couple who had narrowly escaped being her in-laws.

Sir Joshua suddenly patted contentedly at his hip. 'Ah, I know. I have it now. This gel's a friend of Jason's from his old Surrey days…'

'Miss Meredith is a friend of Connor's from his old army days,' his wife corrected in her musical tone. She squeezed at Rachel's hand in a way that was oddly affectionate before she let it go. 'Miss Meredith and Connor were once engaged…oh, a good few years ago now.'

The quizzing glass was swiftly levelled at Rachel. 'Demme! So sorry, my dear. Have you found yourself a husband since, Miss Meredith?'

Rachel found her voice at last, aware that people around were smiling, taking their lead from the good humour of this kind couple. 'No, sir. I am still Miss Meredith…' Rachel tailed off, hoping that no one deemed she was being sarcastic, for unpleasantness was the last thing on her mind.

Rosemary Davenport smiled at her, as though she understood and wanted to reassure her no offence was taken. Paul and Lucinda were then included in the radiance. 'I hope we get a chance to chat later,' she told Rachel in her soft accent. 'It would be nice to know how your family do…your parents and your sisters and so on…'

'Thank you, yes, I should like that,' Rachel said,

hoping no mention would be made of Isabel. But something in Lady Davenport's eyes allayed that fear, too.

After another polite bob Rachel slipped quickly forward to take hold of Paul's arm. As the trio proceeded into the vast reception room she heard Sir Joshua demand of his wife, 'Has she always been that pretty?'

A nod must have answered him, for what she next heard was, 'Why the deuce wouldn't the boy marry her, then?'

Chapter Ten

'Well, I can't say I was at all pleased when I heard of the business with Windrush.'

'Indeed, neither was I, Mrs Pemberton,' Rachel said quietly, congratulating herself on managing such monumental understatement. 'Is William here with you?' Wistfully she peered over a shoulder into the crowd of people in the room, hoping to locate her sister's fiancé. Just a promise of his mild, affable person would have cheered her enormously for she was feeling quite bereft.

There was a sultry atmosphere indoors and her friend Lucinda was already flagging from the unremitting heat. Thus her husband had taken her to the terrace for a little reviving evening air. Rachel had declined to go too, for she felt quite a gooseberry and refused to sheepishly follow them about. In order that they would not fret over abandoning her, Rachel had voluntarily transferred herself to the company of June's prospective father-in-law.

Alexander Pemberton was welcoming and entertaining and had regaled her with anecdotes about William as a young and mischievous schoolboy. It was hard to believe the sensible young man she knew, who was soon to be her brother-in-law, was the same character as the cheeky scapegrace being described by his father. Then William's other parent had swept up, dampening the humour and very soon despatching Alexander on an errand. Having won seclusion with her quarry, the woman's calculating regard was making Rachel glumly sure an interrogation was soon to commence.

'William? Here?' Mrs Pemberton imperceptibly opened proceedings. 'No. He has gone off into the country for a day or two. Possibly in the direction of Hertfordshire,' she sniffed with palpable disgust that her son should seek the air close to his fiancée. 'I imagine he will be sorry he missed this evening. Since *the bad business* he and the Earl are quite firm chums, you know.'

Mrs Pemberton's awed gaze was lingering on a spot to their left, forcing Rachel to acknowledge that their host was, indeed, gaining ground all the time. She slanted an oblique look from beneath her thick lashes at a party of gregarious gentlemen just a few yards away. All looked debonair and distinguished; yet it was the shorter gentleman with the unfortunate profile who was holding court. The Duke of Wellington, Rachel had to admit, was rather a disappointment in the flesh, with his lack of stature, hooked nose and that abrupt barking laugh that cut a wide swathe through all conversation at close quarters.

Yet he certainly had a powerful, charismatic aura. The younger men being diverted by his guffaw-punctuated yarns deferred to him quite naturally, if not by dint of rank, from respect or affection, she imagined.

Gentlemen were milling about on the periphery of the elite, awaiting an opportunity to wedge a word or their person into that fêted male circle. Ladies, too, were loitering in the vicinity, their fans snapping open and closed, their figures first posing this way, then that. In their summer-weight gauzes they fluttered hither and thither, like a mist of pastel moths, yet never far from the light as they sought a way to settle without a scald. They trilled laughter at one another, gaily chatted, but kept their eyes fixed firmly on the prize.

Powerful broad shoulders clad in slate grey were again drawing Rachel's eyes. Far from having a physiognomy that was hard to behold, their host looked wonderfully handsome. Reluctant admiration registered in her mind as she discreetly regarded his high cheekboned countenance and ribbons of blue-black hair straying on to his lean jaw and snowy collar. An engaging smile tilted his mouth as he listened to his erstwhile general gesticulating in a way that made his stepbrother, Jason, roar with laughter.

With something akin to resentment she realised that Connor looked undeniably attractive and the females hovering were aware of it too; the majority were directing their best flirtatious efforts at him.

'No, I can tell you I was not happy about the outcome of *the business* at all.'

Rachel's thoughts were jarred back to Mrs Pemberton. Gratefully she gave up on wretchedly reminding herself that she didn't give a fig which women contrived to bump against him or daintily drop down to retrieve a lost fan from close by his foot. Just a moment previously she had watched Barbara West, the Winthrops' niece, pluck from the polished wood floor a scrap of ivory and lace in peril from one of his elegant shoes. She was surely old enough to know better strategies than that! In fact, Rachel thought sourly, she must be about her own age.

'I had every hope that your father's unhappy situation with his estate would at least turn up some benefit for us all,' Pamela continued. 'I was quite sure it would result in the wedding being reconvened at St Thomas's and the reception at your father's townhouse. I know it's small, its appointments rather…rudimentary, but at least it's in London, which is, after all, what most people wanted originally. At the outset I stated that a wedding that takes place in the Season must take place in the metropolis or everyone is horribly inconvenienced. But of course no heed was taken of my views. Now, had I been allowed more of a hand in the preparations…as indeed I offered more than once…'

'You seem very certain it will *not* be in London, Mrs Pemberton. Why is that?' Rachel breathed over the woman's rambling when she had sufficiently conquered her astonishment to do so. Her eyes darted to Lord Devane again.

'Perhaps your papa has not disclosed all to you, so I ought be discreet. It wouldn't do to be deemed interfering. It is, after all, gentlemen's business.' When that dangled carrot elicited no hungry snaps, Pamela speculatively eyed the lovely young woman who was training a look of frowning intensity on their host. She interestedly noted that a casual look from Lord Devane had strayed their way and prompted Miss Meredith's large blue eyes to dart back to her own. 'Have you seen much of Lord Devane since you arrived back in town, Miss Meredith? And I have to say—although I know how some…older ladies foster an arrogant independence—should you not be here with your mother? Or at least your sister?'

'My mother and sister are very busy, as I'm sure you must appreciate. I am here to visit and be of assistance to my good friend, Mrs Saunders.'

'Ah, yes…' Pamela disdained to glance at the terrace. 'I know who you mean. The lady who looks to be in, ah…a delicate condition. I'm surprised she is out of doors.'

'Why? She is in good health, Mrs Pemberton, I assure you, and does not need to be quarantined. In five months she is to have a baby, not the measles.'

Pamela's lips thrust into a knot. Her eyes narrowed on Rachel. 'Well, I'm sure it's not quite *comme il faut*. But as she is here with her husband, presumably he has no objections to the risk to her health or her reputation. Doubtless they will ignore the tattle tomorrow…'

Rachel turned the full effect of her gelid eyes on the spiteful woman. The icy blast had an unexpected effect. Mrs Pemberton, for reasons best known to herself, repealed discretion and divulged exactly what Rachel wanted to know.

'The day after the gambling, William and your father had a meeting with the Earl. It was arranged that the venue for the nuptials would remain unchanged, although, at a risk of becoming a veritable echo, London *is* undoubtedly the place for a wedding at this time of the year. His lordship needn't have done it. And I for one wish he had not. I say he's been far too decent and obliging, when one considers *all* things *past*…and present…'

Even before Rachel looked back his way she sensed he would be watching her. Their eyes held infinitesimally, but long enough for her to read the message there: he wanted to speak to her and his patience was wearing thin in the pursuit of it. From his mannerisms she knew he was excusing himself from the circle of jovial dignitaries.

He was again expecting her to stay still so he could approach her. Despite what she'd just learned of his honestly obliging her family with a dispensation, she once more felt panic making queasy her stomach. Why couldn't she just get this over with! He had stalked her virtually the entire length of the room. Must she let him be vastly amused…vastly irritated by watching her flit like a hunted deer from one thicket of people to another in the hope of keeping him sufficiently at bay?

What a fool he must think her! What a fool she thought herself! The intention in coming here at all had been to do a deal with the dratted man. Oh, why had she *come*?

She had come, she forced herself to calmly acknowledge, because she had not anticipated just how badly that first sight of him would affect her. The first clash of their eyes and all she could see were brown fingers on her wobbly white hand as he mopped spilled tea. All she could hear were his ruthless words, his callous laugh as he left her with her clothes in disarray. All she could feel was the hard pulsing heat of him thrust against her melting body. Her lips had burned, parted as if again under that violent kiss. Through the myriad mingling aromas in his hot drawing room she could detect the powdery perfume of crushed rose petals…the redolence of his woody cologne wafting from her feverish skin.

How could she bear to make a pretence of conversing politely in public with him when privately they both knew of the insults and embarrassments each had caused the other? Why had he made her come here at all? Why had her tormentor not simply sent her the paper to take home? Did he intend humiliating her further before he quit England for Ireland?

A blur of a dark figure was looming on the periphery of her vision. At once she murmured an excuse to Mrs Pemberton about seeking her friends and veered away towards the right and the terrace.

'Miss Meredith…'

Rachel braked her speedy pace and with a deep breath turned sedately about. As a hand was extended towards her, she dropped the skirts she still held from being trampled in her fleet-footed escape, and clasped those elegant white fingers with her own. 'Lady Davenport…I…I was just about to catch up with Mr and Mrs Saunders. I believe they await me on the terrace.'

'Ah; I believe my son was just about to catch up with you. But I dare say he can wait a little while longer.'

Rachel blinked, smiled, searched for a topic of conversation somewhere to be had in amongst the guests. Finding none, she burst out in desperation, 'You look very well, Lady Davenport. Just as I remember you…and no older at all,' she trailed off, wondering if such an observation was diplomatic or wise.

A musical chuckle put her at ease. Her fingers were squeezed, then released. 'Thank you very much, my dear, for that compliment. And to return you one: you look more beautiful than you did as a teenager. I've never forgotten you; perhaps we should have made a better effort to properly get to know one another six years ago. I know we had very different social circles at that time, and you seemed so confident and popular that I didn't want to intrude on you and your young friends and spoil your fun.' She gave Rachel a sweetly rueful look. 'But, for some reason tonight, something has been plaguing me. I hope you won't mind me mentioning it. When you were engaged to Connor, I didn't seem too…haughty or unapproachable…or unfriendly, did I? I would always have been pleased to chat or shop…or take a drive…'

'No! Please don't think it. It wasn't anything like that.'

Rosemary smiled. 'I had to ask; I know that mothers-in-law can be very daunting.' Her tawny eyes strayed sideways to where Pamela Pemberton, her jaw incessantly wagging, stood with her downcast husband.

Rachel understood the subtle indication and gave a wry smile. 'Yes, indeed…' was all she said.

'I remember that my first husband's mother quite terrified me,' Lady Davenport said. 'They were very clannish…very proud people. And Michael was her blue-eyed boy. He looked very like Connor, actually.' A maternal look sought and found her son's sapphire eyes. She gave him a twinkling smile. 'I think Connor would like me to leave you alone.'

'Please don't,' Rachel quietly beseeched without looking around.

'Ah, I see. Yes, gentlemen can be daunting, too. I understand that. I hope I don't sound too much of a coward, but Connor's father fair scared me witless, too. At first.'

'He did?'

Rosemary nodded. 'But only at first. I wasn't used to being kidnapped, or rough-handled, you see. I was the Earl of Devane's daughter and used to being protected and pampered all my life. A handsome, eligible son of an Irish chieftain didn't impress me. But he impressed the local colleens, which was why he hadn't previously found it necessary to learn much about courting etiquette. I soon taught him all he needed to know.'

'Kidnapped?' Rachel breathed, her eyes wide.

'Our marriage settled a feud: a matter of honour between our families that had festered through generations. As I didn't respond to his initial overtures, he forced my hand…if you will. The Flintes were quite barbaric…very dynamic, and the most beautiful people ever. Connor didn't tell you much of his father's fabled background, I take it?'

Rachel shook her golden head, her wide eyes fixed on Rosemary's face.

'I'm not surprised. I imagine he considered some things better left till after you were man and wife. I know he was keen at that time to seem a most conventional, honourable suitor. He wanted to be worthy of you. And he was,' she stated with quiet, adamant pride. 'But Connor could be…wild. He could be very like his father, actually. His grandfather…my father…would despair of him, at times. Yet how they loved one another. He should have had the fairest hands should my father,' she said, her accent thickening with her memories. 'Mother of Mercy, the amount of times he washed them on account of my son!' Rosemary trailed off on a husky chuckle. 'Enough. I've said more than enough. All I meant to say, Miss Meredith, was that I'm glad we've had an opportunity to meet again and talk a while. I see that supper is about to be served. I must go and find Sir Joshua and see to things.' She moved away a little, pausing only to add, 'I hope all goes well on your sister's wedding day. In spite of the unfortunate distaff side, William

Pemberton seems a fine young man. Convey my good wishes to the rest of your family, won't you now?'

'Yes, I shall. Thank you...' Rachel half-turned politely as the woman smiled in farewell.

Gracefully Rosemary moved away, summoning people to go with her and sample delicacies in the supper room. As the room emptied, the only person who appeared to be walking against the flow was the Earl of Devane. Hastily, Rachel turned back towards the terrace, just in time to see Paul and Lucinda emerging through a door at the other end of the room. After a cursory look about, they began to follow the crowd heading in the opposite direction, doubtless assuming she'd already quit the room.

Rachel dithered on the spot for barely a moment before deciding she was ravenous. As she prepared to take a detour to the exit, she felt her wrist taken in a powerful hand and she was jerked about and lead none too gently on to the terrace. She tensed, preparing to throw him off, at the same moment he let her free. Her own violence made her stumble back a few paces; then, with a steadying breath and an indignant toss of her golden head, she swept with wordless aplomb back towards the drawing room.

He blocked her path. 'If you think I'm about to chase you the length of that damned room again, you can forget it.'

'Let me pass,' she demanded, yet a hint of pleading made hoarse her voice.

She heard him swear beneath his breath before a hand touched her chin, tilting it up. She withdrew at once, retreating until she could go no further and her hands gripped the chilly iron balustrade behind. Their eyes met, merged through the moonless dusk.

'Rachel, if I'd been your husband you wouldn't have objected,' he reasoned softly.

'You are not my husband,' she choked out.

'I almost was.'

'Almost is a million miles away. And if you had been my husband and had ever treated me with such…such vile disrespect, I would have objected very strongly. I would have killed you.'

'And if you had been my wife and had spoken to me with such vile disrespect, I just might have throttled you first,' he countered quietly.

Rachel launched herself from the railings and rushed towards the light. 'It's as well then, my lord, I had the foresight to abscond six years ago and give us both a fair prospect of attaining our dotage.'

He easily intercepted her before she was even close to getting indoors. 'Move aside, I'm going home,' she icily conveyed to his figured waistcoat.

'Before we've had a chance to discuss Windrush?'

'There's nothing to discuss,' she stated with a shaky triumph in her voice. 'I have it from Mrs Pemberton that the dispensation you spoke of is already arranged with my father and June's fiancé. I have it that you and William seem quite friendly. I don't believe for one moment even you would renege on your word now it is common knowledge.'

'That's because you've never really known me, Rachel.'

She looked up slowly, with shimmering, solemn eyes. 'Yes. That I can believe. I've never really known you at all.'

'Good. We're agreed on one thing. Do you want to discuss Windrush?'

She swallowed, moistened her lips. 'Are you saying you will go back on your word?'

'I'm saying I've been ridiculously generous and I want something in return.'

'What?'

'Ah, what…' he repeated wryly, self-mockingly. 'Two things, actually. I'll start with the good news. I want you to take a young woman off my hands and on to your staff. She's proving to be a trial through no fault of her own. She's a reasonable housemaid and you needn't worry about the cost of her wages and so on. I'll continue to pay her for the time being. I just want her out of my house…'

'That's the good news?' Rachel asked with silky sarcasm. She returned to her place at the railing. 'You really are the most loathsome man, aren't you? If you imagine for one minute I shall take one of your doxies, swelling with your bastard, under my roof simply to oblige you and minimise a scandal…'

'That's precisely why I do want you to take her under your roof: to oblige me and contain a scandal. For her sake, not mine. Gossip doesn't bother me; soon I'll be overseas. Her brother maintains she's chaste, so she ought not to be increasing with anyone's bastard. But she's uncommonly pretty, which presents problems for her and her brother who's trying to protect her. The usual conclusions are being drawn to my interest in them. Not least because certain individuals are exciting speculation by stirring and spicing the pot. I want to thwart any rumour that I've a fourteen-year-old concubine in Berkeley Square. It'll not help her to gain respectable employment once I'm in Ireland. She and her brother are in my employ simply because they have nowhere else to go at the moment.'

'God in Heaven! Fourteen years old? She's a child, just two years older than Sylvie!' Rachel exclaimed, repelled. 'Wasn't the Italian woman mistress enough for you? Was she too old? Do you really expect me to believe that from the goodness of your heart you've taken to rescuing harlots and housing them in a palace? Do you think me a fool?'

'No, I don't think you a fool and I don't expect you to believe me, Rachel. You of all people I knew would think me a degenerate and a liar. That doesn't matter. This is a deal. You want your sister married at Windrush and I want this favour. A favour that's to cost you nothing. In fact, the Merediths will get two extra staff, gratis, until such time as you might decide to move the girl and her brother on with a character in their pockets. That's my only stipulation; that you provide them with suitable references when you let them go.'

Rachel simply stared at him in confused amazement. Of all the things he might have required of her, making respectable a courtesan and her pimp hadn't figured at all. But he would relish outraging her. He was probably quite piquantly diverted by the fact that the woman who once had been his future wife, the woman who had rejected him, was now coerced into housing one of his whores. He was a vindictive man, that he had admitted. His intention was to even the score between them, he had admitted that, too. In a way she had to admire him for devising such ingenious methods.

His mother's recent revelation that he could be wild had disquieted her; now that description seemed like a fond defence. This was a man who was sunk in depravity. She thought of her schemes to regain her inheritance and felt no guilt at all. Deception *was* the only way. Any residual hope that she might charm or flatter or strike a reasonable deal with this reprobate was gone.

She quickly turned things over in her mind. A glib acceptance of what he was proposing was the way forward. He could only humiliate her on the matter if she let him. In fact, she might turn it to her advantage.

Beaulieu Gardens was, at present, seriously understaffed. Noreen was running herself ragged covering all aspects of household chores. Mr and Mrs Grimshaw, who oversaw things, were too old and set in their ways to keep the place as spick and span as was warranted by an establishment occupied during the fashionable Season. Yet as she was in her father's house with only his tacit permission, she'd not felt able to incur him extra expense by taking on domestics.

Connor watched her eyes flit from side to side, her finely drawn brunette brows meet then quirk as she strove to come to terms with what he was asking of her. He considered again defending himself and reiterating that his dealings with the girl were platonic, but he knew it would achieve nothing but rouse her disgust. Inwardly he smiled; if she was contemptuous of his altruism, he wondered how she would react to knowing what next he wanted. To resume conversation and come closer to that personal issue, he said mildly, 'I'll write to your father and explain the situation before you return home. He won't object to employing the pair at Windrush, I'm sure.'

'Oh, indeed,' Rachel snapped out bitterly. 'I'm sure he'd oblige you by taking in a dozen of your cast-off drabs. Whenever was there something that you did that my father didn't like?'

'Now that brings me to the second thing I want…'

Rachel felt her stomach clench at his drawling tone. It was quiet, cynical, yet so very honeyed. She looked up warily at him, but he seemed momentarily distracted.

'Why is it you despise your own father?'

'I don't,' Rachel gritted tightly.

Connor shrugged. 'You could have fooled me.'

'Yes. I could. He obviously could not. That's why he lost Windrush to your mean thievery and why I now have to be here at all, listening to your revolting catalogue of requirements…'

He smiled as she tailed off into frustrated, resentful silence. 'And one of those requirements is knowing why it is you despise your father.'

'Perhaps because he is idiotic enough to still think so highly of you,' she snapped.

'I thought so. I could change that. Would you like me to? Will you then think highly of me, Rachel? If I make your father hate me?'

'Say what you mean. I've no inclination to unravel riddles.'

The consequence of her snappish, insolent dictate was silence. She seethed inwardly in impotent frustration. He was well aware he could present as many enigmas as he liked. He could give or withhold information, just as he could give or withhold rights to her home. She imagined her parents must even now be beholden to him for still residing there. How he loved to impress on her just how firmly he had her pinned beneath his thumb. As the silence continued she blurted, 'You don't even like my father, do you? He thinks so much of you and you don't even like him.'

'I've no reason to dislike him. He always treated me well.'

'*Well?*' she cried scornfully. 'He used to treat you as his own flesh and blood. I thought perhaps you might have more to say on the subject than that. You and he would spend a ridiculous amount of time together…riding to hounds…smoking in clubs…playing at cards…'

'You were jealous of your own father?'

Rachel gave a hysterical choke of laughter. 'No. I was jealous of you. Never in all my life has he given me much time or attention. Had I been a much-wanted son, things might have been different. But I'm a bitter disappointment. I'm a girl, you see.'

'I do see. You're a woman. That's a fact. Believe me, Rachel, I've always been far too aware of that.'

Rachel felt her face burn beneath his steady, sleepy scrutiny. She swirled about, gripped the balustrade and inspected the gloomy gardens. 'How do I know you're not lying?' she demanded shrilly. 'You've already implied you might rescind your agreement. Do you imagine I'll concede that you dump these people on me without first I am certain there is such a document?'

'Perhaps you'll just have to trust me on it.'

She spun about, laughed scornfully. 'I'd sooner put my trust in a trading justice.'

He smiled sardonically, knowing what he did about his worship, Arthur Goodwin. 'You're still a child, Rachel, aren't you? Beneath that powder and paint—which incidentally you don't need—you're just a little girl.'

'I sincerely hope not,' she silkily demurred. 'Not now I know how your tastes run.'

He walked close to her, halted in front of her with a look of thoughtful contemplation slanting his sensual mouth. 'It always was hard to decide whether to put you across my knee or kiss you.'

'Well, let me solve the dilemma for you then, my lord,' she carefully enunciated, attempting to slip sideways and avoid his closeness. 'If you attempt either I shall scream blue murder and cause this so refined soirée to end in chaos.'

A casual hand was planted on the iron railing, preventing her straying too far. 'I don't think you'd do that,' he answered smoothly. 'Not with your sister's wedding imminent and half the invited guests here tonight. I think you're childish, Rachel, not stupid.'

With both of her hands, Rachel gripped the wrist preventing her escape. Her small fingers curled spitefully over braced muscle, her nails pinned against his cambric cuff. Abruptly she ceded trying to shift him and instead turned about to sweep off in the other direction, only to find that barred by a dark, immovable arm, too.

'Do you want to see it?'

She gazed up through the dusk into his brilliant, preying eyes. 'See it?'

'The dispensation. You said you want proof it exists.'

'Yes,' she gasped quickly, noting his gaze had dropped to her mouth. 'Yes, I do,' she repeated. With brisk businesslike action she stepped against him in a way calculated to make him move reflexively aside. He remained as he was, apart from his hands; they relinquished the metal balustrade to slide about her and keep her close.

Rachel grew rigid, quivering with feverish anticipation; waiting for a cruel, lustful hand to force together their hips, for malicious lips to bruise her own.

Instinctively one of her hands thrust between them, pressed to her bosom as if to shield it from his plundering fingers.

Connor looked down at the splayed fingers and the high-buttoned demure bodice, under protection. A ghost of a smile touched his mouth. He lowered his head. 'Nice dress. Are you wearing it for me?' he taunted softly as his lips cornered hers in a kiss that was both seductive and reassuring.

Rachel waited for his anger, his spite to filter through the sweetness. She wouldn't be tricked by his sophistication just because brute force had previously trampled her defences. Determinedly she steeled herself to remain impassive, unyielding. His eyes were closed, hers were open, watching his face, searching for a warning sign of that vengeful lust she'd endured before. It was sure to come. She'd responded before. Never again…never again, drummed in her mind as her mouth parted beneath the sensual insistence of his and her prepared fist, planted between them, relaxed, flattened against the cool silk of his waistcoat. His lashes raised; somnolent and wary eyes fused before he unsealed their lips. He gave her a smile, the one that June could mimic, the one that was barely there.

'Come to the library, I'll give you the document to take home with you tonight.'

He was back by the door to the drawing room, beckoning her, before Rachel had marshalled strength or sense enough to move.

Chapter Eleven

The first people Rachel saw as they walked in silence into the drawing room were Paul and Lucinda Saunders. The second couple to catch her eye was her aunt and uncle Chamberlain.

Rachel groaned inwardly as she observed her aunt Phyllis quickly whisper in her husband's ear. Then the woman gave her eldest niece the first smile to be bestowed on any one of the Merediths in over six years. Rachel elected to ignore the distinction.

But she was not so dismissive of the interest stirred by their appearance. Gossip might start in earnest if she and Devane again went missing only to once more emerge together. Quickly she voiced her fears. 'It might give rise to unwanted conjecture if we disappear at the same time. Whilst I join my friends, the Saunders, would you please go alone to collect the document, then return in a moment to give it to me?'

'No.'

There was no time for persuasion as her aunt and uncle were almost upon them. Her annoyance at his blunt refusal was limited to her stiffly removing her hand from where moments ago he'd placed it on his arm. Her vexation mounted when she saw Paul and Lucinda were not after all going to come over; now that her kinsmen were accosting her, they had diplomatically diverted to talk to some other people just returned from the supper room.

As her aunt Phyllis creaked close enough to peck her cheek in greeting, Rachel had to stifle the urge to elbow away her father's portly, corseted sister. Her uncle Nathaniel shuffled on the spot looking ill at ease, conscious that his wife's abrupt *volte face* was absurd in its excess. When last Phyllis had shown their eldest niece this much affection, Rachel had been nineteen and accepting felicitations on her engagement.

Her aunt beamed a welcome; Rachel returned her a sickly smile. Once she had been beyond the pale. Now, it seemed, she was to be allowed, nay, shepherded back into the fold. And it was all because of the man by her side. He had forgiven her, taken pity on the unpopular spinster she had become. Thus she was acceptable, even envied for his polite patronage. If only they knew! A surge of anger rose up in her, threatening her composure, as she recalled several occasions over the past six years when her parents or sisters had been snubbed in public by this woman just because once she had jilted Connor Flinte.

Rachel's eyes whipped from her aunt to her sheepish uncle.

'Why, Rachel, how pretty you look in that blue dress. I swear you never fail to suit that colour,' her aunt Phyllis gushed as though there had been no lengthy hiatus in their relationship.

'Thank you, Aunt Chamberlain,' Rachel returned formally. 'I'm amazed you were able to recognise me at all, considering how much time has elapsed since last we spoke.'

Rachel watched with not a hint of remorse as a flush mottled her aunt's jowls. What did stir her compassion was that her uncle visibly winced and stuck his fingers into his cravat, loosening it from his perspiring neck.

Nathaniel cleared his throat. 'Well! Well, then,' he gallantly distracted attention from his wife's ugly confusion. 'And how are your sisters? Busy with sewing their pretty dresses? Young June will be a blushing bride. And Sylvie a picture in her frock. Yes, yes. Capital! Always a sweet little girl. This fine weather is just the thing.' He nodded stressfully at Connor, who made a suave response to these garbled observations.

'A less sultry climate, is needed for the big day,' Phyllis interjected, fanning herself with a plump, glittering hand. 'We ladies won't want to be wilting in our wedding finery from the heat. Isn't that so, Rachel?'

'Are you to come, then?' Rachel asked in mock surprise. 'When first the invitations were sent months ago and there was no reply from you, we imagined you were busy trying to break a prior engagement. But we always knew it was bad timing, not bad manners, that kept you from penning us a line of explanation.'

Nathaniel visibly shrank back in his shoes. This time his wife rallied. Her sharp little eyes stabbed at Rachel. 'Indeed, so. You are right, in that respect. But we are lucky in that we have managed to rearrange our schedule. Now all is attended to, I assure you, my dear. Just this week I dashed off a reply to your parents and had it to the post within an hour.'

'Why…that is good of you, Aunt Chamberlain! I trust the people we steal you from on this occasion won't too earnestly mourn the loss. And of course, Mrs

Pemberton will be honoured. Why, I swear, if I didn't know it impossible, I would have the two of you for sisters. You're so alike!' Her eyes strayed to Pamela Pemberton's bony limbs and long, equine face before settling on the small, round woman close by.

'Some months ago, you say, the cards were sent?' Phyllis rattled off furiously, well aware that characters, not figures were being disparaged. 'Well, I'm sure I have not had mine as long as *that*,' she forcibly protested. 'The post, of course, is not to be relied upon; possibly it was misdirected—'

'I think not—'

'I imagine it was,' Connor drawled over her words, with a hint of finality in his voice that drew Rachel's eyes to his.

She read a warning there. Perhaps he was worried she and her aunt might start a cat-fight right here in his refined drawing room. The notion held great attraction. But for June's wedding dictating decorum, she might have thoroughly enjoyed impressing on this hypocritical cow exactly what she thought of her. Challengingly, she met Connor's deceptively mild gaze. *This is my business*, was the message flashed beacon-like in her limpid eyes.

Don't push me too far, was signalled back in the blue-flame heating her face. A heavy masterful hand curved over her elbow ready to move her on. He nodded politely at her aunt and uncle.

Keen not to let their noble host escape too soon, and desperate to know if her suspicions were correct, Phyllis cooed, 'And will you be attending my niece's, nuptials, my lord?'

'I'm soon to return to Ireland,' was all he said as, with a smile, he steered Rachel away.

Phyllis Chamberlain watched them go with narrowed eyes.

'Good of him to be so kind to her and take her about with him like that.' Nathaniel sighed. 'I've seen her look monstrous forlorn this evening skipping from place to place trying to find someone to talk to. Took her for a stroll in the air, too.'

'*Stroll!*' his wife hissed. 'I swear he's got a touch of rouge on his mouth. What does that tell you?'

Nathaniel looked aghast. 'No! Really? I'd never have had Devane for a poncy dandy! More of a Corinthian, I'd have said…'

With a withering look flung across her fat shoulder at her spouse, Phyllis stomped off to confer with the woman who bore no family likeness to her at all.

'*Witch!*' Rachel burst out beneath her breath when sufficiently far away for no one but her companion to hear the expostulation.

'Hush, sweet, or people might think I'm paying my kind attentions to an ill-tempered virago.'

Rachel slanted him a smouldering look. About to snap that he could pay his attentions elsewhere, she realised that he was leading them towards Paul and Lucinda who were waiting to greet them.

'Supper was delicious. Have you yet eaten?' Lucinda blandly opened the conversation. 'We looked for you, Rachel…'

'No…I…er…was looking for you on the terrace and found Lord Devane. He was also taking the air.'

Paul and Lucinda gamely avoided catching each other's eye or indeed that of either of their companions.

Four people started a conversation.

Everyone stopped and Connor said into the quiet, 'I've a minor matter to discuss with Miss Meredith and

also a few business papers to give you, Paul. Would
you mind if we all went along to the library for a few
minutes and attended to it now? It shouldn't take long.
Might I persuade you to come along, Mrs Saunders?
While I bore your husband, I've a fine collection of
Gothic novels you might like to look at.'

'How wonderful; I'd love to see them. I like to read.'
Lucinda immediately slipped a hand on to the suave
arm Connor offered.

'They're mostly my mother's books, so are probably
quite romantic tales, I imagine…' Rachel overheard
this conversational explanation as he lead Lucinda towards the door. Paul took Rachel's hand, threaded it
through his arm and gave it a brotherly pat. Rachel
glanced obliquely at his pleasant face, sure he was
about to say something. Instead he gave a small, be-
mused shake of the head, then they followed in their
host's wake.

'Come and sit down, my dear; she went in there with
him quite willingly,' Paul Saunders told his wife as she
again tiptoed towards the stately double doors that led
from the huge library into the Earl's study.

Lucinda inclined sideways and bent her small ear
towards mahogany panels. All that was audible was a
sweet melody emanating from the music room at the
opposite end of the house. 'Do you think Rachel
is…well…safe in there with him?'

'If she's not, you'll soon know of it. Rachel won't
scruple to scream,' Paul wryly remarked. He idly
glanced at the documents spread out on the leather-
topped library desk and smiled at the parchment. He'd
already perused an identical set of insurance policies
quite thoroughly some days ago at his office where the

Earl had had them delivered. But he kept up a manly pretence of earnest interest in every conceivable form of maritime disaster.

Lucinda approached a towering bookcase and eased out a tome from the packed shelf nearest to her. 'He truthfully has a fine collection of novels.'

'Good…' her husband said as he watched her buxom figure traipsing to and fro, novel in hand. He pushed back his chair and went to settle himself on the leather couch by the unlit fire. The atmosphere was still warm, and he removed his jacket and sank back into supple hide. He watched his wife from beneath heavy lids; her new shawl slipped absently from her plump arms to the floor as she reached for another book on a higher shelf.

'Come and show me what you've got. I hope Connor's right and it's romantic.'

Lucinda turned, blushing at his husky tone of voice, recognising it very well. She shot a look at the study door. 'Do you think he's proposing again?'

'Possibly…but *what* I wouldn't like to hazard a guess. Come here,' Paul said on a rumble of a chuckle. 'Let's get comfortable, it might be a long wait…'

'Do you trust me now, Rachel?'

Rachel looked at the document beneath her fingers. Quickly she smoothed it, refolded it. 'May I take this home with me?'

'Yes.'

'Thank you.' The document was made smaller, briskly and precisely, so it would fit into her reticule. But it was the other papers, rolled and tied with red tape, sealed with red wax, that again drew her eyes.

She was sitting in his chair, behind his imposing desk, where he had indicated she should sit. He had extracted the dispensation from the top drawer, but omitted to shut it. Instinctively she knew what lay revealed in the shallow recess: he was intentionally tempting her with the deeds to Windrush. Ownership of her home, her inheritance, was close at hand. And just one mantra drummed in her head: possession is nine-tenths of the law. Her fingers itched to snatch them up.

Slowly, impertinently, she reached in and lifted out the scroll. Reverently she placed it on the polished mahogany, then moved it with one fingertip until she could just read: Freehold in Title to the house and demesne known as Windrush...

'You want me to ask for this too.' She looked up at him. He was standing by the huge marble mantelpiece beneath a painting of an enormous, fierce-looking hound. 'Why are you taunting me with the deeds to Windrush?'

'If you're prepared to negotiate for them, then I can tell you what else I want. On the terrace I told you I wanted two things.'

'Perhaps I might not ask for them,' Rachel said, her eyes adhering to his through the candle-flicker.

'You will. Any minute now.'

She flung the deeds back into the drawer and slammed it shut, then stood up. 'You think you're so clever, don't you? You think you can manipulate me, make me dance to your tune. You're wrong...'

'Why didn't you marry Moncur or that other fop...Featherstone, wasn't it?'

The unexpected change of topic brought her pacing to an abrupt halt and she simply stared at him. 'That's none of your business,' she finally said with insolent levity.

'Knowing why you rejected them might be all I want.'

'Is it?'

'Why did you break those engagements?'

With a dramatic show of ennui she began removing pens from the holder and leaning them against the standish. 'Because…because I didn't want to be married. It was a mistake…it was as simple as that…'

'It's a mistake you make too often. Did you love them?'

'No! Yes, of course…I think…' The last pen was flung on to the desk and she threw up her hands in frustration, forming fists. Conscious of her friends next door, and to prevent herself shouting, she gritted through her teeth, 'It's none of your business.'

He'd used Paul and Lucinda as chaperons to get her decently here, just to torment her into an argument. Well, she refused to be provoked. She must keep debate between them calm and reasonable. She gazed at the proud stance of the canine in the picture. It looked untrained…wolflike. Immediately she thought of Rosemary Davenport and her revelations regarding this man and his unruly father.

'I spoke to your mother. She is just as I remember, so very kind and nice. Your stepfather, Sir Joshua, I didn't think looked so well.'

'He's not so well. He's suffered seizures lately. The doctor thinks it might have affected his memory.'

'Oh, I'm sorry…'

'What did my mother say to you?'

Again Rachel considered telling him it was none of his concern. She took a deep breath. This was surely safe ground. Better to loiter upon it than venture to other unknown paths. 'She told me your father was an

Irish chieftain's son, and how he brought about their marriage by abducting her to end a centuries-old feud. She also said you're very like him.'

Connor laughed, picked up his tumbler of whiskey and drank deeply from it. It was some moments after it was replaced that he murmured, 'Did she, now?'

'Yes. She said you were wild and that your grandfather would despair of you.'

He watched a finger trace the rim of his glass. 'Yes, he would,' he said softly.

'Why? What did you do?'

'The things wild young men do that their elders and betters despair of: spend too much money, gamble, whore, fight…'

Rachel hadn't expected him to be quite so honest. 'Oh. I didn't know…'

'No, you didn't know, Rachel. I took great pains at that time to make sure you didn't know. I was quite the gallant young major, wasn't I now? For what good it did…'

She understood the thread of bitterness and self-mockery. Quickly she said, 'Your poor grandfather. I expect he must have desired a different heir. I never knew of that either. You never said you would one day be an Earl.'

'I would have told you if I sincerely thought I had a chance of becoming an aristocrat. I might have boasted of it, for you seemed impressed then by status. Six years ago I was fourth in line to succeed and had my mother's two brothers and one of their sons in good health. It didn't seem possible all would die before me within twenty months of one another. That's why I made a career in the army.' He smiled, tossed off the remainder of his drink. 'That and the fact that my grandfather had a gun pointing at my head when he told me he'd bought me a commission in the Life Guards and to get packed and ready to go.'

Rachel walked closer to him, intrigued. 'Your grandfather threatened to kill you?'

'More bluster than anything. I don't think he'd have pulled the trigger. He was at the end of his tether. I had put him in an awkward position by indulging in one sin too many. He took it personally, for it deeply offended his ethics and sensibilities. He was a good man. An honourable man…'

'What did you do?'

He upended the decanter. A stream of amber flowed into crystal. 'I took a married woman as my mistress. I cuckolded an old and esteemed friend of my grandfather's. He wasn't amused.'

Rachel stared at him in silence, then murmured primly, 'No, I imagine he would not have been.' She cleared her throat, added briskly, 'Well, you must have been young, I suppose. I take it the adulteress was much older than you. Certainly old enough to know better. Perhaps she led you astray.'

'Well, thank you for those kind words, Rachel,' he drawled. Indolent amusement was levelled at her over the rim of his glass. 'Actually she was your age at the time, twenty-five, and I might have been a tender eighteen, but I knew exactly what I was doing. I've kept a mistress since I was fifteen.' Abruptly he swallowed some whiskey.

Rachel looked at him, moistened her lips. 'Oh, I see…' was all she could think to say to that news. And then she did think of something to say. 'You had a mistress when we were engaged?' she demanded, icily polite.

He placed his drink down, turned to face her. 'Well, what would you have done if you'd known, Rachel? Jilted me...?'

She felt the blood suffuse beneath her skin at his sarcasm. 'Well, I'm glad I do know, at last. I don't feel quite so...'

'Guilty?' he supplied quietly as she failed to finish the sentence. 'Feel as guilty as you can. You were the only woman in my life at that time.'

Rachel ceased fiddling with quill feathers and moved towards the door. 'It's time I left. Paul and Lucinda will be ready to go—I know Lucinda is quite tired...'

'Why won't you ask me what I need to give you back Windrush?'

Rachel remained silent, simply stared at the raw-boned beast on the wall. It looked real enough to leap out at her.

'You want that estate more than anything, don't you?'

Almost imperceptibly she nodded.

'All I want is a fair exchange. I want something I once desired more than anything. Do you know what I did on my wedding night?'

She felt unable to jeer that she couldn't give a damn. Her eyes, her voice seemed to be trapped by his. Slowly she shook her head.

He smiled a savage smile that just took his lips back against even teeth. 'Neither do I. I haven't the vaguest idea where I went or how I got so drunk. Suffice to say that when Jason found me unconscious on Clapham Common a day or so later he thought I'd killed myself. Another night there, comatose, and perhaps I would have died. It was two days after he got me home before I came to—a week after that when the fever abated.

The first coherent thought I had was quite uncharitable; I wanted to kill him for not leaving me there.

'For six years on and off I've fantasised about my wedding night. At first it was an obsession…wanting those blasted lost dark hours back; to have them as I was entitled to have them, in passion and pleasure. Later it mellowed into a nagging curiosity about you…about what I'd missed. But it's never gone away. It's always been there, an irritating scar on my mind. I want my wedding night, Rachel. You owe me my wedding night.'

She hadn't realised he'd got so close. He raised a hand. She flicked it off. He raised it again, then again and persevered until she simply stood still, lulled by fingers that circled with tantalising light strokes on the satiny skin of her arm.

What he was suggesting was horrendous, outrageous. She supposed she should swoon in shock. But she wouldn't. It wasn't a shock, or even a surprise. A remote part of her mind had realised as long ago as their tense reunion on that hot apple-scented afternoon, that he would aim to lock her into this ultimate revenge.

'A wedding night, by definition, follows a marriage,' she mentioned with cool logic. 'The ceremony never took place. I told you on the terrace, you're not my husband.'

'I came close enough with just twelve hours to go. Give me my wedding night, Rachel, and set us both free. It started with me wanting you, it'll finish there too. And if you get nothing else out of it, you'll get back your inheritance and the sure knowledge that when your father finds out, he'll want to shoot me down dead.'

'That's what I must do or you'll auction Windrush?' her faint voice asked.

'I don't want a house in Hertfordshire. I'm going home to Ireland. You give me my wedding night and I'll give you your deeds. You'll get the property sooner than you thought. If you agree—and I want your full agreement, Rachel; I want you willing—Windrush is yours, not your father's.'

'And do you think I could do that? Do you think I could keep the estate myself and return home with those papers and boast to my family how willingly I whored to get them? Do you expect me to do that?'

'Return the title to your father, then. Tell him I seduced you. Deal with it as you see fit. Either way he'll hate me. It's what you want, isn't it? For your father to wish me dead?'

'Yes,' she whispered in a hoarse croak. 'And he ought to wish that already.' She viciously slapped away his hand from where it still soothed her. 'How satisfying was it for you to steal a drunken man's house? How proud...how clever did it make you feel gambling with a man who had lost his wits to alcohol? God in heaven, it would have been better sport for you taking candy from a baby. And wouldn't a gentleman have at least given him a chance to win back such a valuable stake?'

'I did offer him the chance.'

'Are you telling me he lost to you twice?'

'No, I'm telling you he passed out before the cards were dealt again. He couldn't stand up or see straight Rachel, let alone tell a diamond from a spade.'

'He couldn't see the knave in the pack either, could he? Even when sober he couldn't see that,' she jeered in raw rancour.

Connor laughed, shrugged negligently. 'Don't worry; he'll see him now. And he isn't going to like it that I've stood his scheme on its head.'

'*His* scheme?'

'He might have been under the influence, but he was sober enough not to want to risk a second game. He didn't want Benjamin Harley to get Windrush. He intended I should have the estate. He didn't stake it until I sat down at the table and once I had it he didn't want it back. So I obliged him and took your birthright, fair and legitimate. But the only way I'll take you is the way I've just described. That's as far as I'm prepared to fall in with his plan to resurrect our relationship.'

Rachel felt the blood drain from her face. 'What are you saying?' she whispered, horrified.

'I'm saying, my one-time love, that your father is labouring under the foolish hope that I'm still besotted with you. He thinks I'm the honourable fool I was six years ago. He thinks if he puts you in my way and in my debt enough, I just might marry you and provide the Merediths with a happy ending. That won't happen.'

'No, it's too late for that. Far too late for that.'

'I'm glad you agree.'

'I do,' Rachel breathed, sweetly courteous, as she came close to him again. 'The only way the Merediths would ever have been assured a happy ending was if your stupid grandfather had found the courage to pull that trigger when you were eighteen.'

Her hand flew up, cracked resoundingly against a lean dark cheek. Immediately she flew backwards away from him. 'But that was quite satisfying,' she bit out before turning proudly for the door.

An arm curved about her tense body, jerking her off

balance and back against him. Immediately she fought his hold, then swirled about in his arms. The pearls twined into her hair scattered on to the floor like glimmering hailstones as five dark fingers supported her scalp. Slowly, deliberately he kissed her, plundered the mutinous soft lines of her lips with ruthless seduction until she was whimpering with tense frustration. Just as she succumbed to the sweet torment, allowed his tongue to tease hers, he took his mouth away.

'That wasn't very satisfying,' he breathed against her quivering flesh. 'So let me know by midweek if you want to negotiate on my terms or the estate will be auctioned at the beginning of July.'

Her large, glistening eyes raised to his, seeking some compassion beneath the fringe of preposterously long lashes. There was nothing but a diamond-hard glitter.

'And that's an end to it? It's enough that you finally humiliate me in the most sordid and basic way? You won't then feel inclined to find other things you want?'

'I won't humiliate you and I won't renege on my word. There's nothing else I want but peace. I told you: it started in lust, it'll end there too.'

'And that won't humiliate me?'

'No.'

He caught her wrist this time before her hand made its mark.

Wrenching herself free, she backed off two paces, then swept with wordless dignity to the door to find her friends to take her home.

'There's a rider approaching,' Sylvie called over her shoulder to her mother.

Gloria Meredith joined her youngest girl at the morning-room window. She squinted off into the distance at a dark blurry shape moving at some speed towards the house. 'I must purchase some spectacles. My eyesight is not what it was…'

'It's William,' Sylvie advised with a laugh and turned to look at June, sitting, feet curled beneath her, with sewing in her lap.

It seemed a moment before June's dreamy expression registered that the stuff of her reverie was, in body, in the vicinity. She started to her feet. 'William? Here? In Hertfordshire? Are you sure?'

'Well, come and look,' Sylvie ordered with a scowl for her dithering sister. In Sylvie's opinion, June didn't suit being in love. She wandered about like a witless idiot most of the time. Only yesterday she'd sat on a needle that June had forgotten she'd left idly poked into the arm of a chair. Of course, June had been so distraught at the sight of the small puncture mark on her little sister's thigh that she had sobbed and wept until Sylvie, in desperation, had apologised for bringing it to her attention, for she'd barely felt it, she'd insisted graciously.

June flew to the window and peered out. A smile of sheer rapture lit her face and in a swirl of pretty tiffany skirts she was gone from the room.

June encountered her father in the hallway in the process of shaking hands with her fiancé. William had his attention immediately on the alluring sight of his betrothed as he pumped his prospective father-in-law's arm. Edgar Meredith, with a little smile for the young couple, made his excuses and ambled off to his study.

'I'd no idea you were coming to Hertfordshire before the wedding,' June breathed.

Her fiancé managed a passably casual shrug. 'I found myself at a bit of a loose end in London. Philip Moncur and Barry Foster and some others have gone off to Brighton. They wanted me to accompany them, but I can't say I fancied it. I can't say I've fancied seeking my parents' company too much either these last few weeks…Father's well enough on his own…' A meaningful grimace followed the remark. 'So I thought a bit of country air was the thing; a constitutional before all the excitement starts in earnest. I've been staying for a few days at the King's Arms. It's a quaint place. Good food and ale. Decided today I'd just drop by on a visit…see how you all do…'

That was all the standing on ceremony that June could bear. With a little sigh she propelled herself into her fiancé's embrace. He hugged her tight. 'I don't think I can endure another day without you, let alone three weeks,' he whispered hoarsely against her soft hair.

June happily disengaged herself, took his arm and led him towards the morning room. 'Well, you must,' she said archly. 'And you will probably be quite disappointed to have left London. A friend for you was on her way into the city, just as you were heading here. Rachel is not long ago returned to Beaulieu Gardens. She will be upset to have missed you. Perhaps you passed each other on the road, unawares.'

Soon they were ensconced in the morning-room chairs with the warm sun slanting to beatify their faces. Sylvie had wandered off to change her clothes and take a ride on her pony. Thus, just Mrs Meredith played gooseberry to the lovers.

'More tea, William?' Gloria called, holding up the pretty pot.

'Yes, thank you, Mrs Meredith.'

Gloria attended to his cup, slid a glance between the

couple. The young man seemed to have trouble detaching his eyes from her daughter's sweet countenance. I have one child settled, she stressed for herself before her anxious thoughts again returned to Rachel.

She just wished she'd come home, for no good would come of chasing what was lost. She knew that her eldest daughter was pursuing her inheritance rather than her friendship with the Saunders. Her husband knew it too. Not that they had spoken of it; in fact, since the day he had returned to tell them of his grossly selfish behaviour, they had spoken little at all. Just essentials, over the running of the household or the wedding preparations brought them close enough to exchange a few frosty formal words. Gloria sighed depressively. It went unnoticed. With a murmured excuse about seeing to the luncheon, she withdrew.

William sipped from a delicate china teacup that looked imperilled by his big fingers. He frowned. 'Why has Rachel gone back to London so soon?'

June sent a circumspect look towards the door as though fearing they might be overheard. 'It's the business with Windrush: Papa losing it to Lord Devane,' she informed little above a whisper. 'Rachel was furious. I've rarely seen her so angry. She and Papa were at terrible loggerheads. She insists we be married here and has gone to do battle with Lord Devane over it all. I told her that it would not matter if we married instead in London…'

William's frown deepened. 'Well, I'd rather be married here at Windrush and told Devane so. He wasn't put out by allowing us to keep to our arrangements. He has no use for the place, after all.'

'What do you mean?' June asked in surprise. 'That

Rachel is gone on a fool's errand? Had you already approached Lord Devane over it all?'

'*He* approached *me*…and your father. As soon as Edgar was lucid enough to understand what was being said we all met the next day. Why did your father not tell you that, I wonder?'

June looked shocked. She shook her fair head. 'I don't know. Surely it would not have slipped his mind. Perhaps the alcohol affected his memory.'

William's curious expression turned bleak. 'I hope there is not some deviousness in it all.' He sighed. 'It seems strange to me, for unless I'm much mistaken, I'd wager a fortune that Devane is still much taken with Rachel.'

'I think so too,' June agreed. 'And can't see why he'd be mean enough to ruin things for us.'

'I'd as soon start married life without being central to all this skulduggery, my love.' William sighed. 'No good ever comes of such underhand behaviour: withholding information and harbouring secrets and so on. It is something I cannot abide…'

June looked alarmed at his vehemence. Her large hazel eyes attached to his for so long that he rose and, crouching by her chair, asked, 'What is it, dear?'

'I don't want us to have secrets either. There's something I must tell you, William…about Isabel…'

Chapter Twelve

'Faith, it's you back. Now, what might you be after wanting this time?'

'The same as last time.' The repartee was ready but there was little confidence in Sam Smith's demeanour today. In fact he barely raised a smile and twitched a bit beneath the steady glare directed at him from beneath brows like rusty arches.

Noreen Shaughnessy crossed her arms over her starched bosom and pointedly examined two sets of scuffed boots planted on her recently scrubbed steps. Her eyes belligerently widened, daring the young couple not to scarper.

The brash whippersnapper was easily recalled from the time he'd delivered that letter from Himself. The small female tucked behind him was a stranger. As Noreen slyly cocked her head to get a better look at his timid companion, she noticed there was a fancy-crested coach at the kerb with a solitary battered travelling box atop it. It was a rich man's rig bearing a poor man's luggage, and she recognised the coachman. He'd been driving the vehicle that brought her mistress home—with the earl of Devane escorting her—the first night they arrived in town. This was his lordship's coach and this, she'd believed, was one of his lordship's servants. So why was he here, with his chattels, delivered to their door in such style?

Noreen had her hunches. In fact, she'd done little else but brood on her suspicions for weeks past. Since they'd arrived in town and Miss Rachel insisted on immediately confronting the Major, Noreen knew something big was brewing. When he'd come back the following morning, looking like the handsome prince from a fairy tale, and her mistress acting for all the world like an excited girl set on hooking her beau, Noreen had put her faith in dreams: Windrush regained, things back as they should be. As they *would* be, but for the master acting like a proper fool. Then the front door had slammed like it was surely coming off its hinges and she'd been summoned by her white-faced mistress to sweep up the bits of clock and best china that marked the dream's departure.

Yet she'd seen the way the Major looked at her; and she'd seen the way Miss Rachel looked right back, with her chin high and her nose high…and that hunger in her eyes, as though something miraculous was just within reach but she was scared to reach out and grab lest it turned right round and bit her.

Now he was a hero and a lord to boot, but he was a man first. An influential man. And Noreen guessed a lesser fellow might feel entitled to impress all that on a woman who'd left him, practically at the altar, looking like every sort of fool. No one could deny Major Flinte had had cause to feel bitter and angry six years ago. And if he were biding his time for the perfect opportunity for tit-for-tat, it wouldn't come any sweeter than now. With Windrush gone to him, and Miss

Rachel determined her sister's wedding go ahead as planned, he sure enough held the whip hand…

But Noreen knew the Major was a decent man, an honourable man. It was one thing, she realised, that she and the master had in common: their lasting faith in the Major's honest goodness. He wouldn't ruin a woman he'd once loved. He just wouldn't, Noreen would stake her life on it…

'Your mistress is expecting us,' Sam Smith announced proudly, erasing the contemplative grimace from Noreen's countenance. 'We're taken on, Lord Devane says so…'

Gently he drew forward the girl from where she hovered behind him. 'I'm Sam Smith and this is me sister, Annie. I'll introduce you to Noreen, Annie…'

'Don't you be after taking liberties! And how is it you know me name?' Noreen barked.

'Sure and it was your mistress said it, Noreen,' he drawled in a fair approximation of her brogue. 'Miss Meredith called you that last time I was here with that letter from my master. My master as was, that is.' He rocked high on his toes, expanding his chest, keen to appear unconcerned about this abrupt downturn in his and Annie's prospects.

Noreen blushed again at the memory of him teasing her that day. 'It's Miss Shaughnessy to you. Or you can call me ma'am. God's own truth! It's a jackanapes you are. You're naught but a kid!'

A few days ago Noreen had tried not to look too relieved…or offended…when Miss Rachel told her new staff were to be taken on. But, in her heart, relief reigned, for she knew she was doing too much. Vera and Bernard Grimshaw, the old retainers who oversaw the place when the family were away, were as much help as a sack on the back. He was afflicted with arthritis so badly he could scarce move out of a body's way, and she was deaf as a post and too fat to do much more than loll about eating what she'd just took out the oven. Which left herself working dawn till dusk, and then some, which was more than a mortal could stand.

But she'd never have guessed this cheeky devil might some day be a colleague at Beaulieu Gardens. He looked big and ugly enough to do a full share, but that sister hiding behind looked like she might be as much use as fat Vera when it came to getting down and putting black on a grate or a scrubbing brush on a step. Noreen found herself again trying to peer beneath the girl's lowered bonnet brim. Weak and weary or shy and retiring, it cut no ice with Noreen. If she was here to work, work she would.

Sam recognised the inquisitiveness levelled at his sister and smiled thinly. Women never liked Annie. Poor little cow never had to say or do anything. They just never liked the look of her.

'Say hello to Miss Shaughnessy, Annie,' Sam ordered gruffly, tilting up her head to cure Noreen's curiosity.

His sister obeyed him, and solemn eyes set in a perfectly sculpted oval face regarded Noreen.

Noreen gawped, entranced for a moment by the wistful child. Then she slid a suspicious glance at the youth who was by no stretch of the imagination a looker.

The girl had a clear, pale countenance. The wispy tendrils of silky hair that had slipped free of her bonnet glowed like rich thick sherry. Her eyes, or what could be seen of them beneath those dropped black lashes, were huge and velvet brown. Sam had a good mop of chestnut hair, it was true, but there any similarity ended. His eyes were a shade of grey and his skin was lightly dusted with freckles; something else to hold against him. Why should his be unremarkable whereas hers were ugly blemishes? 'Your sister, is she now?' was directed snappishly at Sam.

He sighed at the sarcasm; automatically a protective arm curled about Annie's shoulders. He proffered their references, penned that very morning by Joseph Walsh. On the master's instruction, of course, burned like acid into his consciousness. 'She's me sister,' he stated curtly. 'Go and tell your mistress we're here.'

With a sullen, sideways look Noreen did as she was told.

Thankfully Rachel found it easy to be kind and gracious to this couple who had been forced upon her by her enemy. She'd feared she might snap and snarl at them. But now they were here, in her morning room, she felt more curiosity than irritation. She also felt an overwhelming sense of shame as she studied the girl. The idea that this awkward, nervous child might be any man's mistress, let alone likely to tempt the urbane Earl of Devane, now seemed utterly ludicrous. Yet she had accused him of being perversely interested in her!

A better presumption would have been that the Italian soprano would risk laughing herself hoarse at the very idea that this gauche maid was her rival.

Annie was indeed exquisitely pretty, but excruciatingly shy. Her brother seemed to be her rock…her universe. On being ushered, by Noreen, to an audience with her, one of Annie's small hands had latched on to one of Sam's sleeves. Still the girl stood slightly behind him, gripping, as a talisman, that piece of dark material.

Her sad eyes were lifted to his face, unwaveringly seeking reassurance. Once in a while, she darted a look at Rachel, flinching if their glances grazed, as though expecting a blow or a harsh word. As their eyes skimmed together again, Rachel gave her a welcoming smile. Annie looked startled and shuffled further behind her brother.

'Your sister seems very…nervous. Do I frighten her?'

'All ladies frighten her, m'm.'

'Why is that?' Rachel asked, astonished.

Sam felt ill at ease. He should have kept his bitter comment to himself. Too late. Bluntly he expanded on it. ''Cos of their gentlemen liking the look of her, which case they don't…'

Rachel studied him in silence for a moment, then transferred her attention to the girl's pure, pale face. Perhaps she had been a little hasty…or naïve in thinking no woman would view the child as a threat. Sam's cynical attitude spoke volumes: he was drawing on experience. 'Do you mean that your sister sometimes receives unwanted attention from gentlemen? And that their ladies resent it? Blame Annie for it?' Rachel asked gently, aware the youth already regretted his candour.

Sam's lips skewed into a travesty of a smile. One of his hands comforted the bloodless fingers biting into his arm. 'Yes, m'm,' was all he prudently allowed himself to admit this time. He looked directly at Rachel; guessed that a woman's suspicion might soon be kindling in her mind. Much as he hated Lord Devane for crushing his dreams, he had to be fair. If it wasn't for him, Annie would by now be beneath Arthur

Goodwin's paltry protection for a time. And after that time…then what?

All of it was his fault. Her own brother had put her at risk from that fat lecherous pig. He'd lost his temper that day the carriages collided and stupidly drawn attention to himself. But for that folly, Arthur Goodwin might never have bothered them. So he'd tell the truth. Put his lordship straight with this woman he loved. Then never think of him or wolfhounds or a new life in Ireland, ever again. 'Lord Devane was kind and good to both of us. Annie liked him. We both did. We would have stayed with him.'

Rachel took no offence at the bald declaration that Sam and his sister preferred Berkeley Square to Beaulieu Gardens. In truth she would rather they were still in Devane's employ. But not to spite the libertine this youth had championed. What troubled her conscience was that she could never match the prospects they had lost when Devane put them off.

She no longer knew what her own destiny held; she could scarce guarantee their futures. Sam had tacitly confirmed what the Earl of Devane had told her: he hadn't seduced Annie Smith, he had protected her and her brother. From what Sam inferred, she gleaned that degenerates hounded his sister for their own base ends. Knowledge of Connor's generosity, his integrity where the Smiths were concerned, made her oddly angry and uneasy. It was at such variance with the way he now treated her. Yet once she had known him only behave in an honourable way…to everyone. He certainly *had* been the gallant major he so recently scorned in his quiet sarcastic way. She had made him rue his own goodness.

Yet once she had loved him.

When they had been first betrothed she had only to look at him for her knees to turn to water, for her heart to hammer wildly.

But after months in which he seemed to spend more time with her father than with her, she'd come to think of him as dull and boring. Her father thought him a handsome, personable fellow. An engrossing companion…soon to be a son…to take about with him and show off to his cronies. Rachel had grown increasingly resentful of his absence and had also begun to suspect him too weak and placid.

Piqued that he allowed her father to monopolise so much of his time, she would set out to rile him. But nothing seemed to upset his equilibrium. She had flirted intentionally and provocatively with other gentlemen; he'd tolerated it with equanimity. She had failed to keep appointments to go for a drive in the Park or to meet mutual friends; he'd smiled that small smile of forgiveness, conveyed their excuses. She'd yearned for a more lusty, dynamic lover. He'd kept his kisses brief and chaste, his caresses light and respectful. She didn't want a handsome shell of a man with no power and substance…and no passion. She'd teased and tormented, wanting a flash of jealousy, a sign of smouldering desire he couldn't control, sure it was there. Time and again she had attempted to prod into life the tiger she was certain resided within. He was a soldier, an officer decorated, so it was rumoured, for courageous sorties behind enemy lines in the Peninsula. But even his valour was shrugged aside by the man himself. She had been irritated by his modesty when he drawled in that lazy way that he'd found himself in the thick of things primarily by accident. In final frustration, she'd decided he must be a fortune hunter, more interested in her father and his fine estate—which in the fullness of time would be hers and thus her husband's—than he was in his future wife. How very ironic. Now he had that very estate—her pride and joy—and he disdained to keep it. He had no use of it for he had inherited one of his own which was so much grander.

Now when she demanded his tolerance, his respect, the savage in him snapped at her heels. Angry lust or cool contempt was all he now showed her. Yet the caring, gentle man he had been was still alive. That side of him had nurtured the well being of these young people. With a deep sigh she unconsciously yearned for the man she might have had. If only she could have shaped herself an idol from those appealing facets of his character...the bits she chose, how easy it would be to madly love the beast once more...

Astonishment at acknowledging such a thought gave way to horror and must have registered in her face. She noticed both Sam and his timid sister were watching her. Hastily she composed her features.

'So you have been used to working with horses, Samuel?' Rachel burst out briskly, scanning Joseph Walsh's spider-scripted sentences. Somewhere in her anguished mind she wondered if it had been necessary to go to such farcical lengths as to provide references for a couple she had already consented to take on. But Connor seemed a stickler for propriety. Despite his boast that he cared nothing of gossip for himself, for he was soon away to Ireland, she wondered whether he was protecting her reputation or his own.

'Yes, m'm. But I'll work in the stables or the kitchens. Joseph Walsh...' he indicated the letter with a nod

'…was training me up to serve at table, only I never finished learning to be an under-footman…'

'And Annie?' Rachel looked at the girl; this time Annie held eye contact from beneath her luxuriant lashes. 'It says here, Annie, that you have proved yourself competent as a scullery-maid and that you did some sewing for the Earl's housekeeper.'

After a little nudge from her brother, Annie whispered, 'Yes, m'm.'

'Good. Versatile and conscientious people are what we need here at Beaulieu Gardens,' their new mistress said to encourage them. 'Noreen will show you to the kitchens and introduce you to the other staff. You may partake of a little refreshment, then Noreen will show you where you lodge. By one of the clock I shall expect you to start work. Ralph Turner who drives for me, will allocate jobs in the stable or garden, and Noreen will allocate jobs and supervise you in the house.'

Rachel suddenly felt tired, and a great desire to be alone with her troublesome thoughts. She was certainly unable to deal with any incipient personality clashes between her staff that day. Thus she elected to ignore the challenging glance that slanted between her Irish maid and the youth.

Rachel's solitude was to be short-lived. By two o'clock, Lucinda Saunders was sitting with her in the drawing room. Rachel wasn't surprised to see her. In fact, she had been expecting her sooner. It had been a few days since she and Connor had emerged from his study with the space between them seeming solid with ice.

Rachel knew that her friend had been agog to learn what had occurred to cause such a freeze. Possibly the fact that his lordship also had the mark of her hand imprinted on his lean cheek had fired Lucinda's curiosity.

Paul Saunders had interrupted any leading questions his wife attempted to put to Rachel on the ride home. Every time Lucinda had slid the seat to corner Rachel for a gabbled private whisper, her husband had blandly drawn them into a conversation about the fine music or the delicious buffet they'd enjoyed that evening. He'd remained undaunted by his wife's obvious frustration and speaking looks and Rachel was seen safely indoors at Beaulieu Gardens without having scandalised her friends with any sordid details of what passed between her and Lord Devane. But now Rachel knew that Lucinda would not be put off longer from knowing why Connor had been so determined to speak to her alone that evening.

Lucinda launched straight away into, 'I would have been here yesterday but I felt a trifle breathless. I think the babe is trying to find a comfortable spot; either that or he's training to be a tumbler.' A hand massaged at her abdomen as she eased back in the comfy chair. A crafty look was shot at Rachel from beneath her lashes. 'I hope you're about to indulge in some girlish gossip today. You know I'm just dying to know…'

'Would you bring us some tea, Noreen, please?' Rachel interrupted quickly, noticing that her maid was hesitating by the door to help little Alan range his toys on the table.

'I'll see to it straight away, m'm,' Noreen readily agreed.

Noreen had barely shut the door behind her when Lucinda quickly continued, 'My first thought when Connor took you off alone like that was that he might propose. Paul said he wasn't sure *what* he might propose. I know I'm being too vulgarly inquisitive, Rachel, but we are such good friends. Did he ask you to marry him? Did you reject him again? Is that why you both looked so…so…?'

'Embittered?' Rachel supplied with a twist of her soft lips. Should she reveal the shocking, callous way he had treated her? Did it matter if she did? People everywhere knew of the shocking, callous way she once had treated him. All he wanted was what was fair; he'd mocked her, while taunting her with the deeds to Windrush. So she would be fair…and expose his cruelty as once she had shown the world her own…

'He made me a proposition, Lucinda, not a proposal. Suffice to say that I no longer find the thought of being a kept woman at all appealing, or amusing. It was a mean thing to say about Philip Moncur that day, even in jest, for he's a nice enough gentleman. But then saying and doing stupid things seems to come quite naturally to me, I'm afraid.'

Lucinda finally closed her dropped jaw to burble, 'Lord Devane made an offer to keep you as his *mistress*?'

'Well, not exactly *keep*,' Rachel rebutted wryly. 'He made it clear he is soon to go back to Ireland. He doesn't want a lengthy liaison as I understand it. In fact, I think one night might do.' She felt a spontaneous surge of tears thicken her throat, stealing her voice. Quickly she bent to give Alan a watery smile as he surrounded her feet with soldiers. She lifted him on to her lap, stroked at his silky soft hair. With a deep breath she continued huskily, 'He let me see the deeds to Windrush. They were in a drawer in his desk…just inches from my hand. I could have tried to flee with them. I swear that was what he wanted, simply so he could thwart me in it. You see, he has no wish to keep Windrush himself. If I agree to his terms, he'll give me the deeds before he goes overseas. Or he'll sell the estate. It's my choice. Good of him, don't you think?'

Lucinda flinched at her friend's dulcet bitterness. She put a hand to her mouth. Her eyes were saucer-wide as she stared at Rachel. Abruptly her features settled into easier lines. 'He must mean just to horridly tease you, Rachel. It's a joke,' Lucinda mollified.

'No, it's not; he means to punish me at last. He knows I couldn't bear the thought of strangers having Windrush. Yet, oddly, while he has it I accept things aren't hopeless. I never before realised just how badly he was affected by my jilting him. Of course, I knew it was not nice for him…' She choked a little despairing laugh. 'How feeble that sounds. Of course it was not *nice* for him. Oh, I just mean I never realised before how much he suffered. Really *suffered*. No wonder his stepbrother, Jason, hates me. I'm surprised now his mother was so civil to me. I imagine she knew how terribly low it brought him.' Conscious she'd probably been imprudent in disclosing so much, Rachel requested quietly, 'I'd rather you said nothing of this to *anyone* at the moment. Once June is married and Lord Devane has gone overseas, if you must, then tell Paul.'

'I should not have asked you,' Lucinda wailed. 'I should not have been so prying.' Suddenly brightening, she confided with wrinkled nose, 'I suppose I could prevaricate a bit if Paul asks too soon…' Her conscience clear on that score, she happily resumed the topic. 'Now I understand why you slapped his face! I couldn't credit you would do so just to rebuff a marriage offer. Oh, I can scarce credit it. Connor seems so gentleman-like, so…so…'

'So decent?' Rachel supplied ironically.

'What will you do?'

'Agree, of course.'

Lucinda's round jaw sagged. Back she flopped in her chair. 'You'll *agree*?'

'While I scheme at something else entirely.' Rachel felt family pride again rampage through her, bringing its own relief. Niggling guilt about her own actions were swept aside by a torrent of filial indignation. 'He shan't win in this,' she hissed. 'Had he just insulted me, perhaps I might have accepted it as condign. June and William can be married at Windrush, of that I have his promise…signed and sealed,' she added significantly. She paused, took a calming breath. 'Thereafter I suppose I would have resided here permanently with my parents and Sylvie when Windrush was sold.' An encompassing glance took in the pleasant drawing room, watched the brocade curtains twitch in the mild afternoon air. 'June will, of course, move to William's villa in Richmond, although they talk all the time of buying a country retreat…' She tailed off.

Sorrow for her papa and his meddling plucked at her heart. He had risked being made to look a fool for her. He had put his trust in the morality of a man who would not shrink from abusing that trust. A surge of righteous anger made her blast through her gritted white teeth, 'The arrogant conceit of the brute! He has the gall to say to me that my father intentionally lost Windrush to him because he hoped it would throw me back in his path. He actually said he intends to foil my father's plan to make him revive our betrothal! There will be no happy ending, the egotistical devil told me.

As though *I* would deem a hateful *mésalliance* with him as a happy ending! It is too much that he also spites my papa! When I *think* how well my father liked him. He still *does* like him. Papa has no idea Connor mocks him behind his back! Oh, where on earth is Noreen with that tea!' Rachel exploded in a stifled cry as she jumped to her feet.

She swished to open the door, only to spy her maid further along the corridor, just disappearing in a busy rustle of starched, white cotton, through the arch that lead to the kitchens below. Rachel sighed on a frown, wondering what errand had superseded her request for tea. She sorely needed some refreshment and some distraction.

Noreen slammed the heavy kettle on to the hob. Wafer-thin porcelain, silver spoons, sugar and cream jugs were all assembled quickly, deftly, without her once raising her eyes above table height. Her mouth was pursed to stop her lips trembling. Her eyes blinked rapidly to disperse the wetness. It wasn't sadness, it was God's own wrath, she promised herself as the hot prickling behind her eyes became unbearable. Quickly she cuffed at it.

Sam Smith placed down the fork he'd buffed to a whitish gloss. He picked up another, turned it this way and that in front of his face while his eyes slid past the utensil to his supervisor. If she was aware of him, seated at the far end of the scrubbed pine table, polishing silver, she gave no sign. The cups and saucers were shuffled aimlessly about on the tray again as she glared at the kettle. Sam knew she was already willing it to steam so she could make the tea and be gone.

'Vera and Bernard are gone out to her sisters along

the street. She's ailing bad, so Vera says. But she'll be back in time to get the dinner on the go. Annie finished dusting the parlour and morning room while you was gone. I told her to start upstairs…'

Noreen nodded wordless acceptance of this mundane information. Nothing much penetrated her misery, her despair. *Handsome prince!* she scoffed at herself beneath her breath, a sob of bubbling rage lodged in her chest. He was the villain of the piece. The ogre. The devil incarnate. And serve her right for knowing it. Eavesdropping was a sure way to learn of disaster.

Abruptly she grabbed the sputtering kettle, tipped it in a clumsy motion and gave a little yelp as she received a small scald from a splash of boiling water.

Sam got up from his stool and came over to her. 'Show me what you've done to y'self…'

Noreen ripped her stinging hand from the comfort of his. 'Don't be after doing that. Mother Mary! I've had worse damage than that…'

Sam grasped her hand again, fended off the other as it made to knock him away. He looked into Noreen's rapidly blinking eyes, watched her quivering lips compress into a tight line. The angry weal was barely discernible on an already work-roughened red thumb. 'T'ain't that bad, you're right,' he said. 'Not bad enough to make a tough old bird cry, anyhow. Did you catch a worse roasting off the mistress over summat?'

Noreen glared at him through an increasing blur in her eyes. 'No, but you will, I'm thinking, if you don't keep your thoughts and your hands to y'self.'

Sam let her go; went to sit back down at the table. He picked up a spoon, polished it slowly, with long strong strokes. 'Vinegar's sweeter 'n you are, Noreen

Shaughnessy. What was it happened to you to make you so sour? Lose a man, did you?'

Noreen stared at him. Then she laughed, hysterically, throwing back her ginger head and swiping at her eyes again. 'So like a man, I'm thinking. Anything wrong with a woman's life, it must be a big strong man let her down. I don't need a man. Never have done. And I told you before, it's none of a stripling's sympathy I'm needing.'

'It's none of a stripling's sympathy you're getting,' Sam countered quietly. He studied her over the gleaming spoon, continued looking even when she challenged him with fierce bloodshot eyes.

'So you've not got a sweetheart waiting for you back in Hertfordshire. Windrush is the Merediths' estate, ain't it?'

'It was…' Noreen said, a strange caustic note honeying her brogue. *But it's not lost yet, is what I'm thinking,* she told herself, nodding.

Sam was attending every mutter and gesture, so she added quickly, 'I got a sister back there. To be sure, that's enough plucking at me heartstrings that I need. She's more'n enough family for me.' With an air of finality, she clattered the tea things on to the tray.

'What's her name?'

'Mary.'

'Younger 'n you?'

Noreen failed to respond, but cursed irritation below her breath.

'Problem, is she?'

'What's it to you?'

'Nothing. I've got a sister of me own gives me enough problems.'

'My sister don't do tail-trading, if you're about to see them as alike.'

'Neither does mine,' Sam said, his voice cold.

'You're thinking I'm a fool, then?' Noreen mocked. 'A pretty young thing gets put off by that godforsaken villain when she toils like the devil snaps at her heels? He's tipped you out and on to us, before Annie loses that sweet shape and folk get to knowing he's the one swole her belly.'

'You're thinking wrong. She ain't carrying and he ain't a godforsaken villain. Lord Devane's a good man.'

'Is he now?' Noreen queried silkily. 'We'll see…' She turned away to attend to the tea. Insouciantly she remarked, 'Shame she ain't a pro. Girl looks like Annie could put you both in Swell Street, I'm thinking.'

'Shame 'ud be if she were a pro,' Sam curtly returned. 'She's a good girl. She'll stay that way. She'll stay fed and clothed and decent, for as long as I do.'

Noreen raised her eyes to look at him. 'Where's your ma and pa?'

'Dead.'

'Mine too.'

'Thought so. Just you and Mary, then, is it? No other kin?'

'Is it me family tree you're after getting?' Noreen asked sarcastically.

'No; an' it's not lifting your skirts I'm after either, if that's what you're thinking.'

Noreen dropped the tray back to the table. Her face flushed crimson, her mouth fell open, but no tongue-lashing could force past her dazed shock.

'Yeah…I do mean what you think. You think I'm just after putting you on your back, don't you, Noreen

Shaughnessy? Well, let me tell you, I might be a bit brash and I might talk a bit bawdy, but if I want a tumble I can go straight back to Whitechapel and take a fancy I know who don't bristle like a cornered cat every time I look her way.'

Noreen made an agitated attempt to straighten cups and saucers and mop milk from the tray. 'You go back there then. Find yourself a little girl to play with. Sure and you're never old enough for a real woman, anyhow. You're not a man, you're just a kid.'

Sam smiled, then he laughed, with quiet male satisfaction. 'She's not a little girl. Men as like little girls make me sick…make me sick to my stomach. She's a woman…older 'n you, I'd guess. But I saw you a week ago and I'm looking now. You're what I want, heaven help me if I know why. I'm man enough for you, Noreen Shaughnessy…and you know it…'

Chapter Thirteen

I assume that you have in mind a suitable venue to consummate the happy event. Please let me know where and when, and at the risk of being too indelicately eager, might it be soon? Early settlement of the transaction would be appreciated, if for no other reason than it will hasten my going home and your going overseas.

Connor read again the acerbic few sentences set out in neat ladylike script. She hated him and she wanted him to know it. Her despising was couched in every prettily formed word. It was in her refusal to begin with the courtesy of an address to him or finish by signing even one of her initials. He was beneath contempt. Yet she would acquiesce. Like hell she would.

He folded the consent to her ravishment, recently delivered with pomp on a silver salver by Joseph Walsh. A laugh scraped at his throat at that absurdity. He slumped back in his chair and closed his weary eyes.

'What's funny?'

'Nothing. Nothing at all.'

Jason Davenport prowled aimlessly about the room.

By the magnificent mantel he stopped, gave the Irish wolfhound posted over it a glare. Two fingers prised his superbly folded cravat from his perspiring neck as, indignantly, he looked through the windows at a late afternoon in May that was unremittingly hot and still. He abruptly tipped a shot of whiskey into a glass in irritation. 'Just five hundred then…till next month when my allowance is due…'

'No.'

'You're a tight-fisted bastard. I know for a fact you won fifteen hundred last night at White's. Harley made a point of telling me. He's still steaming over losing Meredith's estate to you, you know.'

'Yes, I know,' Connor said distantly, gazing at him over a steeple of tanned fingers.

'Was it Harley instigated the rumour you'd been bedding the Smith girl under your own roof?' Jason asked with casual interest.

'No. But he quite cheerfully backed it once it was up and running.'

'Where have you hidden them? I've not seen sweet Annie or her brother in days.' Jason grimaced a look of genuine alarm at Connor. 'God! There wasn't any truth in it, Con, was there? You haven't set her up somewhere in Cheapside? She's just a baby. Mind you, if she still looks as delectable in a few years' time, I might be interested in taking her on myself…' His voice, one eyelid, lewdly lowered.

Connor propped his fists on the edge of the desk. Slowly he pushed himself to his feet. 'Jason…do me…and you…a good turn. Remove yourself from my sight for a while, there's a good fellow, before I see you across the street with the toe of my boot.'

'Three hundred?' Jason hastily changed subject, apparently deaf to his stepbrother's threat to summarily eject him. 'How can I show my face at the Palm House without a penny to my name? I'll look a fool, starting straight off with markers.'

Connor shrugged, turned him a classic profile as he gazed into his garden. 'I think, Jason, you mistake me for a person who cares a damn about your credibility.' He suddenly speared a steely blue stare at his stepbrother. 'You've not approached your father again for money…have you?'

Jason cleared his throat with whiskey. 'I said I wouldn't,' he gasped hoarsely as the liquor stung. He paused reflectively, 'I know your stables are overstocked…I've a rather nice set of silver ice pails just come into my possession, taken from Frank Cornwallis following a rubber of whist. They're corkers! I'd say they'd look pretty good in a house like this. They set me back the money he couldn't find. At just two hundred and fifty they're a bargain.'

Connor gave him a smile. Lengthy black lashes screened the afternoon glare as he debated whether to kick him out anyway or suggest they go and find a couple of obliging jades and stay drunk until dawn.

He slumped back into his chair and slowly unfolded the paper. It didn't read any sweeter third time around. He jerked open a drawer in his desk, dropped in Rachel's note. He was about to close it again when the stone sparked sunbeams. Without removing it from where it nestled, concealed amongst parchment, a dark thumb brushed the sapphire's faceted surface. Why he'd removed it from the jeweller's box in the safe where it had reposed, feeling the need to look at it, he'd no idea. But now with slow deliberation he found a loose end of red ribbon binding the deeds to

Windrush then threaded it through the ring's golden shank and tied it. He smiled at the rank symbolism in what he'd done, then with a curse slammed shut the drawer.

His head bowed, supported by massaging fingers sunk deep in his glossy ebony hair. He must have been insane to have started this, for he hadn't the vaguest idea now how to bring it to a dignified close without looking every sort of idiot. Did that matter? She already thought him every sort of idiot.

Perhaps he should ask Rachel if she had any ideas how they could put this interlude behind them and carry on with their lives as though they'd never again met and engaged in such pointless, hurting vitriol. It was ironic: but for that blasted incident with the carriages jamming the street he might never have seen her. He might have made it home to Ireland in blissful ignorance of the soulful, indomitable woman she'd become. Hardly, he mocked himself, her father would have made it his business to ensure that their paths crossed at least once before he escaped. He was an astute father who knew his daughter. The man understood him, too…too well for comfort.

Rachel had always been a fashionable beauty. Now, her elegant sophistication was hardened with a grit she used to veil an increasing vulnerability. The melancholy she felt over Isabel was quite apparent to those who loved her; and it was likely to pluck at the heart of a man who'd once cherished her as much as he had.

She was unpopular. She'd outraged the *beau monde* by jilting him on a whim and so tardy it was scandalous. But it was failing to show proper humility, to beg forgiveness, that made those people so pitiless in their displeasure. No matter that she faced the world with a credible air of insouciance, being disliked wounded her…added to her distress.

At nineteen she had been surrounded by friends, showered with countless social invitations. She was accepted now into company under the umbrella of a family outing, but it was only the Saunders who welcomed her for herself. She could look quite isolated in a crush of people. The poignancy of watching her concealing her unhappiness on the Pembertons' stairway, even now, clawed at his insides.

But Rachel was too proud to feign amnesia over past slights to snatch herself a companion. Her aunt Chamberlain's specious cordiality had disgusted her, and he knew he'd played a part in it. Had he not been accompanying Rachel she might have remained ignored by the woman. Perhaps that was just something else she resented: his power and influence, his celebrity. And to him it was nothing against having her respect…having her…

What he had instead was her permission to take her to bed for one night of coerced lovemaking.

'All your moody moping about is to do with that blonde baggage, the Meredith woman, isn't it?' Jason slurred into Connor's reverie, emboldened by the alcohol he'd steadily consumed and peeved that his bargaining for cash was being ignored.

Jason was barely aware Connor was out of his chair, but he certainly knew of the one-handed vice constricting his throat.

'Be careful…be very careful, Jason, what you say next,' his stepbrother threatened through touching teeth. 'And while you're listening carefully: I'm sick to death of you and your selfish spendthrift ways. Your father's ailing…possibly due to you worrying the life from him. My mother's an unhappy woman…because she's anxious over her husband's health.'

Abruptly he released his brother's neck as he noticed Jason's complexion turning puce. He backed off, offered two broad palms in conciliation. 'Just be careful, Jason, what you say. That's all.'

Jason massaged his crushed windpipe. He gulped a nervous laugh. 'Steady, Con,' he wheezed. 'I only said it to rile you. For all our sakes, get it done, will you? Reinstate the blasted betrothal; it's what you want and she's not now so silly as to reject an earl at her age.'

The depleted decanter shattering into pieces in the vacant grate let Jason know that possibly his stepbrother had a different perspective on things.

'I'll never ever get engaged again,' Connor told him with a smile that scintillated devilishly.

Jason retreated circumspectly from the frustrated man barely a yard away. In his white linen shirt, cuffs shoved back to display sinewy brown forearms, and with his raven locks long, unkempt, framing dark savage features, Connor looked as perilous as a Barbary pirate fired with blood-lust.

Jason shrugged carelessly. He put a hand to check his cravat and an end of cloth came loose in his hand.

'Sorry,' Connor condoled. 'It must have taken you some time to perfect that work of art.'

Jason unwound it slowly. 'Too damned hot for it anyhow.' He grinned, shoving the luxurious bandage in to a pocket. 'Pax, then?'

Connor grimaced wry agreement.

'Fancy a night at Mrs Crawford's? I'll forgo the Palm House until I've a bit more blunt.'

'Sure, why go with a little when you can take your whole allowance and lose the lot,' Connor remarked drily on turning to the large casement window. It was gripped at with tense long-fingered hands and he stared sightlessly over his gardens.

'Don't lecture, Con. You're in no position. When I think what fantastic tales I've heard about you at eighteen! God! You were a veritable bandit!' Jason said in awe and admiration.

'True…but you're not eighteen, Jason. You're twenty-six, by my reckoning.'

'I'm just off to see Cornwallis,' Jason hastily said, unsettled by that fact. 'He reckons he's got a sweet nag running on Epsom Heath tomorrow at two o'clock.' He slipped out of the study door, shaking his head, his handsome countenance creased in disgust. Love! He swore effusively beneath his breath. He'd sooner gamble his life away! At least you stood a chance of winning…

He stalked the marble hallway, his footsteps echoing eerily. He'd find Cornwallis, and a way of pawning him back his silver ice pails. A snip at two hundred pounds…

'How are you settling in here at Beaulieu Gardens, Sam?'

'Well enough, m'm, thank you.'

From her position seated at the small escritoire by the window, Rachel looked at the young man she had summoned to the morning room. He stood before her politely, respectfully. 'You have found the work environment…harmonious?'

'Yes, m'm. Noreen…er…Miss Shaughnessy is very fair with the chores.'

Rachel watched, interestedly, as a ruddiness stained the youth's cheeks. 'And your sister Annie is happy?'

'She likes it here very much, m'm. She and No-reen...er...she and Miss Shaughnessy get along right well.'

'Noreen has already said Annie works very consci-entiously and that she has some aptitude for sewing. Noreen's sister also is an accomplished needle-worker.'

'Noreen's mighty proud of Mary's lace work. Be all accounts it's better'n what some fancy Frenchie can do,' Sam boldly recounted on a wide smile. He grew quiet on noticing his mistress's amused surprise.

'Noreen has cause to be very proud of Mary. I think she's probably justified in her comments, too,' Rachel said, realising the overweening Madame Bouillon's handiwork had obviously come under her maid's crit-ical eye.

Of course, it was heartening to know that her rather cool maidservant was warming to her new colleagues enough to divulge some of her family background. A trenchant look settled on Sam. He was quite a strapping lad and, if a little immature of countenance, still quite appealing. Perhaps Noreen thought so too... Quickly she reigned in her galloping thoughts. 'You are not missing your last position in Berkeley Square, then?'

'Not as much as I thought I would, m'm.'

'If I recall correctly...were you not driving a dray when first I saw you? I believe your vehicle locked wheels with a hackney cab near Charing Cross?'

'The jarvey's rig caught on to my uncle's wagon,' Sam bluntly corrected. 'He were trying to push ahead; wouldn't wait his turn in the queue. You told him so. I thought you were right brave to speak up to that slimy...to his worship Arthur Goodwin.'

Rachel was aware of the antipathetic sneer in his tone as he referred to the magistrate. She gave a little smile. 'Well, that answers my next question. I was just about to enquire whether you recalled the incident.'

'Oh, I do,' Sam said, nodding significantly. 'I ain't ever going to forget it.'

'It has made such an impression, I suppose, because you met Lord Devane there. Afterwards, did you seek him out to employ you and Annie?'

'I did,' Sam admitted proudly. 'I make no bones about saying that I hoped I'd see him again. I reckoned him a particular gentleman that day for helping. So when I spotted him coming out of a posh house…' Sam hesitated, remembering the fancy piece who'd been hanging on to his neck that night. He cleared his throat. 'I saw him and said as we'd be honoured and glad to serve him. I knew Annie 'ud be safe and happy with such a master. Then he put us off…' A spontaneous look of disappointment corrugated his features but he continued jauntily, 'And I was grateful he took the trouble to place us with such a fine lady as yourself.'

Rachel inclined her blonde head in gracious acceptance of the compliment, feeling churlish, for she'd certainly not wanted them here at first. Mainly she was pondering on how she could steer the conversation to what she really wanted to discover about the *particular gentleman*. 'You must have become used to a steady routine in such a grand house.'

'Yes, m'm.'

Rachel smiled, took a golden ringlet soft on her cheek and twirled it about her finger. 'The master…Lord Devane…probably kept you to a routine…to coincide with his own. Did he dine at home most evenings?' she asked with a casual look about.

'Yes, m'm, I think…'

'But you're not sure?'

'Not really…'

'And is he usually to be found at home, for a while, after dinner?'

'Most evenings, I think… Well, not Wednesday. I know he would regular go out quite early on a Wednesday, with his brother, Mr Davenport, in that flash curricle.'

'Wednesday… Today's Wednesday,' Rachel remarked faintly.

'It is, m'm,' Sam concurred, with a searching look that transformed into a frown.

Rachel recognised his burgeoning conjecture. 'Good, I'm glad you are settled here,' she briskly said. 'Although I'm not able to definitely offer you a permanent position in Hertfordshire—that will need to be agreed with my father—if it comes about, it seems we will deal well together.' With a small smile and a nod she lowered her eyes. 'Thank, you, Sam. You may return to your duties.'

As Rachel heard the door close she squeezed shut her eyes. Today! If she was to do it at all, she *must* do it today! Or wait a week. She could not! She must return home. June's wedding day would soon be upon them. Her mother would be wondering what on earth she was about to stay away at such a vital time.

Connor had had her consent to spend the night with him, but she had yet to receive an answer as to where to go and when. She imagined such clandestine affairs were conducted at isolated spots out of town: possibly a hunting lodge, or a cottage or a country inn—for obviously they could not cohabit at either of their residences. She now knew he'd had improper liaisons, so he would be experienced in arranging discreet trysts. She was confident he would think her submission genuine. *You want Windrush more than anything, don't you?* he had mocked her. And she had readily agreed. He thought he had her bested. It would be seen who was bested when the game was done! And it seemed it would be done tonight.

She knew the layout of his house now; she knew exactly how to find his drawing room, his library, his study from the hallway. She knew exactly where the deeds were kept: in a desk, in a drawer, opened with a key that had a rather pretty Sévres inkstand as a repository.

She knew his butler too. Joseph Walsh knew her and had seen the Earl pay her particular attention. Whatever the man thought of that privately, publicly he now treated her with the deference due to one of his master's close acquaintances. And the fact that Lord Devane *had* paid her such particular attention at the Pembertons' *musicale* and again at his own soirée, must lend a certain authenticity to her story.

When she returned home with the deeds to Windrush and a tale that her former fiancé had taken pity on her and presented her with her inheritance as a parting gift before he went overseas, who would deem it utterly implausible or incredible? Many distinguished, respectable people had witnessed him seek her out and stay with her—including his parents. He had voiced to her aunt Phyllis his intention to be back in Ireland very soon; disposing of Windrush quickly and effortlessly before he went might not seem such odd behaviour in the circumstances. Parting with it in such a magnanimous, if eccentric, way might not either. He was rich, he had no use for it, and as everyone was wont to impress on her, from serving lads to her own papa, he was an honourable generous man… *'And so say all of us,'* she found herself quietly, hysterically chanting in morbid glee. It might be a simple scheme, but she couldn't see a problem with it being a success…

'Sweet Jesus! Tell me again exactly what she said,' Noreen whispered, gazing up anxiously into Sam's face. She drew him to one side in the kitchen, away from where Vera was rolling pastry on a floury table. The woman was stone deaf, but Noreen knew it was vital to prevent this news being overheard or spread about.

She had never imagined just how important it would prove to be, tarrying to pick up one of the little lad's soldiers from the floor in the hallway on the day Mrs Saunders came for tea with the mistress. At first she'd wished she'd never overheard one word. Now she was grateful she'd been intrigued enough after a moment or two to snoop long enough to hear it all.

'Be still,' Sam ordered Noreen, who was jigging agitatedly on the spot. His callused fingertips soothingly abraded her forearm. 'Miss Meredith wanted to know when Lord Devane is likely to be gone from home. 'Course she didn't say it quite like that. She tried to make out she was more likely to want to catch him in. As if she might drop by and visit him, like…'

'She wants him *out* of the house, is what I'm thinking.'

I could have snatched it up and fled. I swear he wanted me to. Just so he could thwart me in it… The words reverberated in Noreen's suspicious mind. Miss Rachel wanted Himself elsewhere so he *couldn't* thwart her in it! 'Can I trust you?' Her anxious eyes scoured Sam's face. No man in her twenty-five years had ever treated her the way he did, with a desire and a deference that made her feel at the same time fragile as glass yet strong as an ox.

'If you need to ask, perhaps you can't,' he returned shortly.

'There's things you don't know about the mistress and that blackhearted divil.'

'Don't say so about him. He's a good man…'

'There's things you don't know! Isn't it meself's heard the truth about him from Miss Rachel's own lips?' she hissed. She threw a chary look at the old woman still making a pie. 'So, before I tell you all about it, what I'm after finding out—*are* you man enough for me, Sam Smith? Will you trust *me* when I tell you God's own truth? Will you do what I'm wanting you to do? For if she's planning what I think she's planning and it goes wrong… Mother Mary! It'll ruin things as will never be put right. Not for her…not for her sisters. And Miss June soon to be a bride!'

The silence seemed long, too long. Noreen's pleading eyes fell from the strength of consideration in his. She gathered her uniform in her trembling fists and made to sweep proudly past.

His answer came in one unconditional word. 'Yes.'

'Miss Meredith!'

As the elegantly attired blonde woman smiled at him and inclined her lovely head in greeting, Joseph Walsh immediately ushered her into the hallway. He'd taken a ticking off last time from his master for not showing this woman liberal hospitality and he didn't intend repeating his mistake by keeping her waiting any longer on the doorstep.

After that bizarre incident when she'd arrived looking oddly dishevelled and belligerent, he had made it

his discreet business to discover a little about Miss
Meredith. Now he knew that this lady and Connor
Flinte had once been betrothed, and from the way the
man acted when she was about, Joseph wouldn't at all
be surprised to soon see them as a couple once more.
Thus he refused to ponder on whether the lady thought
it wise to test her appeal or her reputation by again
arriving alone and unexpected at her admirer's residence.

'Lord Devane desires my company,' Miss Meredith
brightly, nonchalantly declared, thus reinstating the
butler's nonplussed expression. 'Are my friends, Mr
and Mrs Saunders, yet arrived?' she added to Joseph's
amazement.

The butler coughed, struggled admirably for composure. 'Why, no, Miss Meredith. As far as I'm aware
they're not...*expected*?' he ventured. 'Lord Devane is
not...er...presently at home...' he told her with a finger
at his lips and a deepening frown, as though fretting
that he must have mistaken or forgotten some instruction from his employer. A sudden idea occurred to him,
causing an abrupt elevation of his peppery eyebrows:
perhaps the fault lay with Lord Devane. A prior arrangement might have slipped his lordship's mind. He
might have succumbed to routine—or pressure from his
stepbrother—and gone carousing as was customary on
Wednesday. That thought was given tenability by the
fact that, unusually, both gentlemen, not just the
younger, were inebriated by six of the clock when they
had quit the house and sped away in that racing curricle.

Thus Joseph didn't quite know how to tell this
lovely, soft-eyed woman that it seemed she'd been
stood up because the Earl of Devane was too drunk to

remember he'd invited her or her friends to call. Hastily he reminded himself that dealing with such trials and tribulations as the Quality felt entitled to wreak was part and parcel of the duties of any butler worth his salt. With an air of confidence, he reassured her, 'I'm persuaded he might soon return…' In his mind, Joseph already had volunteered one of the footmen to scour the likeliest haunts for sight of his master's unmistakable equipage gracing a seedy kerb.

'Might I wait?' Rachel indicated the hallway chair where she had sat before. That occasion seemed aeons ago, so much had occurred in the interim.

'But of course! Come along to the rose salon and find a comfortable chair,' Joseph told her solicitously. 'That pretty room is a favourite with Lady Davenport,' he politely imparted on leading her to a door along the echoing corridor. 'When Mr and Mrs Saunders arrive I shall have them join you. I'll fetch some tea…'

'No! Please don't trouble yourself, Joseph,' Rachel cried quickly. 'I have not long ago dined,' she sweetly added in mitigation to her blunt refusal of refreshment. If her scheme was to have a chance of success, she needed to be left alone, not have him rejoin her after an unknown interval.

With a polite bow Joseph was again by the door. As it closed after his retreating figure, Rachel gripped at the pink-cushioned, gilt-framed chair behind and stiffly lowered herself into it. For a moment nothing registered other than dazed relief at actually having got inside on such a flimsy pretext. She had done it! 'Please don't ever let Joseph get into bad trouble for admitting me,' was the next thought that emerged prayer-like through her quivering lips.

Her fingers clenched on the golden chair arms, slid-

ing damply. Obliquely she realised just how much in
shock she was. Her heart was hammering so fast and
hard beneath her ribs that she was amazed the butler
hadn't noticed her quaking and become suspicious
enough to expose her straight away as a fraud. She put
a hand against the satin-covered spot beneath a rounded
breast, pressed it as though to forcibly constrain the
vibration rocking her fingers. She breathed deeply to
calm herself.

Encouragingly she reminded herself that she might
have been economical with the facts, but not once had
she actually told a lie to Joseph to gain admittance. His
master *did* desire her company, the lustful brute, and
she had only enquired whether the Saunders had arrived, not that she expected them to do so.

Thank goodness poor Joseph had been too flum-
moxed by it all to directly ask whether she was invited.
On the periphery of her nervous exhilaration, content-
ment registered: Joseph had unequivocally accepted her
right to be here. Lord Devane's interest in her, his patronage, *were* common knowledge.

Suddenly her environment intruded on her thoughts.
She took a swift, encompassing look about the perfectly proportioned square room. It was indeed
pretty…feminine…with its dusky-pink drapes and fur-
nishings and the thick creamy rug that spilled over the
floorboards, stopping short of the wainscoting so that
a narrow perimeter of polished wood was displayed.
The furniture was fashioned from rich red mahogany:
dainty long-legged pieces that complemented the
room's elegance. That was the most admiration she lavished on her sumptuous surroundings.

All her intelligence was then devoted to preparing
for the work in hand. She would wait a few more

minutes; give Joseph Walsh time to go about his duties before she dared put a foot back into the corridor. She must perfectly time her sortie for there would be one chance only to achieve what she'd set out to do.

She had chosen her clothing carefully. Her gown was of a sombre night-blue sarsenet, her stole, black lace. She hoped the sun would soon fully set, for the duskier it became the less likely she was to be spotted darting along the corridors. Not that she wanted it dim enough for the servants to be scurrying about lighting tapers. Should she be discovered roaming the house, her audacious escapade must be aborted and her store of excuses delved into.

She shied away from such a predicament, determined to remain positive and optimistic. She looked at the clock on the wall. Twenty minutes past eight. It was still quite light outside although the last sunbeams had disappeared. In fact, it was a beautiful early summer evening. Through the open fanlights she could hear a chorus of blackbirds piping in the dusk, sense a balmy air soft on her skin. For a moment the mesmerising movement of billowing pink velvet held her attention.

Sharply rallying her thoughts, she quickly darted out of the chair and gained the door on noiseless feet. She pressed an ear close to the panels. There was no sound but the fast pump of her own blood deafening her. One small hand slid clammily about the massive brass knob and noiselessly eased open the door an inch...then another...then another, until she had a clear view of the vestibule and was confident it was vacant.

On the point of slipping through the aperture, she suddenly heard footsteps and male voices. Hastily she shrank back and pushed the door into the frame until just a gap of an inch or two remained.

Joseph Walsh and a liveried footman were walking in the direction of the great doorway as though having emerged from the bowels of the house. The footman appeared to be listening to Joseph's explicit instructions then, with a final nod, he was on his way out of the house. Suddenly Rachel knew why. Of course! The butler, confused by his master's odd absence when he had guests, would try and find him to alert him to the oversight and bring him home.

Rachel screwed up her lovely face in alarm and exasperation. Closing the door fully, she leaned back against it, thinking...thinking...

Logically, it would be some little while before Lord Devane's whereabouts was located. There was still time. She must simply act without delay.

Having waited, heart in mouth, the few minutes she calculated it would take Joseph to disappear towards the kitchens, Rachel again opened the door a crack.

She was wrong! Joseph hadn't disappeared at all. This time the sight that greeted her drained the colour from her face and a sharp indrawn breath grazed her throat. She watched, stunned, through the minute opening as the butler pushed the great door closed having just admitted a new arrival. Joseph would, of course, know this man, for a short while ago they had been work colleagues...

Sam Smith and Joseph Walsh were conversing amiably as they strolled in the direction of the rose salon and thus missed the moment the door clicked fully shut.

Rachel waited tensely, straining to anticipate the moment those cracking footsteps would stop and the door would open. The uneven tattoo drumming on marble came closer…closer…then passed, faded away. She remained perched on the edge of the gilt chair, her fingers clenched on its brocade seat. She sat statue-like for some minutes, barely breathing or thinking; just expecting to hear the beating feet again as the men returned to confront her.

After several minutes of echoing silence, the first anxiety that burrowed into her numb mind was that Sam Smith might be here to alert her to some disaster or other that had occurred in her absence at Beaulieu Gardens. As her logic stirred, she dismissed it. If that were the case they would have entered the room. And, anyway, none of her servants knew she was here. She had deemed it prudent to keep this visit to Lord Devane's residence strictly to herself. The fewer people involved in this night's work, the better it must be. A hackney cab had brought her here and she intended returning with her booty in the same manner.

Why should Sam Smith not visit his old colleagues? He had made it clear he enjoyed his time working at this house. He and Joseph looked quite gregarious, as though they enjoyed a chat. He was on the staff at Beaulieu Gardens now, but once Sam's chores were done for the day, what remained of his time was his own to spend where and with whom he would. It was just a bizarre coincidence that tonight of all nights he should choose to pay a visit to the house his new mistress was intending to rob.

Rachel's eyes darted to the mahogany clock in the corner. The time was approaching fifteen minutes to nine. She must make a move; revive her courage and carry out her mission, or take the coward's way and slink away home.

Determinedly, she again approached the door and opened it a crack. She placed a foot outside, then, muttering in frustration, withdrew it almost immediately as she heard indistinct male voices shouting from somewhere in the depths of the house. Was she never to be out of this accursed room! Through the small gap Rachel frowned despairingly at the hallway, but could see nothing although the commotion seemed to be increasing in volume. Other voices were joining the babble, both male and female, until the whole house seemed a swelling cacophony.

Rachel stood petrified to the spot, a mixture of hysteria and curiosity racing through her as she watched liveried servants converging on the hallway from all directions. A pair of whispering maidservants sped past her fractionally open door, sending a draught to cool her feverish skin. In amongst the voices shouting loudest she recognised both Joseph Walsh's faint Irish intonation and Sam Smith's abrasive cockney.

And then she realised why she could hear her own servant's protestations above so many of the others. He was under arrest! She could see him quite clearly now, held by two burly footmen with Joseph apparently giving him a good scolding. The middle-aged butler's arms were waving about, then one of his hands suddenly formed a fist that was shaken menacingly close to Sam's face.

Rachel opened the door wider, placed a foot outside. Quickly she slipped through the aperture, shut the door silently behind her, cutting off her retreat.

Why on earth were they setting about Sam? was the first thought to penetrate her daze. Why was nothing ever simple? was the second. The third had her taking a circumspect look about. Whatever it was Sam had done, he had quite spectacularly created a diversion that could only help her...if she chose to make use of it.

With a deep, inspiriting breath, and one last glance at the mass of black uniforms milling in the hallway, she flew in the opposite direction.

Chapter Fourteen

'Miss Meredith! I've been searching for you!'

Rachel swiftly stepped back from the open drawer, just curbing a guilty impulse to slam it shut. Instinctively she concealed the gun by gripping it in both hands behind her. On legs that felt boneless, she walked away from the massive mahogany desk to demurely face Joseph Walsh.

Joseph shook his head in regret. 'You have heard the awful commotion and come to investigate. It is a strange coincidence indeed that I've discovered you here, where it started.'

'I…I certainly heard a commotion. It started in *this* room?' Rachel managed to casually converse, even though her mind was racing now as fast as her heart.

Joseph strode closer to her, an assiduous look softening his frown. 'Little wonder you were alarmed enough to go exploring. The chaos the rogue has caused! He tried to escape. But now Weekes and Crewe—two of my strongest, fittest footmen—have him safely apprehended. You need not fret that we still have a criminal on the loose beneath our roof.' Suddenly Joseph's expression was utter dismay. 'Heavens! Was it not yourself, Miss Meredith, who was good enough to employ Samuel Smith and his sister when they left here? And I furnished them with such glowing characters to take with them! Lord Devane will be furious, knowing he has introduced to a friend such felons. Although I can't too hastily besmirch the girl's character. *She* might be honest.'

'What do you mean...*felons*?' Rachel whispered, although a horrifying inkling was already in her brain as her eyes darted unbidden to the empty drawer she had so vainly rifled. When she had surreptitiously slipped into the room she had realised straight away that something was amiss. The drawer was already unlocked and pulled out a little way, the key still in the escutcheon, and all that reposed within was the fancy pistol she had stupidly removed to facilitate her fingers searching the rear of the receptacle. Now she had the weapon still clutched behind her back and no chance of replacing it without arousing Joseph's suspicion.

'Samuel Smith has repaid his lordship's kindness, his generosity in giving him and his sister honest employment, by returning to rob him! He wheedled his way in by saying he wanted to collect a forgotten item of clothing for his sister. I have to say I was suspicious. We had not come across even one stocking of Annie's left behind. I thought I'd give him rope enough to hang himself. I let him go alone to fetch what he wanted while carefully observing him. I caught him slipping from the scene of the crime concealing his lordship's possessions.'

Miss Meredith visibly winced and blanched at that news, inducing the butler to sympathetically say, 'Alas, I can see how that has affected you, ma'am, and no surprise. You're fretting that perhaps your own home is no longer secure. Even as we speak the sister might be filching your own valuables.'

'What did he take?'

The sharp query sounded like impertinence but the accompanying sob-like breath from the lady stirred Joseph's pity. Miss Meredith was obviously in shock, and, with one of the iniquitous brood beneath her own roof, entitled to know what sort of swag might interest a family of thieves. 'Smith had in his pocket legal documents and a gem. A magnificent ring, taken from right there!' A finger shot out to indicate the empty drawer. While his eyes were trained dramatically on the spot too, Rachel hastily turned aside, relieving her cramped, aching hands of the gun by slinging it into her reticule.

'Ring?' she croaked once the concealment was accomplished.

'A sapphire enclosed with diamonds. Quite wonderful…' was all the man imparted as though still much in awe of it.

'And where are they now? The missing items?' Her attitude was far too brusque. But controlling her voice or her body seemed beyond her capability. She was quivering from head to foot. She could feel her frozen lips trembling even as the brittle words tumbled out. A million fantastic thoughts seemed to whirl in her head of why Sam was here and why he had stolen the deeds before she could. Was it possible that he had also taken a ring that sounded so very much like the one Connor had given her on their betrothal six years ago? *Was* Sam a thief? Had his prime target been the jewel and he had simply taken the document, too, because it was to hand? How could she feel righteous? What depths had she sunk to in her obsessive need to get what she wanted, if not common thievery? Had Sam left the document behind, *she* would have attempted to smuggle it from the room. Farcically, she instead found herself forced to appropriate his lordship's weapon.

Her answer came simply, wandering into her stormy thoughts to becalm them. Sam was not a thief…he was her guardian angel. Suddenly she knew, almost certainly, that he had done it for her…to protect her. Somehow he had discovered her plan and valiantly tried to save her from her own scheming.

At that moment an agitated maidservant burst in, drawing the attention of both the room's occupants. The girl's saucer-round eyes gawked at her superior before she allowed herself some sliding peeks at the beautiful stranger with him. 'Pardon me, Mr Walsh, but Mr Weekes says as the constable is arrived and that the magistrate is coming too, fast behind him.'

Joseph nodded at the girl and with a sketched curtsy she was gone in an excited rustle of black and white cloth.

Joseph held out a reassuring hand to Rachel. 'There! The authorities are even now taking charge. I can see how distraught you are, Miss Meredith. But all will be well, I promise. Lord Devane will soon be back to attend to the matter. Smith has been caught red-handed and must be punished. The items you were asking about are quite safe. They are put securely by as evidence.' He gave her a kindly look. 'I understand how anxious you must be to get home and check on Annie Smith and your own belongings. You need only say and I shall have one of the footmen immediately hail you a cab.'

Rachel's stiff lips stretched in an approximation of a smile but she felt simultaneous tears of forlorn frustration prick her eyelids. She had risked all, yet mean fate had allowed her nothing. All it handed back to her as a finale to her shambolic scheming was an opportunity to bolt for cover like a whipped dog. She could go and leave Sam stranded, alone, to face an inquisition. If she acted now, she might yet elude lies, if not deceit.

Soon Connor would be home. On learning of her presence here tonight, he would know just why her impromptu visit coincided with the attempted theft of the deeds to Windrush. He would know why she had cravenly scampered off. Would he hound her for aiding and abetting? See her in a magistrate's court tomorrow alongside Sam? Or would he simply despise the lowly trickster she'd become and let things lie for lack of hard proof? Perhaps knowing her amateurish antics had been so easily thwarted would be enough revenge for him.

Her eyes blinked rapidly, clearing away the teary film. A young man who hardly knew her had put himself in peril for her sake. She could not live with her conscience if she did not at least try to ease the burden on him. She had no idea how that might be achieved, but she knew she must speak to him at least, free him at best. 'I should like to see my employee, Samuel Smith, please, Joseph.' Ignoring Joseph's cautionary look, Rachel walked, head high, to the door of the study.

'You may leave us.'

The constable looked as though he might protest but a thick imperious finger flicked indicating the man remove himself. 'Go. I must confidentially question the accused. I shall call if I have need of your assistance.'

With a final peer over his shoulder, the beagle dragged his flat feet along the hallway to idle with a knot of servants who were still loitering, while Joseph Walsh was busy elsewhere, loath to yet relinquish such awesome diversion.

Sam Smith brashly cocked his head, then his chin dropped and he was gazing at his wrists and ankles, bound with rope in front of him. He shifted on the hard wooden chair he'd been forced down upon opposite the rose salon. Lamps were now lit and a beckoning mellow blush was tinting the space beyond that half-open door. 'Should I be honoured you've come in person to escort me to gaol?' Sam asked with hollow cheekiness.

'Indeed you should, my good man,' his worship, Arthur Goodwin, replied. His voice sounded as silken as the official robes in which he swished about. His head, thatched with mousy hair only at the sides, was free of the ribbed judicial wig and appeared a greasy dome beneath the flaring wall-sconces. 'You're keeping me from my supper, from my well-earned repose with my dear lady wife. But I'm not angry. Oh, no, no. Indeed, I own to being quite delighted that we meet under such…auspicious circumstances. Sweet fate has had a hand in this night's work,' he murmured contentedly as he walked away a little. He turned to amusedly study his cornered prey, savouring how best to apply the torment he intended to inflict.

This youth had led him a merry dance in his pursuit of that angelic-faced wench. He'd been insulted, sneered at. A member of his majesty's judiciary, a man of some wealth and status condescended to notice this slum-scum, yet they had the brass neck to spurn his patronage! And he knew their motives: to drive up the price of the fragrant miss. Now the whelp would pay! So would that doe-eyed *demi-vièrge* when he finally had her nailed beneath him… A thick finger wiped a beading of sweat from his bulbous top lip as he ruminated on his favourite sport: roughly deflowering pubescent girls.

'I was unexpectedly kept late in sessions and thus was fortuitously at the court house when Weekes arrived with the news that one Samuel Smith had been taken red-handed, stealing from the Earl of Devane. Do you know what my first thought was on walking into this grand abode? I would forgo a month's worth of dinners and conjugal rights to see you thus: trussed and branded a thief and, I'll warrant, so very...*very* keen to bribe me to be lenient with you.'

Sam Smith raised his hate-filled eyes to the smirking pasty face thrust close to his. 'Go straight to hell, you evil bastard. I'll not ask any favours of you.'

Arthur Goodwin bared his grained teeth in a grin. 'Oh, I think you will. Because it's up to me now whether *you* are going straight to hell. You're not so young or so stupid as to be unaware of what mire you are now steeped in. But just in case you are stupid, let me enlighten you as to the details of the case I've just come from this evening.'

Sam contemptuously turned his head to stare at the gaggle of servants some way along the hallway. They gawped right back, tearing their eyes away only long enough to nod and whisper words at each other. He felt furious at himself for getting caught. He felt furious at himself for not having given sufficient consideration to the consequences of getting caught. He felt ashamed of himself because, for the first time in his life, since his ma had died, he'd put another woman before Annie. He'd been thinking only of Noreen when he got himself embroiled in this. Even now, he found himself thinking of Noreen. He wasn't man enough for her.

He'd failed her. He'd let Annie down too. This slimy beak was about to crow over just how badly he'd let his young sister down.

'This evening, just an hour since, I despatched a young man—about your age, I'd say—to Botany Bay. Now he's enjoying his supper of bread and water in custody. Tomorrow he'll be on his way to one of the prison hulks. Have you heard of the hospitality they offer? I'll be pleased to educate you as to what you can expect on even the best of those overflowing sewers. Shall I acquaint you with that young man's crime?' He walked close to where Sam fidgeted on the chair and circled round him. A finger and thumb came out, fondling one of his ears before viciously twisting the cartilage. Arthur Goodwin bent his mean lips close to where his fingers savaged. 'First *I* would like to know something. How is that sweet little sister of yours?' He tightened his grip. 'Come, tell me how my lovely Annie does. I can't hear you...'

Just a small whimper bubbled from Sam's compressed lips as his torturer's fingernails nipped into his skin.

'That young clerk—soon to be enduring a living death whilst awaiting his time to sail away to a different underworld—embezzled a thousand pounds from his master during his time as his clerk.' Arthur Goodwin shot a look at where the exhibits of Sam's crime lay on a table. 'I'd say the sapphire alone is worth more than two thousand. The theft of valuable documents has yet to be added to the sum. How are *your* sea-legs? Or perhaps I might choose to have you dance the Newgate jig. What will tender Annie bargain with, do you think, to save your neck being stretched?'

Sam Smith ripped himself from the magistrate's grip

and lurched to his feet, sending the man reeling back a few paces. His chair clattered on to its back. Sam followed: forgetting that his feet were cuffed, he over-balanced. From his position, sprawled at the corrupt justice's feet, he spat up at him, 'She's safe from you. She's where you won't get your filthy paws on her.'

'Samuel? Are you hurt?'

Sam Smith and his worship, Arthur Goodwin, whipped around startled countenances as they heard that soft, urgent call.

Sam pushed up on to an elbow then wobbled his way to his feet. 'I'm well enough, m'm,' he said gruffly, unable to meet Rachel's eye, or that of Joseph Walsh as he hurried after her slender figure hurtling along the corridor.

'I wish to speak privately to my servant,' Rachel burst out breathlessly to Arthur Goodwin. She turned to Joseph, puffing up behind her. 'Unbind Samuel's feet, please, Joseph, so he might move more easily to the rose salon.'

'I don't think that's wise, Miss Meredith,' Joseph ventured as though talking to a peevish child. 'Come, I shall have one of the footmen hail you a cab. It is time, surely, you were safely away home. The magistrate will be giving this rogue a thorough scolding, to add to the one he received from me. You need not fret he will go hence without reprimand.'

Arthur Goodwin plumped out his chest beneath his robes, keen to keep in evidence his authority over the prisoner. 'Indeed, sir, you are correct. Now, it is time to remove the villain into proper custody. Watson!' he barked at the beagle, whilst running an assessing eye over Rachel. Not that she interested him in the way Annie Smith did. He supposed she was pretty enough;

but too old and far too sure of herself to perk up the lecherous bully in him. What kept his sly eyes trained on her was that he recalled seeing her before. She'd been immodestly pert then too.

She'd had far too much to say for herself on the afternoon the hackney he'd hired had locked wheels with the dray Smith had been driving. In his opinion, what she'd needed then was a man to slap her down. Just as she did now. Perhaps Devane was the man applying for the job, he inwardly smirked. He recalled the way the Irishman had seemed fascinated by her. If they weren't well acquainted before that incident, they obviously were now. The lady seemed quite at ease here, giving her orders…

But what might she be doing in his lordship's house, in his absence, and with apparently no chaperon present? And she had said that the youth was one of *her* servants? So the Smiths had left the Earl's employ…

Arthur Goodwin had a devious detective's mind. It raced to an unlikely conclusion, but one he nevertheless very much liked. Had she been distracting Joseph Walsh whilst her man was robbing the house? With a very thoughtful purse to his lips he strode over to examine the recovered booty lying on a table. 'Are you acquainted with a property known as Windrush, Miss Meredith?'

'Yes,' Rachel returned tartly before turning her attention to Joseph. 'Please free Samuel's feet or I shall do it myself.'

With a sigh, Joseph bent to untie the knots.

'This is most irregular! Just a moment, Miss Meredith!' Rachel heard the magistrate remonstrate as she ushered Samuel within the pretty pink room.

She turned in the doorway to bar his fat body with

her willowy figure. 'I *will* have five minutes alone with my servant.' She closed the door in his ugly, sweating face.

Once within the room, Rachel looked soulfully at Sam. He avoided her gaze, making her despairingly throw back her head and blink hot-eyed at the ceiling. 'Did you mean to steal those deeds, Sam?' she burst out.

'Yes, m'm.'

'And the sapphire ring, too?'

'No!'

Sam looked directly at Rachel. 'I'd no inkling a ring was tied to the ribbon round the papers and that's the honest truth. It were pushed underneath it in the drawer. I just snatched up the scroll and ran...'

'Why?'

'Get out of there as fast as I could.'

Rachel gave a sobbing laugh. 'No. Why did you steal papers that are worthless to you?'

'They're not worthless to you.'

'You did it for me?'

'No, m'm,' Sam said quietly, incurably honest. 'For Noreen.'

'You stole the deeds to Windrush for Noreen?'

After a silent moment of inner turmoil, Sam burst out, 'Noreen overheard you telling your friend about Lord Devane wanting a mean revenge on you. She guessed from what you said that you meant to have back the deeds to your home by fair means or foul. I told her when we talked this morning you seemed keen to know when his lordship was likely to be out. So we hatched a plot, then waited to see if we guessed right in thinking you might try to slip away and come here. Noreen said I must get to the deeds afore you did; she's awful scared over consequences for your whole family. I followed you and hid in the street. I clocked one of the footmen talking to Joseph by the door, so I hopped up the front steps all casual, as though I were just passing, like, and thought to stop by to fetch Annie's shift. Joseph Walsh told me his lordship was out, so I knew there was only one reason why you'd worked your way in.' He paused to rub at the bridge of his nose. 'I got to his study quick as I could to save you getting there first. Noreen told me where the deeds was kept. She overheard you telling your friend that too.' He blushed, shuffled his feet. 'Noreen wasn't eavesdropping, she only stopped to pick up the little boy's toy in the corridor and heard things said about Lord Devane as are hard to believe.' He shook his head in sad perplexity. 'His lordship's always been good to me, and Annie. That trading justice out there wants to ruin Annie, you see. He'd love to see me out of the way to have a free run at her. I told Lord Devane that Goodwin had us cornered with nowhere to go and he took us in. And there's no truth…just spite…in them rumours that he did it out of lechery. He's never laid a finger on Annie.' He sighed. 'Noreen's told me about your sister Isabel, too. She told me everything…'

'Everything…?' Rachel echoed.

'Yes, m'm. And that's why I did it. You see, I understand more'n any man the miseries caused by rich gents as won't never take no for an answer. Goodwin 'ud see me swing, then leave Annie with her belly swole, and she not yet fifteen. Men like that make me sick, for there's plenty of willing women for those with their wallets bulging too…' He reddened again at his coarseness. 'I got to ask this, Miss Meredith: Noreen's said if anything happens to me over this, she'll look after Annie. You'll keep them both on, won't you?'

Before Rachel could conquer the lump in her throat sufficiently to allay his fears on that score, the door sharply opened, making Sam gasp nervously. Flowing robes breezed in, then Goodwin's portly figure emerged, with Joseph Walsh close behind. This was it, then, Sam realised. He was to be taken away, perhaps never to see Annie or Noreen again. He knew he would face a noose or transportation. Within days he might be gone. With a stricken look, he realised the gallows might be preferable to that living hell the trading justice had described. He'd heard of those floating prisons and knew that Goodwin hadn't exaggerated the vile conditions on the hulks. Suddenly he felt so very young and wished he'd seen more years than seventeen.

'You have had your five minutes, Miss Meredith— it is time to take the guilty party away.'

Rachel tilted her chin as she said clearly, 'But we are not yet ready to leave.'

Joseph's chin dropped on to his chest and as he fully digested her meaning, he visibly wilted, looking as though he might collapse.

Arthur Goodwin simply smiled. 'How unnecessarily honest of you, my dear. You would have got away with it. Although, I must admit I had my suspicions. A strange coincidence indeed, I thought, was your presence here at the very moment one of your servants infiltrates to pilfer goods of so…obscure a value. A petty thief might take the ring, although any fool would know such a memorable piece would be difficult to pawn. The deeds would be of no use to him whatsoever. Then I thought…suppose the villain didn't realise the ring was attached to the scroll and simply grabbed it up and fled? I have been racking my brain over it all and I seem to recall gossip that the Earl of Devane recently won an estate in Hertfordshire at cards. I would hazard a guess that estate is Windrush and that you reside there? Also, where are these friends of yours, the Saunders? You told Mr Walsh they would soon be arriving. Would you say they are yet delayed? Hmm?' The jibe was accompanied by a leering smile. 'Let's away before Lord Devane arrives home. I doubt that upstanding gentleman will want to be bothered with the likes of you two…'

'He already is bothered, Goodwin…' a voice drawled from the doorway.

The stunned silence in the rose salon seemed interminable. Connor was positioned in between the wide door frames, in casual stance with feet apart and one hand thrust deep into his breeches pockets. The neck of his shirt was gaping where at some time during the evening his neckcloth looked to have been rudely removed. An elegant charcoal tailcoat was pegged carelessly on a finger over one shoulder. His complexion had the drawn pallor of prolonged overindulgence and his eyes looked as though at any time they could fully close. In short, the *upstanding gentleman* looked the embodiment of a dissolute aristocrat.

Connor glanced over his shoulder into the hallway. Idly he drew his hand from his pocket, to plant it on the door frame. What he then said proved he was drunk, yet still alert to proceedings. 'Joseph, am I overstaffed?' he softly slurred.

Joseph Walsh goggled at him, unable to speak although his lips did move.

His lordship's dark brows arched quizzically. 'Am I?' he enquired with dangerous ennui.

'I don't think so, my lord,' Joseph finally forced out.

'Pray, tell me then why I have just encountered at least seven servants looking for all the world as though they have damn all to do but stare at me? Should they be abed then, is that it?'

Joseph swallowed, shuffled. 'I'll…er…see to them, shall I?'

'Do that,' Connor advised with a significant small smile. 'See to them before I do and put you out of a job as well.'

Joseph hastened for the door, taking one last fascinated peer at the people frozen in a tableau in the cosy room. Connor allowed him to pass into the corridor by turning a powerful shoulder, then with a weary push away from the frame he was walking into the room. His low-lidded eyes levelled on Arthur Goodwin.

Look at me, Rachel pleaded silently. Please look at me. He obeyed her silent summons and eyes as crude and hard as flint-stone abraded her in an insolent head to toe summary. Oh, my God! No! He's *very* drunk and *unbelievably* angry, she inwardly wailed.

Arthur Goodwin stepped forward, bowed precisely. 'I'm afraid that mischief has been done tonight in your absence, my lord. But the stolen items are recovered and the perpetrators must be dealt with.'

'Sure…and they will be. By me.'

'A crime…a theft has been committed, it must be dealt with by the proper offices, my lord…' Connor was informed in a soothing, unctuous tone.

'What's been stolen?'

Arthur Goodwin bustled officiously for the door and returned in a trice with the deeds and ring still attached. He presented them to Connor, together with a clearer view of his shiny balding pate as he bowed low. 'This was found in that villain's possession. He attempted to fight his way free and escape with them. Your butler witnessed the whole business.'

'It's my fault…my doing. Samuel was simply here because of me…' Rachel's voice quavered but she kept her chin high as she unflinchingly met Connor's stare, waiting for his disgust. For a missed heartbeat she thought he might simply turn and walk away, hand her over to the fat magistrate after all. Although her proud, frightened eyes remained engulfed by his, she was obliquely aware that his stepbrother, Jason, had just sauntered into the room to prop himself negligently against a wall.

One end of the scroll beat a soft, slow tattoo on to a broad palm as Connor strolled towards her. Despite herself Rachel found she could no longer meet his eyes. The closer he came the weaker she felt. The arrogance she needed to keep her strong was draining away; shame was swamping her, cowing her. She was base and cowardly. Had she adhered to their bargain he would have given her those papers…privately, discreetly. But she had wanted everything: the prize, the victory. She'd wanted to best him in this hurtful game they played. She'd wanted to falsely win because she'd lost what she really wanted…him.

Now everything was gone, including her family's reputation and June soon to be wed. Obliquely her dazed mind understood the magnitude of that, obliquely, too, she realised it would be tomorrow before the full horror of it properly sank in. The humiliation of defeat must first be dealt with. Her slender pearly neck bobbed as her throat worked, swallowing, swallowing, as she strove to cope with the impossible. Her eyes jammed shut; still a tear escaped to hover on her lashes before, in a brisk movement, she averted her face and swept it away.

Connor arrested the hand as it made to return to her side, curled her fingers about the deeds, then brushed a kiss on a cool cheek in a gesture that was almost obeisance.

'No crime has been committed. You're wasting your time here, Goodwin.'

Rachel sensed the warm alcoholic breath stir the hair close to her ear. Dewy eyes slanted up at him through her lashes then quickly flinched away from the sardonic humour, the promise of retaliation she read there. She'd prodded the tiger in him into life. This was what she'd wanted, wasn't it? A man who would meet her provocation with a passion he couldn't…wouldn't control.

'I find that hard to believe, my lord,' Arthur Goodwin protested with a frantic, possessive peer at Sam Smith. Already he sensed his sadistic grip on the boy and his sister being loosened. The youth's incipient joyous smile made him blurt out angrily, 'She admitted involvement in the crime.'

'She? Do you mean my future wife?' Connor turned a steel-eyed quizzical look on the magistrate. 'And what do you find hard to believe? My word? Are you calling me a liar? I shall explain myself once only: I have just presented my bride-to-be with her wedding gifts. Obviously she's been a mite impatient and came to collect them herself. I should have guessed she would…the minx.'

Sam's smile blossomed until he had to prevent a guffaw by thrusting his cuffed hands against his teeth. Connor arrowed a threatening look his way, and the youth quickly examined the floor.

'I'm sorry you were brought here on a fool's errand,

Goodwin. Waste no more time, get away home.' When that command brought no immediate response, other than the magistrate's skin to bloom maroon, Connor added on an icy stare, 'I should like to be private with my future wife. As the servants seem to have taken an unofficial holiday, would you show his worship out, please, Jason?'

Jason Davenport took one decisive, if tipsy, step towards Arthur Goodwin. It was enough to have the man, hands balled at his side, stomping towards the door. A malevolent glare, replete with frustration, was launched at Sam Smith. Sam responded by making a very lewd gesture with both fists that transformed into a prayer-like steeple as his saviour slanted him a warning look.

'I'll deal with you another time. Get along home,' Connor told the grinning youth who, losing no time, skipped obediently for the door.

Rachel moved that way too; much as she knew she must apologise, beg forgiveness, make known her gratitude, and a million other humbling things, she couldn't. Not while he was in this mood, not while he was so intoxicated that she could detect an aura of sweetish incense emanating from him.

She'd barely managed a stealthy step when he arrested her by taking her face in a firm, punishing hand. 'Not you, sweet. You stay here so I can deal with you now.' Her chin was released in a flick and then, with a surprisingly fast and steady stride, Connor was at the door. He closed it, leaned back against it and surveyed her, unsmiling.

'You mustn't punish Sam; he did it for me…and Noreen, my maid. They've become close…' When that elicited no response, she blurted out the next thing that came into her head. 'I sent you a letter…you didn't reply.' Stupid, stupid, she castigated herself. What a stupid subject to introduce while he was like this...

Her papa would get drunk and be either too jovial or too maudlin. She had never been sure how to approach him when under the influence of alcohol. He could be sulky or bellow; he might badger the family to play at silly games and tricks. So she would simply take her mother's advice: stay out of your father's way until he is again himself. Her mother was an intelligent woman. 'Might we speak of this tomorrow...please?'

A hard sardonic smile was all that denied her polite request.

'Did you want me to reply to your letter?' Connor suggested in a voice that Rachel was sure sounded yet more slurred.

'Yes...no...'

'Well, which is it, my dear? Yes or no?'

'This is a nice room. But rather...feminine and fragile in shade and design. I imagine that is why your mother likes it. Joseph says it's her favourite.' She had walked away as he advanced, moved to examine a dainty demi-lune table inlaid with boxwood. She placed down the deeds and her fingertips brushed its satiny surface.

Connor moved to a different table. Finding a glass, he removed the stopper from the decanter.

'What are you doing?' Rachel gasped, horrified.

'Pouring a drink.'

'But...you must not! You're drunk already!'

He laughed; laughed in a harsh, guttural way. Slowly he turned to face her, holding the glass and decanter out appealingly. 'Be fair, Rachel. Are you going to allow me anything? I mustn't punish Sam Smith. I mustn't have what I fairly won from your father, I mustn't have my wedding night… Now you're telling me I mustn't have a drink either?'

Rachel moistened her lips, wishing desperately she could be away from him, just till he was himself again. Just till he was that fine honourable gentleman she'd rejected. Yet oddly she desired being closer to him too. She wanted to go to him, comfort him, put her arms about him and hold him, for despite his dark irony she could sense his pain…pain she had caused him six years ago that still festered and tormented him.

'Choose one,' he said with a menacing softness which killed her empathy. 'Choose one thing I can have or I'll choose. Come, sweet, tell me what I am allowed…'

'I'm not speaking to you when you're drunk,' Rachel quavered.

He smiled a devilishly contented smile. 'My choice too. Something we can do that needs no conversation.' The decanter and glass were returned to the table and his jacket, still slung over a shoulder, was abruptly discarded on to a chair. He turned and walked towards her with slow deliberation.

Rachel backed into the demi-lune table, and felt the forgotten pistol within her reticule bump against her leg. She brought the bulky bag closer to her where it was easily accessible. 'You're being silly, Connor.' She had meant the reprimand to sound authoritative but it burst out through chattering teeth. She carefully positioned herself behind the dainty chair she'd sat on earlier. 'Stay where you are or I'll scream. If I do scream, Joseph Walsh will come to my assistance. It will simply cause more upset tonight and you will not want that,' she sensibly explained as though talking to a fractious child.

'Scream, then. After tonight's escapade, Joseph will be as deaf as the rest of the household. You deserve punishment and they all know it.'

Rachel stepped sideways, put a pink-and-cream striped sofa between them. She lifted her chin, her anger dominating her fright. 'Well, think of your dignity and sophistication then, sir,' she whipped at him icily. 'Did you not once tell me how bored you had become with fornicating against chairs and walls?' That did bring him to a halt. Rachel watched his raven head tip back, his white teeth displayed in a velvety laugh. His deep blue eyes levelled at her from between a mesh of dusky lashes. 'We'll use the table. I've no objection to that. Besides, I'm drunk, Rachel, as you rightly perceived. My dignity and sophistication have suffered already tonight. Why worry now?' he taunted softly.

Rachel pivoted away from him so fast that her golden hair flagged out behind her. Slowly she turned to face him, her lovely face flushed as she raised the gun in two white, unsteady hands and levelled it at his head.

Chapter Fifteen

'Are you going to shoot me, Rachel?'

His easy drawl let Rachel know he deemed it highly unlikely she'd find the courage.

Her tongue tip darted to moisten her lips and her shaking hands tightened on the silver-inlaid grip. 'Are you going to force me to it? If you're sensible and let me go now, I shall meet you tomorrow, when you are lucid and more yourself. I realise there is much that is vital and needs to be aired…much that I must say to you. I *will* apologise then…I swear.'

'Something vital occurs to me that ought to be aired now. May I say it?'

Rachel nodded jerkily, trying to ignore his amused, mocking tone.

'Is it loaded?'

A jerk of his dark head indicated the gun and startled, she looked at it too. 'I don't know,' she admitted, too honest. 'It's your weapon. I found it in your desk drawer. Don't *you* know if it's loaded?'

'I confess I ought to. I'll guess it's not. There, if you shoot me, it'll be my fault,' he reasoned softly as he approached.

Rachel steadied the pistol with both hands, bringing it up and extending it threateningly. She backed away to the wall, two fingers crossed in position, hovering on the trigger.

'You think my memory is suspect along with my character, Rachel? Pull the trigger, then. It's the only sure way to find out.' The flimsy cabriole-legged settee was sent skidding sideways on its castors by a booted foot. Her protection was reduced to the slender barrel of the flintlock and the slow tears that dripped down her cheeks.

Connor put up dark fingers, curled them about the wavering muzzle, stabilising it as easily as once he had steadied crockery she couldn't control.

Rachel removed her hands, relinquishing the weapon to him, and covered her wet face. 'It isn't loaded...is it?'

'Let's find out...'

The deafening report had her muffling a shriek and jerking against the wall. Her fingers slid from her face to cover her ringing ears. Cordite clung acridly in her nostrils. Stupefied, her wide eyes flicked to Connor's critical gaze, followed it to the magnificent chandelier. One candle had been reduced to a smoking stump. The rainbow light was pendulating entrancingly and thus dodged danger as a clump of ornate plaster suddenly detached itself from the ceiling and landed with a dusty thud on the carpet.

She barely twitched. 'Were you aiming for that particular candle?' she asked almost normally, but for a hoarseness stealing volume from her voice.

'No. Just its flame.'

Rachel looked at him and he looked back. He smiled at her, really smiled at her, and with a lazy lob the gun bounced on to the seat of the striped settee. 'I could do it clear-headed,' he boasted impishly. A dark hand rose to cradle her chin, slid to a cold shivering cheek, stroking away the wet with infinite tenderness. 'I'm permanently afflicted with the vices of a misspent youth, I fear. It's one of the reasons I never introduced you to my too-truthful grandfather. He would have felt it his duty to tell you so. And I was scared you'd leave me…'

The door opened and Joseph, eyes wide and swivelling, hovered uncertainly in the doorway. Connor moved away from Rachel and elevated enquiring eyebrows at his startled butler.

'Pardon me, my lord; I thought I heard an explosion. Like a gunshot…'

'Yes, you did. Miss Meredith finds the rose salon a mite too feminine in style. We're adding a few masculine touches… Have the carriage brought round,' he tacked incongruously on to the end as he collected his jacket from the chair and shrugged, superbly nonchalant, into it.

After a comically aghast look, Joseph roused himself enough to scoot away to do his master's bidding.

Connor stared at the vacant doorway before sending Rachel a sideways look. 'If I've terrified you, I'm sorry. I was about to add I didn't mean to…but that would be a lie. I think I did, at first…' He gave a wry, private smile. 'But you'll be relieved to know I'm more myself now.' He paused, looked up at the ceiling as though contemplating the damage.

'You seem to have sobered up somewhat,' Rachel ventured softly.

'Army training. The sight of a weapon pointing

one's way, the sound of gunshot, can usually be relied on to restore the faculties to a soldier.'

He started to speak, stopped, and his dark fingers pinched at the tension between his eyes. 'Come, I'll take you home,' he stated quietly.

Several times on the short journey through the streets to Beaulieu Gardens, Rachel had glanced at Connor, hoping to engage him in conversation. He had seemed to deliberately avoid her eye. He lounged in the corner opposite, gazing impassively out into the dusk. She guessed it to be approaching midnight and the streets seemed unusually quiet. No night watchman shouting, no vagabonds darting to the coach to cling on and beg for pennies, few other vehicles rattling alongside to convey revellers home.

She lifted a corner of the leather blind that blocked her view from her side of the coach and glimpsed familiar landmarks. Within a minute or two she would be home. He would stop the coach and set her down and she knew she would never see him again.

She had meant what she'd said about meeting him tomorrow so she could properly apologise and thank him and so many other things, but he would avoid doing so. She knew that as simply as she had known Sam Smith had risked his life to protect her and to safeguard her family's reputation.

The carriage was slowing; Connor seemed to stir himself as though just realising they had reached their destination.

Rachel folded her hands on her lap, looked at his beautiful, carved profile through the sombre interior. 'Shall I see you tomorrow?' she asked, although she already knew the answer.

'No.'

She nodded, bit down on her lip. Despite knowing what she proposed was highly improper, she said huskily, 'Would you come in with me so I might say what I must?'

'No.'

She swallowed, blinked at her fingers straining awkwardly in her lap. 'May I delay you a few moments then and say it now? Please?'

Connor looked at her at last, but she couldn't see his eyes and she wanted to. She so wanted to see the look in his eyes, but his face was hidden in shadow.

'What do you want to tell me, Rachel? That you're sorry and ashamed and grateful? I know that.' He leaned forward, rested his elbows on his knees and speared five fingers through his raven's-wing hair. 'If it helps salve your conscience, I feel that way too. I'm sorry I once wanted to hide from you my past. I'm ashamed I wanted to coerce you to sleep with me, and I'm grateful you brought me to my senses by pulling a gun on me before I did something neither of us would have ever got over. Go home. Go home tomorrow to Windrush and your parents...'

'Windrush belongs to you.'

'I gave it to you. I gave you the deeds in front of witnesses. I don't want it.'

'I can't take them,' she gasped on a suppressed sob. 'I left them behind on your table.' She fumbled for the door handle, wanting to be gone before she was dismissed.

'You wanted Windrush so badly you were prepared to risk gaol. Now you've suddenly given up on it? What about Isabel and her son?'

Rachel swivelled back on the seat, a frantic hand

swiping tears from her eyes. 'What? What did you say?'

'You heard what I said, Rachel. I think you wanted Windrush as a refuge for Isabel and her son. Did you?'

Rachel felt her heart slowly pounding in dread. Nevertheless she answered simply, 'Yes. After June and then Sylvie were married, some time in the future, when there was no more need to bow and scrape to society's idea of etiquette, when my parents were lost to me and no one left but me to please...I thought it would be so nice to have Isabel home...and my nephew. I know it might never be, but still I dream of it sometimes...' The silence lengthened and she added softly, 'My aunt Florence is not in good health, she is quite old now and almost blind and Isabel has no one else in York. She's twenty-four and lives almost as a recluse, but never complains.' Her golden head bowed beneath the pain. 'She never complains. Who told you? My father?'

'No. William Pemberton came to see me today, having just returned from visiting your sister in Hertfordshire. He thought I should know.'

Rachel's head dropped further towards her hands. 'June *told* William? She should not have. Not yet.'

'She should *not* have? They're soon to be man and wife but she should *not* have? She should have kept her secrets and risked letting lies and deceit taint their lives as I let it ruin ours?'

Rachel snapped her head up to look at him, barely seeing his face behind the blur. 'It...it was a private matter. Just for family. And we've not lied; we've let others draw their own conclusions about Isabel's absence. We're guilty of failing to correct conjecture, nothing more.'

'I thought my past was just for the family to know. It was to be kept private that I'd been a wild hedonist who'd challenged an elderly man to a duel over his wife: a woman I lusted after but had no right to. You sensed that something about me was bad. You were right to be wary and reject me. And you couldn't have foreseen your sister being violated in York.'

'She says she was willing. Had she been forced, I think my parents might have been more able to bear the shame.' She shook her head in despair at that. 'As it is they would rather join strangers in believing her dead. There *was* an outbreak of scarletina in York; neither of us was ill but we remained quarantined for some time to be sure we would not bring the infection home. By the time it seemed safe to travel Isabel knew she was pregnant, although she would divulge none of the circumstances, even to me, and we were always close. It was assumed she'd not returned with me to Hertfordshire because she'd succumbed to the disease. When the months passed and still no sign of her, and her pictures were put away, and people saw how mention of her made us all cry…' Rachel's voice trembled into silence. She stared at her clasped fingers, knowing she must alight and go in now, for she'd said far too much. But what was she betraying? He knew the essence of their secret. Why shouldn't she tell all to this man who'd been a catalyst to the disaster? The temptation to share those six years burdened with Isabel's shame and isolation was overwhelming.

'Sylvie thinks that her sister is dead. She was only six then, too young to understand; now she's twelve but my mother won't tell her. She fears she is too immature, too forthright to be trusted to keep the confidence. She might jeopardise her future happiness and security with an unguarded word. The Saunders don't know either. June and I were forbidden by my parents to speak of it, even to close friends. The deception is now too well entrenched in history to be remedied. My parents are in an awful predicament. They love Isabel still, but with three other girls to settle, what are they to do but discreetly give her financial help? If our disgrace became public knowledge, there would be no weddings and no respite from supporting four spinster daughters. Isabel understands all that and refuses even to move closer to Hertfordshire in case the scandal is uncovered and she blights us all. Yet it was I who did that. My selfish folly at nineteen has caused untold suffering to so many.' Rachel blinked rapidly at the leather blind at the window, lifted a corner to stare blearily at her home. 'I…I don't know why William has told you,' she suddenly said. 'I pray he tells no one else. Should his mother hear a whisper of it…' Rachel's voice cracked on imagining the chaos that would ensue. 'I trust I can count on your…on your—'

'Decency? Discretion?'

Rachel caught sight of a brief flash of white in the coach's murky interior. His mordant tone betrayed the smile as sarcastic. 'I'll beg you to say nothing, if need be,' she informed him quietly, proudly.

'I know you consider *me* a villain, Rachel, but I was under the impression William has always found favour with you. Would such an upright character have told me if he suspected I might repeat it?'

'I can't imagine why he told you.'

'Well, I'll tell you why: he was warning me that if my dealings with you over Windrush resulted in the same sad condition befalling you as has afflicted Isabel, I'd have him to answer to.'

Rachel's audible gasp made him grunt a laugh. 'Had the possibility of a wedding-night baby not occurred to you, sweetheart?'

'Of course I knew of the…the risk. But for William to imagine I might…I would…'

'It wasn't your morality he was doubting, it was mine; and my powers of seduction. Perhaps I should be flattered,' Connor wryly remarked. 'And you need not fear his mother will learn anything from him. His firm intention is to marry June and protect you as his sister.'

'He's a fine man. My father should be grateful to have secured such a son.'

'I'm sure he shall be.'

'Yes.' After a pregnant pause, Rachel murmured, 'You have put yourself in an awkward position, sir.'

'I have?'

'You implied we were betrothed. You said it in front of witnesses.'

'I'll never ever get engaged again. I've said that in front of witnesses, too.'

'You said I was your bride-to-be, you gave me wedding gifts. The magistrate heard. So did Sam and your butler.'

'I'll jilt you. What could be better? It'll close the circle.' He jerked backwards into the squabs. 'I'll gazette a notice that we're to be married at the end of this week, then publicly jilt you. You'll have an avalanche of sympathy, I'll be despised. We'll be even. It'll cure everything. You can take the deeds to Windrush home with you. It would be the least a breach-of-promise attorney would extract and I won't contest it.'

She gazed at him through a mist of dignified tears.

'Yes. I understand. Thank you. That should cure everything.'

She had sat a full minute longer with him in the dark, unwanted, delaying him. Quickly she felt for the door handle before the swelling hurt in her chest exploded. She conquered it long enough to blurt, 'You're wrong in thinking I had an intuition you were wild and that was why I jilted you. I swear I never knew. I believed you were honest and ethical...tediously so. You played your part well. I ran away because...'

'Because...?' he prompted, dulcet yet demanding.

'I hoped you would follow me,' Rachel murmured, a tiny watery laugh choking in her throat. 'I thought if you truly loved me you would come and get me.' With that she was out of the coach and running for her door.

She banged on the knocker, her body shivering with anguished sorrow. Within a moment Sam Smith, buttoning up his waistcoat, was peering through a crack at her. He pushed the door wide, solicitously ushered her in and was closing it when a hand and a booted foot stayed it so powerfully that he was sent staggering back a few paces. 'Go to bed. Now!' Connor ordered the lad. Sam didn't hesitate in obeying. With a subtle look and a nod he was gone towards the servants' quarters and Noreen's snug, welcoming arms.

'Whose servant is he?' Rachel demanded querulously, shaking from head to foot. She self-embraced, chafing at her arms to warm them. 'Yours? Mine?'

'Ours,' he said as he stalked her back against the front door.

She turned her head, avoiding those penetrative, glittering eyes. 'Go away, Connor, I'm tired. I shall go home tomorrow, I'll be out of your way, for good, I swear.'

'Say that again.'

'I'm going home, tomorrow, I swear,' she gasped, trying to pass him, but he trapped her with flat palms slamming against the timber either side of her head.

'Not that! Tell me again why you ran away.'

She turned her head, shielding her distress. 'No,' whispered out of her.

'Tell me…' a mellifluous voice threatened.

'I wanted…I wanted you to follow me. I wanted you to properly love me…' she cried.

'Properly love you?' he gritted with such guttural passion that she cringed. 'What I felt for you then Rachel, was very proper and God knows I loved you.' His head lowered as his savagely taut lips steamed warm breath against her neck making her head angle languidly. 'Do you know what it took to be so gentle and respectful and restrained when what I really wanted to do was—' His eyes abruptly closed, his jaw tightening until a muscle jerked by his mouth. 'You drove me mad. I thought I'd go insane with wanting you, yet I stayed faithful. I didn't take a mistress, fearing you'd suspect me a philanderer if you learned of her existence. I was rarely tempted; it was only you I wanted. For four months I was celibate. I continued waiting, tolerating your teasing, your flirting, your provocation.' A hand jerked her averted face up to his. 'Now you say I didn't *properly* love you? I've never loved anyone more properly in my entire damned life!'

'You loved her…'

'Who? Maria Laviola?' Connor asked, his incredulity tinged with amusement.

'No…' Rachel saw genuine incomprehension in his eyes. He had no idea who she meant. 'The wife of your grandfather's friend. You loved her, surely?'

'Perhaps I did, at first, if I was capable of such an emotion at that time. But it was hardly proper. Bernadette was married to a nobleman and satisfied with her situation until I happened along and coaxed her into a liaison. I was arrogant, egotistical and covetous of many things. The fact that she was initially reluctant and needed wooing was probably an inducement rather than a deterrent. To my shame I can still recall feeling quite relieved when my grandfather brought the affair to an abrupt end after six months, for she'd become unattractively clinging and possessive…rather a nuisance. Her husband welcomed her back but I knew, as did she, that their life together was irreparably damaged by scandal and suspicion; scandal and suspicion that I had caused. I knew all that yet it bothered me little at the time. Within a month I'd found someone to replace her. I began returning her letters, unopened.'

Rachel watched self-disgust curl his lips as his eyes shifted to bleakly stare at the wall. He had his own conscience to salve, she realised. Connor Flinte, a heroic, decorated Major in the Hussars, with an earldom and a fortune and a reputation as an admirable, honourable gentleman, was tormented by a youthful folly of his own. He had acted as rashly, as selfishly in adolescence as had she. A pale hand tentatively smoothed his saturnine expression. The wonderful sensation of warm abrasive skin beneath her fingertips emboldened her to slide the hand and comfortingly cradle his cheek. He turned his head so his lips brushed a reciprocating caress on her palm.

'At eighteen I thrived on challenge…confrontation. I'd been spoiled as a child by a rogue of a father who knew at thirty-six he wouldn't ever be forty. For three years, from when I was thirteen years old and the physician told him his lungs were too badly inflamed to cure, until I was approaching my sixteenth birthday, and he died, he tried to give me a lifetime's affection and attention. He indulged me with too much money, tolerated my excesses; praised them sometimes. He instructed me in the ways of the world and its baser pleasures, led me to believe anything in life was attainable if you were prepared to grasp every opportunity and live for the moment. And he told me constantly that I was like him. And I am, aren't I? He abducted the woman he wanted; I would have coerced you into bed. Gallant charmers, the Flinte men...' he remarked satirically. 'Blood will out, I suppose...

'Despite his failings he was a charismatic character. I loved him. So did my mother; she adored him, despite knowing of his weakness for women and riotous living. He idolised her, too; she was the only woman that mattered in his life, the only one who could to any degree control him.' He stole a look at Rachel. Her wide-eyed, rapt attention was all the encouragement he needed to continue enlightening her about his early life.

'After the business with Bernadette, I enjoyed a year or so more of debauchery before army discipline and my grandfather's quiet homilies tempered my licentiousness. Throughout my wild youth my grandfather had persevered in bestowing on me his wisdom. Despite my best efforts to ignore such worthy education, it had rooted in my mind, and maturity had helped me to appreciate it. When a brat I thought him a sanctimonious old miser who'd preach about abstinence and duty. Still I loved him. Now I thank God that his influence on me was as great as was my father's. He threatened to kill my father on numerous occasions. It was only my mother's constant mediation—and her physical presence—that kept them from each other's throats. I expect your father might have dealt the same way with me. He would have joined forces with Pemberton in tracking me down had I managed to seduce you.'

'I wouldn't have let them near you,' Rachel whispered. 'Not now I know.'

'What do you know, Rachel? That I'm pitiable?'

'I know you love me. You still love me, don't you?'

He flinched as though she'd scalded him, dropped his arms to his sides. 'How do you know that?' he hoarsely demanded, stepping back a few paces.

'Oh…suddenly I just know,' she said softly. 'There are those little loving things you do quite naturally for me, such as keeping me company when I'm sad and alone, or mopping spilled tea from my skin when I'm agitated and make a mess. You comforted me when I cried for Isabel and intervened when horrid Pamela Pemberton and my aunt tried to be mean to me. Then there are those important things you do to protect me, such as stopping those belligerent men fighting and arguing in my presence when their carriages got stuck. You saved me from vile Arthur Goodwin and from gaol by lying about our relationship. In doing so you have put yourself in quite a quandary for, despite saying you will never ever get engaged to me again, you have implied the reverse is true. Then there's other ways in which I can tell you care: I can see it in your eyes, hear it in your voice, I'll feel it soon when you kiss me. I know you love me, Connor. You can't escape.' She laughed softly as he spun on his heel, as though he might seek a way out.

'I meant what I said. I'll never ever get engaged

again…know that too.' His tone was as poignantly bashful as was his stance.

She smiled a soft, womanly smile of triumph and peace. 'Neither will I. But it doesn't alter the fact that you love me. I know now that you took Windrush from my father simply to prevent that weasel Lord Harley having it. Had he won that night, he would have taken our home and never given one moment's thought to the havoc and distress caused us by its loss. You immediately granted us a dispensation so June's wedding plans would not fall foul of my papa's silly plot. You've returned us Windrush and taken nothing in its stead…not even your wedding night. And all this you have done for me…just for me. Because you love me.' Her voice cracked on an emotional sob as she strove to conquer for a few more moments the need to go to him, to put loving arms about him. There was still a little more to say.

'You asked me why I jilted my other fiancés and I didn't properly answer you. I couldn't because until now I didn't know myself. I couldn't settle for Philip Moncur, or Mr Featherstone, or any man who wasn't as good…as wonderful as you. I was waiting for you to come back. I knew in my heart some day you'd come and get me.' She watched an unreadable expression tauten his lowered face. 'It doesn't matter that you'd rather stay single, Connor,' she coaxed, wanting him to look at her. Slowly she approached him, slid her silken arms up about his neck, putting her soft feminine curves boldly against the hard, masculine lines of his body. 'I've come close to you, Connor, and I'm looking at you because I really care what you might answer. It doesn't matter that you won't marry me. I'll settle for my wedding night…again and again. I'll still love you in the morning.'

Connor tilted his head, looked sideways at her. A lopsided smile transformed into a choke of laughter then two possessive hands suddenly girdled her waist. His arms, the turn of his body, fastened her to him. 'Now, what are you going to do if I take you up on that?'

Rachel flushed, chuckled, laid her head on his shoulder, abrading her cheek with his soft wool jacket. 'I visit Isabel every Michaelmas with Noreen accompanying me to York. She knows the truth about Isabel, for she and her sister have served us for a very long while. Every time I see Isabel she seems more serene. She has her memories, she has her son. She says she is content. I should like that: to be serene and content. I don't mind if you make me your paramour. Just don't go away and leave me, Connor. I beg you…don't do that.'

His face lowered to hers and in a husky, sensual tone he repeated, 'And I still want to know, Rachel…what are you going to do if I call your bluff?'

'You won't…'

'I'd like to…'

'I know…but you won't…'

'I might…'

'You won't…'

'You're very sure of yourself, and me, Miss Meredith,' Connor drawled in a voice of gravelly velvet. 'That string you've had me dangling on for six years…did you have it specially forged?' His lips descended, touched hers with teasing lightness that put her on her toes to protract the contact. With a groan he succumbed to her teasing little kisses, sliding warm parted lips to pay homage to her enthusiastic seduction.

Breathlessly Rachel dropped her head back and looked at him from beneath a fringe of silky lashes. There was one more thing she wanted to know. 'Did you love her?'

'Who? Bernadette?'

'No! The Italian soprano. The shameless lightskirt who displays her underwear in public, and flirts with all the ogling gentlemen, and glares at me from those odd-shaped black eyes.'

'Oh, her…' Connor said, amused by her bitchiness. 'I take it you'd be disappointed if I said I did?'

Rachel flushed, aware she'd been a mite too obvious in her jealous dislike.

'No, I didn't love her, Rachel,' Connor reassured gently as he smoothed a rosy cheek. 'In fact, I'm not sure now I even liked her very much once I discovered how sly and unscrupulous she could be.'

At Rachel's frown he explained, 'When Sir Percy Monk made it his business to inform her that I had a beautiful new scullery maid, she helped the pervert to instigate a rumour that Annie Smith was beneath my roof in the role of concubine. Sir Percy was annoyed that Annie had fled from the brutal attention of his son and his household and found shelter in mine. That deviant thinks his money can buy any vice he wants. He approached me to buy her back. Presumably, when Maria found out how determined I was to keep Annie, she began fretting that a fourteen-year-old girl might supplant her. It was for that reason and others that I shan't bore you with that I ended our relationship. I expect she's already accepting comfort from Benjamin

Harley, or Sir Percy, and that wouldn't at all worry me. She means nothing to me…nothing at all.'

Rachel had detected the note of disgust in his voice as he spoke of the Italian woman's mean plotting. She looked up at him and in a small contrite voice said, 'But the Italian woman was much more devious than me…wasn't she?'

He laughed deep in his throat and stooped to tenderly kiss away her fears. 'You're not devious, sweetheart…you're just a beautiful schemer…'

Chapter Sixteen

'I've brought you something from London, Papa.'

Edgar Meredith looked at the parchment placed on the table. He put down his pen, closed the ledger he'd been poring over, and five mottled fingers covered the slender white digits still settled lightly on the deeds to Windrush.

'I trusted you would, Rachel,' Edgar said quietly, his eyes fixed on the document. 'I knew you'd get them back, just as you knew I gave them away. We're too alike, you and I, with our plots and plans. I risked a lot, but I never doubted you putting things right. You're a good girl, Rachel; you deserve to be happy. I should so like to see you truly content.' With a sigh, he enclosed that one elegant hand in both his square venous ones, bringing it to his lips to fondly salute her. 'Welcome home, my dear. I've missed you.' A laugh and a little shake of the head preceded, 'We have our squabbles and our upsets, I think it will be as well for us to keep apart...but I miss you so much when you're not here.'

'I've missed you, too, Papa. I've missed you and

mama and June and Sylvie.' Rachel smoothed a hand over her father's dry cheek, stooped to lightly kiss it.

Edgar looked up at her then. Searched her lovely face for the truth as he interrogated her, 'Do you believe me now when I say that Connor Flinte is a good man?

'Yes, Papa.'

'You are friends?'

'Yes, Papa.'

'Then it was worth all the heartache, the wondering and waiting to discover how you fared, just to hear you say that. Men of such calibre are scarce, you see, my love. We must not toss such good friends lightly aside.' He nodded to himself and Rachel could see that he was garnering the courage to probe further.

'Did he…that is…are you once more engaged?' he asked in a tone that was poignantly flat, lacking hope.

'No, Papa. Connor will never again be betrothed. He was quite adamant about that.'

'Well…that's understandable, I suppose. Yes; 'tis a great shame for such a fine gentleman to face a lonely future, nevertheless…' Edgar exhaled heavily in disappointment. With a final pat he rested his eldest daughter's curled fingers on the leather-topped library table. Picking up the deeds, he began rolling the cylinder absently between his palms. 'I shall settle then for you being friends and expect no more. All I really wanted, my dear, was that you would not hate him, or think him mean and selfish. I hoped you would come together, just the two of you, and have an opportunity to say those private things, one to the other, that have long needed to be said. There was unfinished business between you. I might not be as canny as I would like, but I know such loose ends must be tidied lest at some time they trip one of you up.'

Rachel smiled at the top of her father's head. She began to speak but he added gravely, 'Lord Devane has returned to us our home, your inheritance. He need not have been so magnanimous. Even the most honourable of gentlemen would think long and hard about relinquishing such a valuable asset for nothing in return. We are again much obliged to him.'

'Connor is obliged to you, Papa, and wants to tell you so. He did desire something in return: your daughter. He gave the deeds to his wife. He gave them to his Countess as her wedding gift.' Rachel brought her left hand to lay on top of her father's on the parchment. The magnificent sapphire winked lambent blue fire at him, almost obscuring the golden circlet nestling below it.

'I've brought you something else, Papa. Something you've long wanted, more than anything. I've brought you your first son.'

Edgar swivelled in his chair, staring in stunned silence at the tall, imposing man who'd been observing the emotional scene from a respectful distance. He choked a small noise of mingling astonishment and joy. 'You are wed?'

'Yesterday. We married at St Thomas's. A London wedding; Mrs Pemberton would have approved. Fortunately she was not there. Just Noreen Shaughnessy and a man called Samuel Smith witnessed our wedding. It was quite wonderful,' she said huskily with a lingering, loving look at her handsome husband. 'Indeed, the whole day…and night, was quite wonderful.'

Uncaring of the tears that dripped off his nose, Edgar

strode to Connor, unselfconsciously embraced him before pulling back and manfully pumping at his arm. He walked, head high and proud, to open the door. 'I must find you mother at once.' The words bubbled in his throat. He was about to quit the room when he turned about, approached his daughter and, with eyes squeezed shut, hugged her to him as though he would never let her go.

Two pairs of blue eyes, one pale, one dark, clung, merged, over Edgar's thin, quaking shoulder. As the door closed quietly after Mr Meredith, a soft Irish voice murmured, 'I think he's pleased.'

'I think you're right,' the man's dutiful wife concurred.

'We need a honeymoon, Rachel. We deserve a long honeymoon. We should travel…I'll take you anywhere you want…' He shrugged, grunted a laugh at his choice of words that put a blush in his bride's cheeks.

'After June's wedding, I should like to see Ireland, and your estate in Waterford. I think perhaps one of my sisters might like that, too…I so hope she will…'

At Connor's quick glance, she coaxed huskily, 'Wolverton Manor is a long way from London and malicious tongues. It's a long way from York, too… A person could start afresh there…if need be…'

'Have you decided against Windrush as a refuge for Isabel and her son?'

Rachel walked close to her husband, looking up alluringly, pleadingly at him through a web of luxuriant lashes. Her arms encircled his broad neck, stroked at his nape, at his raven's wing hair. 'I can't wait so long to be with her again. Visiting York but once a year, for fear more trips might risk suspicion, is no good. It might be a decade before Sylvie is wed and Isabel can come home. I'm happy…so very happy—let me share some of it with her. I owe her so much.'

She knew that his intelligent mind was weighing the practicalities of such a move. To persuasively distract him, she murmured huskily, 'So you'll take me anywhere I want, will you?'

His rugged face dipped close to her porcelain cheek. Warm, wooing lips hovered close to a corner of her soft mouth. 'Just name the place…'

Rachel pressed into him, her body and mind afire with memories of those new and exquisite pleasures he had showed her in his hard, masculine bed at Berkeley Square, just last night. It seemed so excruciatingly long ago…

'The King's Arms in Staunton Village.' She nominated a cosy, quiet little inn. 'We could go now,' she breathed raggedly. Her eyes lowered beneath the fond amusement in his. Rachel pressed her rosy face against his shoulder. 'We could eat there…'twill save Mama bothering finding us a meal…as we are unexpectedly arrived…'

'Of course we'll dine there, all afternoon. I promise you a banquet…anything your heart desires,' her husband teased. Suddenly brisk, he took her hand and led her to the door. With an urgency which now gave his wife cause to smile, he ordered, 'Let's go…'

*   *   *   *   *

Copyright © Harlequin Enterprises Limited 1997
All rights reserved

Modern Romance™
...seduction and
passion guaranteed

Tender Romance™
...love affairs that
last a lifetime

Sensual Romance™
...sassy, sexy and
seductive

Blaze
...sultry days and
steamy nights

Medical Romance™
...medical drama on
the pulse

Historical Romance™
...rich, vivid and
passionate

29 new titles every month.

*With all kinds of Romance for
every kind of mood...*

MILLS & BOON®

Makes any time special™

MAT4

MILLS & BOON®

Historical Romance™

THE GENTLEMAN'S DEMAND
by Meg Alexander

Widow Sophie Firle's life was in danger—she was
to act as bait to catch the smugglers who'd
murdered her husband. An attractive stranger,
Mr Hatton, promised he would reward her
financially for her trouble, and Sophie had no
choice but to agree. But the plan involved Mr
Hatton moving into her home and posing as her
admirer—and he proved *remarkably* convincing!

Regency

AN INFAMOUS PROPOSAL by Gail Mallin

The idea of seducing Luke, Lord Kildare, into
proposing to her was as absurd as it was
undignified. But Ianthe Garland could see no other
way to save her home. Ianthe remembered Luke
with fondness, and it went against the grain to
deceive him so. She made up her mind to risk
losing Northwood—and then fate stepped in…

Regency

On sale 4th January 2002

*Available at most branches of WH Smith,
Tesco, Martins, Borders, Eason, Sainsbury's
and most good paperback bookshops.*

1201/04

MILLS & BOON®

STEEP/RTL/9

The STEEPWOOD
Scandal

REGENCY DRAMA, INTRIGUE,
MISCHIEF... AND MARRIAGE

A new collection of 16 linked
Regency Romances, set in the villages
surrounding Steepwood Abbey.

Book 9
Counterfeit Earl
by Anne Herries

Available 4th January

Available at most branches of WH Smith, Tesco,
Martins, Borders, Eason, Sainsbury's, Woolworths
and most good paperback bookshops.

MILLS & BOON

FOREIGN AFFAIRS

A captivating 12 book collection of sun-kissed seductions.
Enjoy romance around the world

DON'T MISS BOOK 4

outback husbands—
The fiery heart of Australia

Available from 4th January

Available at most branches of WH Smith,
Tesco, Martins, Borders, Eason, Sainsbury's
and most good paperback bookshops.

FA/RTL/4

FREE
2 BOOKS
AND A SURPRISE GIFT!

We would like to take this opportunity to thank you for reading this Mills & Boon® book by offering you the chance to take TWO more specially selected titles from the Historical Romance™ series absolutely FREE! We're also making this offer to introduce you to the benefits of the Reader Service™—

- ★ FREE home delivery
- ★ FREE monthly Newsletter
- ★ FREE gifts and competitions
- ★ Exclusive Reader Service discount
- ★ Books available before they're in the shops

Accepting these FREE books and gift places you under no obligation to buy; you may cancel at any time, even after receiving your free shipment. Simply complete your details below and return the entire page to the address below. *You don't even need a stamp!*

YES! Please send me 2 free Historical Romance books and a surprise gift. I understand that unless you hear from me, I will receive 4 superb new titles every month for just £2.99 each, postage and packing free. I am under no obligation to purchase any books and may cancel my subscription at any time. The free books and gift will be mine to keep in any case.

HIZEC

Ms/Mrs/Miss/Mr ....Initials ....
BLOCK CAPITALS PLEASE

Surname ....

Address ....

....

....Postcode ....

Send this whole page to:
UK: FREEPOST CN81, Croydon, CR9 3WZ
EIRE: PO Box 4546, Kilcock, County Kildare (stamp required)

Offer valid in UK and Eire only and not available to current Reader Service subscribers to this series. We reserve the right to refuse an application and applicants must be aged 18 years or over. Only one application per household. Terms and prices subject to change without notice. Offer expires 30th June 2002. As a result of this application, you may receive offers from other carefully selected companies. If you would prefer not to share in this opportunity please write to The Data Manager at the address above.

Mills & Boon® is a registered trademark owned by Harlequin Mills & Boon Limited.
Historical Romance™ is being used as a trademark.